METHOD OF MURDER

Tessa, who had seated herself on the other side of Trevor, leaned across him to say to Daisy, "I like that outfit. That violet color becomes you. Those earrings too. You don't get dressed up often enough."

Jonas eyed Tessa. "Are you saying I don't take her out on enough dates?"

"If the shoe fits . . ." Tessa teased, never one to mince words with either of them.

Instead of being insulted, Jonas laughed. "I'll keep that in mind. More dinner dates in expensive restaurants."

"You'll be able to afford it after that sale you and Elijah are going to have," Trevor said. "You ought to be auctioning off the furniture. You'd make more money."

"Ever the pragmatist." Tessa bumped Trevor's shoulder with her own.

After a pause, Trevor said, "I do come bearing news."

Suddenly all attention was riveted on him, and the music faded into the background.

"What?" Daisy asked.

"The autopsy on Hiram was completed. The coroner suspected something beyond the stun gun killed him. It did. Hiram was killed with an insulin overdose. The autopsy revealed two injection sites. Apparently the stun gun was used to immobilize him for the injections. The killer knew exactly what he or she was doing . . ."

Books by Karen Rose Smith

CAPRICE DeLUCA MYSTERIES
Staged to Death
Deadly Décor
Gilt by Association
Drape Expectations
Silence of the Lamps
Shades of Wrath
Slay Bells Ring
Cut to the Chaise

DAISY'S TEA GARDEN MYSTERIES
Murder with Lemon Tea Cakes
Murder with Cinnamon Scones
Murder with Cucumber Sandwiches
Murder with Cherry Tarts
Murder with Clotted Cream
Murder with Oolong Tea
Murder with Orange Pekoe Tea

Published by Kensington Publishing Corp.

MURDER WITH ORANGE PEKOE TEA

Karen Rose Smith

KENSINGTON
PUBLISHING CORP.

www.kensingtonbooks.com

KENSINGTON BOOKS are published by

Kensington Publishing Corp.
119 West 40th Street
New York, NY 10018

All Kensington titles, imprints, and distributed lines are available at special quantity discounts for bulk purchases for sales promotion, premiums, fund-raising, educational, or institutional use.

Special book excerpts or customized printings can also be created to fit specific needs. For details, write or phone the office of the Kensington Sales Manager: Attn.: Sales Department. Kensington Publishing Corp., 119 West 40th Street, New York, NY 10018. Phone: 1-800-221-2647.

The K logo is a trademark of Kensington Publishing Corp.

First Printing: September 2021
ISBN-13: 978-1-4967-3397-9
ISBN-10: 1-4967-3397-5

ISBN-13: 978-1-4967-3399-3 (ebook)
ISBN-10: 1-4967-3399-1 (ebook)

10 9 8 7 6 5 4 3 2

Printed in the United States of America

My husband and I will be married fifty years this summer. I'm dedicating *Murder with Orange Pekoe Tea* to all the couples who strive for their happily-ever-after.

ACKNOWLEDGMENTS

I would like to thank Officer Greg Berry, my law enforcement consultant, who so patiently answers all my questions. His input is invaluable.

CHAPTER ONE

The wail of sirens blared. A police SUV jumped up over the curb, heading straight for the side of the canopies where the protestors stood in disarray. A second patrol car parked at the curb while doors swung open. Red, blue, and white strobe lights dotted the dirt, the canopies, the cookies, and the spilled tea.

Daisy Swanson viewed the scene in disbelief.

One Hour Earlier

The summer Sunday afternoon was peaceful and friendly. Daisy hoped that building a homeless shelter would be good for her Willow Creek, Pennsylvania community. A conversation between two men standing nearby the canopies set up in the middle of the field where the shelter would be built alerted her that all might not be as calm as she believed.

"I hope there isn't trouble," the first man, around fifty in a polo shirt and plaid shorts said.

About the same age though balder, the second gentleman who had been into Daisy's Tea Garden a few times assured him, "Willow Creek residents are too contained for overt confrontation."

Hoping that was the case, Daisy had scanned the stretch of land where dandelions, milkweed, and long green and yellow grass sprouted in no particular pattern. In the next second, she swiveled toward the two yellow-and-white-striped canopies that sheltered tables with iced as well as hot orange pekoe tea in tall silver urns. A red cooler with loose ice for scooping rested on the ground next to the table.

Daisy's Tea Garden's goodies spread in circles on vintage plates painted with roses, daisies, and hydrangeas. Daisy had layered snickerdoodles, chocolate espresso cookies and whoopie pies in an assortment of flavors from chocolate with peanut butter filling, to spice with cinnamon cream filling, to red velvet with vanilla cream filling on each platter. She'd set pots with pink, purple, and yellow petunias around the tables to create a festive atmosphere. The daytime temperature in June in Pennsylvania could easily climb to ninety. Fortunately this late afternoon was a balmy eighty.

Suddenly Daisy felt the tap on her shoulder. When she spun around, her blond ponytail whipped over her shoulder. She instantly recognized Lawrence Bishop, a science teacher at Willow Creek High School who also served on the town council. Lawrence was in his late forties. His hair was still thick, although gray laced the brown. He had a long face and thin lips that looked much more pleasant when he smiled.

He was smiling now. "It was so good of you to host this spread for the community. I hope the town council decided to pay you enough for it."

"Daniel can be greedy with the budget sometimes."

Daniel Copeland, also a member of the town council, was an assistant bank manager so she understood his reasoning in portioning out budgeted funds. "I told him I would do it at cost if he would pay the labor for Iris and Pam to help me serve."

Lawrence looked over the spread again. "I think we got a good deal. I like the idea that you're serving hot *and* iced tea. And the cooler with bottles of water for those who don't want tea are effective too."

In her dealings with Lawrence before, she'd realized he usually had a down-to-earth outlook. "I think we all have to contribute something to make the homeless shelter a reality," she responded.

"Having a benefactor donate the land certainly helped the project. Now if we can just raise the funds for the building . . ." His voice trailed off. After a moment, he continued, "If the fundraising doesn't get off the ground because of all those people who don't want the homeless shelter in Willow Creek, I'll be sorely disappointed. Unfortunately, they can be quite verbal."

Daisy caught a whiff of a man's strong cologne along with the scent of sun streaming down on the baked earth surrounding the tents. "I know there are people in Willow Creek against the shelter. But there are many passionate residents *for* the shelter to counteract their voices."

Without an explanation, Lawrence waved to somebody on the other side of the tent. Leaning toward Daisy, he asked, "Do you have a minute to talk to my daughter and her husband?"

Daisy glanced over her shoulder and spotted a couple making their way toward her . . . or toward Lawrence.

Keeping his voice low, Lawrence explained, "I convinced Piper and her husband to come to this social to divert her attention and his from their problems."

Anyone who had children knew there were always problems. Daisy's two daughters, Violet and Jazzi, brought her boundless joy but also daily complications.

Keeping his voice low, Lawrence asked, "Did you read about what happened at the Hope Clinic?"

The Hope Clinic had opened its doors in Willow Creek a few years ago. It was a fertility clinic. Last month, it had experienced a mechanical problem, losing eggs and embryos that had been frozen and crushing the dreams of many couples using the clinic.

She listened intently as Lawrence explained, "Piper and Emory are heartbroken. The clinic lost their frozen embryos. I want them to become involved in the fundraising endeavor to move on from what happened. I thought you could explain your enthusiasm for it."

Daisy felt a wisp of a breeze on her neck and she was grateful for it. She'd been scurrying around all day, and taking a few minutes in conversation with Lawrence's daughter and her husband would be a welcome break. Her Aunt Iris, her partner in Daisy's Tea Garden that was located in an old Victorian in town, was walking toward the tent from their van with a fresh tray of whoopie pies. Daisy caught her eye. She gestured to Lawrence and the couple who had stopped to talk with them.

Iris nodded that she understood and she'd handle any

of the serving decisions that had to be made. As Daisy quickly scanned the crowd, she saw that many residents were seated on folding chairs, a drink in their hand and a paper dish with a pastry on their lap. The buzz of chatter was everywhere. Anything that brought the community together was good. That's what Daisy's Tea Garden was all about.

Turning to the couple, she let Lawrence introduce them. Piper looked to be a little older than her daughter Vi, maybe around twenty-five. Her auburn hair curled over her shoulders and around her oval face. Her bangs were blunt-cut above very green eyes and freckles spread across her cheeks. She was wearing a pin-striped sundress. Her husband Emory was about five-ten, stocky, and looked as if he might lift weights. His peach-colored polo shirt stretched across his chest. With his khakis he wore sandals and looked quite comfortable. His dark brown hair was brushed up over a high forehead and cut short on both sides. His mustache was thin and well clipped.

After introductions, the conversation centered on the homeless shelter and the gathering. Piper admitted, "The folks who came out for this look as if they're interested. I've heard several conversations with women and men who want to volunteer any way they can."

Emory nodded. "I heard one man say this should be a shelter that the community is proud of, not a building where the community hides away people they don't want on their streets."

Lawrence grinned. "That's exactly why I want you and Piper to get involved in the fundraising. It will give you a purpose for a little while as you recover from your loss."

Piper shot her dad a questioning glance.

Lawrence admitted, "I told Daisy. She has two daughters. Her one daughter, Vi, had a baby not too long ago."

"And my other daughter, Jazzi," Daisy filled in, "is adopted." Since Lawrence seemed worried about Piper, Daisy decided to share a little. "After Vi, I couldn't have more children. I was devastated, but when my husband and I came to terms with it, we decided to adopt."

Shaking her head vehemently, Piper insisted, "It's too soon to think about that."

Just then Jonas Groft came up behind Daisy and settled his arm around her waist. "How's it going?"

"I think it's going well," she assured him.

When some people looked at Jonas, they first saw the scar on his cheek and looked the other way. But she saw the former detective who'd given years to an often-thankless profession. He was strong and not only physically strong. His stubbornness, reflected in the angle of his jaw, had sometimes created a bumpy road for their relationship. But his integrity, loyalty, and caring more than made up for that. After all, *she* could be stubborn too.

He'd shoved his black hair back over his brow, but a strand had fallen forward. He was six-feet tall, broad shouldered, and a ballast in her sometimes-tumultuous life. Today he wore a navy T-shirt with black denims. His low boots were dusty from crossing the field several times, helping her carry supplies to and fro. He'd put up the canopies this morning and carried the tables to them.

"You know Lawrence, don't you?" she asked Jonas.

"Oh, yes," Lawrence said before Jonas could and explained who Jonas was to Piper and Emory. "Jonas is a former Philadelphia detective. Now he owns Woods, the store downtown that sells handcrafted furniture."

"Really?" Emory said. "We've been looking for a cabinet for my den."

As Lawrence, Emory, and Jonas talked about the pieces in his shop, Daisy turned to Piper. "If you ever want to talk about adoption, I'd be glad to share my experiences."

Piper's face took on a melancholy quality, and Daisy realized this social event wasn't the type of solution that would help Piper move on from her experience with the Hope Clinic.

After glancing at the men, Piper took a step closer to Daisy. "We don't know what we want to do. We're thinking about joining a class action lawsuit with other couples against the clinic. It's a huge decision to make."

"Yes, it is," Daisy agreed. "How does Emory feel about it?"

"He's more positive about the idea than I am. I almost feel like our marriage, all our plans, and even our lives will be spoiled if we become embroiled in a lawsuit. We'd be wishing for what might have been, rather than what can be. Do you know what I mean?"

"I do understand. Losing the embryos . . . you both might need to go through a grieving period."

"And a class action lawsuit could just postpone what we have to feel and what we *should* feel. I simply don't know."

Piper looked so sad. She reminded Daisy of Vi when her daughter had gotten pregnant out of wedlock and had to make heavy decisions for a young woman her age.

Without hesitating, Daisy lightly clasped Piper's arm. "If you'd like to talk about adoption, lawsuits, or anything else, you're welcome to come by the tea garden. I'll serve you iced tea and a whoopie pie on the house."

That idea brought a smile across Piper's lips. The smile rapidly slipped away though as Piper looked toward the other side of the tent. Daisy saw the young woman's attention was suddenly captured by a man in white linen slacks, white shirt, and straw hat. He seemed to be enjoying a cup of hot orange pekoe tea.

Always curious, Daisy asked, "Do you know that man?"

"I sure do. His name is Hiram Hershberger. He's the lawyer representing the fertility clinic. He's the enemy in our eyes. A group of us that were affected by the mechanical failure has met several times. I'd better distract Emory. I don't want him to feel he has to have a discussion with the man. Nothing good can come of it."

Daisy watched as Piper moved away, threaded her arm through her husband's and guided him toward the trays of cookies. Lawrence gave a wave to Daisy, signaling that he'd talk to her later.

However, Jonas came toward Daisy and swung his arm around her shoulders. "Not long now before we can pack up and go back to your place for a while." The message in his eyes said he'd like to kiss her right here, right now, but that he'd wait.

Daisy and Jonas had come to an abiding understanding that they were a couple. They'd been through hard times together and apart and then back together again. Now they felt bonded in a deep way that had produced *I love yous* from them both. They hadn't talked much yet about the future, but in the present, they wanted to be together as much as they could . . . with family, without family, alone, or with friends.

Jonas motioned to the crowd and the location of the

party. "When the chamber of commerce decided to have a celebration here to have the community socialize on the property where the shelter will be built and try to form a united front, I was skeptical. But I think it *is* working. I've seen the volunteer signup sheets for the many committees. Now we just need the fundraising to get started."

Strolling along the table, Daisy and Jonas picked up glasses of iced tea. "For plastic glasses, these are pretty spiffy," Jonas kidded.

"Spiffy? If you think flowers on plastic are spiffy for this social, wait until you see what I come up with for our Fourth of July tea garden event."

As Jonas laughed, Daisy heard someone calling her name. That was common at an event like this. Running Daisy's Tea Garden with her aunt, she'd met most of the residents of Willow Creek at one time or another. Some of them she'd gotten to know fairly well. She was glad to see the man approaching her this time was Gavin Cranshaw. He wasn't just a friend, he was an in-law . . . her son-in-law's father.

Gavin was lean and tall with a square jaw that noted determination similar to his son's. His sandy brown hair was already blonding in the warm weather. A contractor, he was tan from working outdoors. Gavin had had wonderful news lately. He'd won the bid to build the homeless shelter.

After giving Daisy a hug, Gavin shook Jonas's hand. At one time, Jonas had been jealous of Gavin, but they'd settled all that.

Gavin blew out a breath. "I feel as if I've been glad-handing everyone since I got here. Daniel Copeland thinks I need to speak with anybody who could be influential in raising money for the shelter."

Jonas asked, "Do they still have plans to hire a professional fundraiser?"

Gavin slipped a hand into the pocket of his navy slacks. "As far as I can tell. I simply wonder if a town the size of Willow Creek can raise enough money to actually build the shelter. If they can't start building and complete the project quickly, prices will go up and we'll need to raise even more money."

Jonas suggested, "Is scaling back the plans and the cost a possibility?"

Gavin shook his head. "Only if we have to. We should know within the first two months of raising money how it's going to go. I'm simply concerned about who the mayor will hire to head the fundraising effort."

"There's a public relations blitz planned," Daisy reminded him.

Gavin looked directly at Daisy. "Do you think Arden Botterill really has the know-how that it takes to do the marketing for the shelter?"

Daisy shrugged. "She says she does. And she volunteered. The council won't have to pay her."

Arden owned the shop called Vinegar and Spice. Daisy wondered again what Arden's background was and if she'd submitted a résumé to the council. Then again, since she was volunteering, the men might not have looked any further.

Gavin said, "I see the mayor over there. I haven't connected with him yet today. I'd better do that before I leave. You two have a good evening."

After Gavin moved away, Jonas pointed to the TV truck and camera crew from the Lancaster TV station. A van with a satellite dish was also parked at the curb on the other side of the field. That one was from Harrisburg. "It looks like we've garnered some attention," Jonas noted. "You could be on the news tonight."

"I hope I'm not. I'm hoping they skip over the refreshments under the canopies and talk to pro and con residents about the shelter, not making it all one-sided."

Jonas nodded toward an interview with Daniel Copeland taking place nearby. "I would think this is community news that the general population would take an interest in."

Daisy studied Daniel and the camera crew. "I hope that's why they're here."

Suddenly Jonas nudged her arm and pointed in another direction to the field behind the canopies. Daisy saw he was focused on the two dogs playing there. One looked like a cocker spaniel and the other appeared to be a Scottie. The Scottie hunkered down, front paws forward and his back end up. The cocker in the position of power just stood staring at him. After a yip from the Scottie, they started chasing each other around the field.

Daisy swerved her attention from the dogs to Jonas and saw that he was watching them intently.

After a moment he asked, "What do you think about me adopting a dog?"

Daisy was aware that a friend of Jonas's had recommended that Jonas adopt one when he was going through a tough time. She didn't know if he'd taken his friend seriously, but maybe the idea had taken root.

She didn't want to sway him one way or the other. "What breed are you thinking of?"

He gave her a lopsided smile. "You know me too well. You believe I've been thinking about this ever since Detective Rappaport mentioned it."

"Maybe I do. Am I right about that?"

Jonas towered above her. Lean and muscled with a stern jaw, he could look fierce. That look had shadowed him since his job as a homicide detective in Philadelphia and his experiences with it. But *she* knew the man behind the rugged attempt to hold people at a distance. If he was uncertain about something, which wasn't often, he brushed his hair up over his forehead. The sunlight, beaming through the side of the tent, illuminated the silver strands at his temples as his green eyes grew darker. Recently he'd told her he secretly liked the idea that she could sometimes read his thoughts.

"When Rappaport first mentioned it," Jonas said, "I really did think he was joking. He was making a point that I wasn't getting along with anybody else so I might as well adopt a dog to have as a friend. But the more I thought about it, I realized how much I *do* like dogs. I even did shifts as a canine handler back in Philadelphia. I don't care about any particular breed. I'd like to adopt from the animal shelter at the edge of town. I want to feel as if I'm saving a life."

Daisy knew that sentiment was typical of Jonas too.

"The thing is . . ." He hesitated. "I haven't made a decision because I wanted to talk to you."

"*You're* the one who would have to walk a dog and care for it. This has to be what *you* want to do," she advised.

"I'm well aware of that," he agreed with a smile and a twinkle in his eyes. "But do *you* like dogs?"

"I do. Ryan and I talked about adopting one when the girls were small, but our lifestyle didn't seem to be a good one for caring for a dog. By the time Vi and Jazzi were both at school, we knew we would be away all day. It just didn't seem fair to the animal."

"I'd like to adopt a dog who's gentle enough to take to work with me," he confided. "My yard at the townhouse isn't huge but your property could be suitable for a dog to run and fetch."

Daisy considered the next few years, surprised that's where her thoughts were going. Her daughter Jazzi would be leaving for college in a year. Daisy liked the idea of a dog around the property, especially as her grandson Sammy grew older.

"It's plenty large for a dog to exercise, maybe with humans having fun too."

Jonas took her hand and she could see in his expression that he was happy they usually thought alike.

Although Daisy liked spending this time with Jonas, she knew she should check on the pastries. Did she still have enough in the van? She hadn't been sure what quantity to supply, but since the tea garden was five minutes away, she could fetch more if she needed to.

Nevertheless, she was enjoying standing here with Jonas, watching the dogs play in the field, thinking about the future.

The breeze lifted a stray strand of hair along her cheek and tossed it across her lips. She was about to brush it away when Jonas released her hand and did it for her. His finger was rough from woodworking and slightly callused.

The tingle she always felt around Jonas lifted the corners of her lips. He smiled back, his eyes dark with a desire to be alone with her later.

Conversations swirled around them. Friends and neighbors picked up a dish of cookies and whoopie pies, cups or glasses of tea. Daisy's elbow brushed again against Jonas's as the day seemed almost perfect. She had a business that she enjoyed, family and friends she loved . . . and Jonas.

Then like a sudden storm enveloping the gathering, everything changed. Daisy didn't see a black cloud moving overhead. However, she did hear a negative buzz begin to sweep over the crowd. It began from the field on the south side of the plot of land closest to Market Street, Willow Creek's main street.

Protest chants reached her ears from at least a dozen persons marching toward the canopies. At first glance, she couldn't tell if they were men or women. Even though the day was summer-like, the protestors were wearing hooded sweatshirts, boots, and camouflage-patterned inhalation masks.

She felt Jonas's arm shoot to his belt for his phone. She suspected he was calling the Willow Creek Police Department.

As the group drew closer, their shouts increased in volume. They shouted in unison—*No homeless shelter in Willow Creek. No homeless shelter in Willow Creek. No homeless shelter in Willow Creek.*

As much as their shouts coursed over the field and sent shivers up Daisy's spine, their boots on the ground sounded a menacing warning too. The protestors marched closer. She took a step back and clutched Jonas's arm.

CHAPTER TWO

Jonas curled his arm around Daisy's waist and pulled her away from the canopied tent. Before she could voice a thought, she watched him—keeping true to his cop training—hurriedly return to the tent and do the same with others, clearing them away from the tables and pointing to the field far from the protestors.

Horrified, her hand covered her mouth as the protestors marched through the area, upsetting cold and hot tea urns, flipping the cookie tray, and jostling aside anyone or anything in their way until the whoopie pies fell onto the table too. With fear clutching her chest and disbelief invading every thought, Daisy was so grateful that neither of her daughters had attended the gathering today. Checking for her Aunt Iris, she spotted her farther back in the field with Russ Windom, the man she was dating. Her aunt gazed on the spectacle with astonishment.

The protestors' chants continued as they disrupted the community assembled to celebrate the building of the homeless shelter.

Then the police arrived.

After the siren stopped and the patrolmen and Detective Rappaport spilled from their vehicles, Daisy felt a modicum of relief. Detective Rappaport, who Daisy knew from investigations they had clashed on and eventually worked on together, jogged toward the first line of protestors. Officer Bart Cosner put his hand on his weapon and pointed the protestors away from the canopies and back into the fields from which they'd come. Two more officers rounded the canopies and shouted at all the persons wearing inhalation masks to remove their masks and move into a line.

Most obeyed.

Jonas, who had returned to Daisy, held her shoulder and leaned close to her. "They're removing their masks. I don't think they're violent, just noisy and disruptive."

"Look, though." Daisy pointed to one of the hooded figures. He was arguing with Detective Rappaport and apparently wouldn't remove his mask.

He shouted, "I want my lawyer. Hiram Hershberger is right over there." The man pointed to Hiram enmeshed within a group of men.

With a pained expression on his face, Hiram Hershberger crossed to the protestor with the mask.

As the protestors quieted down, the residents of Willow Creek that had been gathered for the community social began chattering. Watching carefully, Daisy saw Hiram convince the protestor to remove his mask.

Daisy asked Jonas, "Do you know anyone protesting?"

Jonas looked over the line of men. "I'm not certain about most, but the man with Hiram is—"

Jonas's words were cut off as a woman brushed against Daisy's arm. When she turned to see who it was, she saw Rachel Fisher and her husband. Rachel and Levi were New Order Amish. Daisy and Rachel had been friends since childhood. It had been an unlikely friendship, English and Amish, but they'd connected. They'd run through cornfields together, played tag near the family farm, and even swum in the pond. Rachel and Levi owned Quilts and Notions, a store downtown not far from the tea garden.

Rachel directed their attention to the man with Hiram. With his hood lowered and his mask removed, Daisy could see that the young man had blond hair and was a young adult. His blue eyes were intense on Hiram's face as Hiram spoke to him as if he were giving a lecture.

"That's Eli Lapp!" Rachel said. "He's a fence jumper."

Daisy had always understood that a fence jumper was a young person who had left the Amish community when he was in his teens, often during *rumspringa*—a time when Amish youth tasted the world and decided if they wanted to commit to the faith. Some New Order Amish were shunned if they left the community. That depended on the family and the *Ordnung*—the set of rules—governing their district.

Levi cut in, "From what I understand, Hiram has helped Eli out of sticky situations."

It looked as if the officers intended to walk the protestors to the police station since there were too many to fit into their patrol cars. But it seemed that Eli and Hiram were getting special treatment. Bart showed Eli into the back of the PD's SUV. Hiram signaled that he'd be along in his vehicle.

"Are they arresting him?" Daisy asked. She knew it was a silly question that Jonas couldn't answer, but she thought she'd ask it anyway.

"My guess is that Rappaport wants to scare all of them. I guess Eli is receiving special treatment because he has his lawyer with him. They'll get to the bottom of why this was happening and the motives behind it."

"The motives seem clear to me," Levi said. "They don't want a homeless shelter here."

"Or," Jonas suggested, "all of those young men were paid for this performance. Someone might not want to be identified with the protest yet they don't want the homeless shelter here. The detective and Bart will figure it out."

Slowly everyone began moving back toward the canopies.

Iris came up beside Daisy. "What do you want to do?"

Making a sudden decision, Daisy suggested, "If you can take care of the tea, set more iced teacups up, I'll go to the van and bring the remainder of the cookies and whoopie pies. We can have new trays arranged in no time."

Daisy looked up at Jonas. "Can you try and convince people not to leave yet? I hate to see this shut down when it was going so well. People are talking to each other, discussing what the shelter might do for Willow Creek. We desperately need volunteers and I don't want anyone to be scared that the project isn't going to happen."

"I'll talk to the mayor. He can make an announcement. I'll assure everyone there's still time to enjoy tea and cookies and talk."

With Daisy's clogs sinking into the ground a little, she stood on tiptoe and kissed Jonas on the cheek.

Daisy and Iris spent about fifteen minutes making sure the tables were ready for another round of service. Rachel accompanied Daisy to her work van to help carry cookies to refill the platter.

Rachel said, "I don't know what's gotten into Eli. Hiram definitely had an influence over him."

"I take it you don't think it was a *good* influence?" Daisy inquired.

Rachel's expression was distressed. "Hiram left the community. Eli left. That's never good."

The district Rachel came from was tight-knit. Hers was one with a bishop who expressed a little more leniency than others in the area. Still, the district practiced the old ways, even though Rachel used a gas-powered oven and a cell phone for work purposes and emergencies. Rachel, like others in her community, felt that the old ways helped them stay closer to God. Daisy admired so much about the Amish community. In these times it was hard to keep families together, whether Amish or English.

As they stepped down from the van, Rachel asked, "Has Jazzi considered the colleges she wants to look at this summer? You're going to take a couple of road trips, ain't so?"

"Later in the summer," Daisy said. "Jazzi is still deciding where she wants to apply. But if she wants to apply for early admission for next year, she's going to have to decide soon."

"Your heart is probably half sweet and half bitter over the idea."

Daisy looked over at Rachel, noticing details such as her white heart-shaped *kapp*, her hair pulled tightly into a bun, her *kapp* strings floating down the front of her apron. They were different in so many ways, yet so much the same in others. "You can see my heart."

"For certain sure I can. You're a *mamm* just like me and *mammi*." Levi's mom lived with Rachel and her husband and their children. That was the way of the Amish too.

Daisy and Rachel carried the trays of baked goods toward the table. Daisy donned latex gloves that she'd brought along to arrange the cookies and whoopie pies as attractively as she could. She was pleased to notice that many of the residents of Willow Creek had lingered. Jonas had made sure that the tea urns were positioned the way they should be. All looked as if it had never been disturbed.

However, near the brace for the canopy, Daisy heard men's voices growing louder. When she glanced up, she noted that Hiram was still there. He was arguing with Emory.

The news crews still circulated and Daisy could see that the argument had caught not only the attention of the local reporter—Trevor Lundquist who dated Tessa Miller, her kitchen manager and best friend—but also the eyes of one of the camera crew.

Emory's voice burst from him like a ball from a cannon. "You are a miserable man for defending the clinic. Someone should make sure you can't do it."

Lawrence suddenly approached his son-in-law and pulled on his shoulder. Then Lawrence held onto Emory's arm so he wouldn't swing back to the lawyer.

Hiram looked a bit embarrassed and raised his arms and hands in a what-can-you-do-about-it gesture.

Lawrence walked Emory a good twenty feet away but Emory was still glaring back at the lawyer.

From beside her, Jonas approached Hiram. "Everything okay?"

Hiram glanced sharply at Emory. "Just another hot-head who doesn't understand what lawyers do."

"I imagine any of the clinic's clients could be upset with you when they see the clinic as the cause of their issues," Jonas pointed out.

"I can't discuss the case," Hiram grumbled. "And I need to get down to the police station to rescue a young man from himself."

After Hiram had stalked off, Daisy said to Jonas, "I suppose he's talking about Eli."

"I suppose so. I was surprised at what Eli was doing today."

"You know him?"

"He's come into the shop now and then to apprentice on how to make furniture. I really had never taken him for a rabble-rouser, or even someone who would stand strongly against something. He seems mild mannered, cooperative, and is quite good at woodworking."

Daisy scanned the crowd that was still gathered under the tents and around them. "I guess everyone has buttons that circumstances can push. But what about a homeless shelter pushed Eli's?"

"Maybe it has something to do with his fence jumping," Jonas said with a shrug.

"Maybe. But I'm wondering if Rachel is right that Hiram influenced Eli to leave his Amish community."

* * *

Two hours later, as Jonas drove Daisy home, they talked about what had happened. Daisy was still shocked that protestors had invaded their gathering.

Jonas didn't seem quite as surprised.

"Strong feelings on both sides cause cracks in the community," he reminded her. "One side apparently felt they had to take power into their own hands and make raucous noise to be heard."

"Everyone's free to speak at town council meetings," she said. "A few voices dissented there, but not so violently. The council listened to their concerns, but they thought the homeless shelter was something the community needed. Last winter they found a camp of homeless men in one of the fields. In a *field*, Jonas. No one should have to sleep in a field in freezing weather."

Jonas reached over to her and took her hand. "One of the farmers I know let a few men use his barn on the coldest nights last winter, but somehow they felt safer in the fields than they did in the barn. I don't understand it. When I was on the streets in Philadelphia, I didn't understand a lot of things. The question is—will they stay in the shelter? That's a valid question. Willow Creek Police Department's not big enough to patrol all the fields along with the streets. These days there are no easy answers, but I have to think building the homeless shelter and providing meals will help."

"I want to think we're a caring community. Do you think the police will arrest Eli?"

"Hiram Hershberger has a reputation for getting people off."

"He could probably say that Eli was just practicing his first amendment right of free speech."

"I suppose," Jonas agreed. "But the camouflage mask and the boots could lean toward terrorist threats. We'll see what develops. The town council can't let intimidation stop the project if they really believe in it."

They were both quiet on the remainder of the drive. They'd taken Daisy's work van to the tea garden to park it in the back lot, and Jonas had driven her home, stopping in front of the generous detached double-car garage. Daisy hadn't finished the second floor of the garage when it was built. After she discovered that Vi was pregnant and that she and Foster were getting married, Daisy had made the decision to have the second floor of the garage finished into an apartment where the couple could live rent-free the first year. They needed help to start their life together, and Daisy wanted to give that help if she could.

At the garage, she glanced toward her home that had once been a barn. After they climbed out of Jonas's SUV and stood in front of the garage, they gazed toward the house. Daisy focused on the multi-paned window that had once been a hay hatch where hay bales had been lifted in and out of the barn. That was Jazzi's room and a light glowed there. A smaller window above that one let daylight into the attic space. A floodlight at the peak of the roof hadn't flashed on yet and Daisy could catch a glimpse of blue plaid curtains that draped Jazzi's window.

The second floor had been divided into two bedrooms with a bath. Before Vi had gone to college, it had suited her daughters perfectly. Now Jazzi had the second floor to herself. Her whitewashed furniture and blue-and-white spread were very different from what was now the guest room, which had a more contemporary design with sleek-

lined walnut furniture and a dark green spread and curtains.

Jonas reached for Daisy's hand, and she liked that this
man, who was somewhat quiet when he didn't want to
share his feelings, was affectionate and showed her how
much he cared. As she peered up at the white-trimmed
windows and dormers, she thought about Ryan's insurance money that had made this new life in Willow Creek
possible. She'd always be grateful he'd been her husband, and Vi and Jazzi's father. She'd always remember
the marriage they had had. But now she could imagine
possibly sharing this house with Jonas someday.

Since she lived in a rural area, rather than a neighborhood, and she'd been a widow with two teenage girls,
she'd had a security system installed. She unlocked the
door and then punched in the security code to turn off the
alarm.

Jonas followed her in the wide front door. There was a
stairway to the rear of the living room that led upstairs. A
huge wagon-wheel chandelier lit up the area which was
open to a dining area and kitchen. The floor-to-ceiling
stone fireplace near the dining area gave a cozy feeling to
the room in summer, winter, fall, and spring.

When Jonas glanced toward the upstairs, Daisy had to
smile. Her two cats had started down the steps to greet
them. Jonas waited for the duo to arrive. Marjoram, the
tortoise shell with unique markings, came right to Jonas
and sat on his foot. One side of her face was mottled in
tan, brown, and black. The other side was completely
dark brown. Colors ranging from orange to cream spotted
her back and flanks while her chest was a creamy tan and
rust. Looking up at Jonas, she gave a small meow.

"I never know if you want me to pick you up," he said conversationally.

She gave another meow and stayed put.

"If I'm reading your sign language right, that's a *yes*. So here we go." He stooped and picked her up, holding her loosely in his arms.

Daisy knew Marjoram was a squiggler. She didn't like to be held long, but Jonas knew that too. Daisy's tuxedo cat, Pepper, came over to her and wound in a figure eight around her ankles.

"I like your greeting but I know what it means," she said to the feline. "Did Jazzi feed you?"

Just then Jazzi jogged down the stairs. She would be a senior in high school when school began again and would have to make many decisions about her life. Jazzi's road had been complicated over the last three years. Adopted, she'd gone on a search for her birth mother. Jonas had helped her, which had solidified a bond between them.

Daisy watched Jazzi's thick black glossy hair swing across her shoulders. It was straight without a wave and Jazzi had bemoaned that fact until she figured out how to make her hair work for her. Her latest style perfectly framed her oval face with her high cheekbones and cute nose. She was wearing a blue-and-white striped T-shirt and denim shorts.

Looking straight at Jonas and Daisy, she asked, "Are we going to cook out?"

"We can," Daisy answered. "It's a beautiful day for it. I just happen to have burgers pattied and ready to go. I brought home potato salad from the tea garden yesterday, and we can make a lettuce salad too if you want."

Jazzi approached them and scooped up Pepper. "I

want. I'd like to go over my list of colleges with you—
the ones I want to go see before I decide if I want to apply
to them or not."

"That sounds like the perfect thing to do on an early
June evening. We can look at the calendar and see when
we can get away."

"I'm available to chauffer too," Jonas said.

"Road trips," Jazzi decided with a grin.

Within an hour, burgers sizzled on a plate on the picnic
table. Jonas had melted cheese on a few and Daisy had
sliced tomatoes to pile onto the burgers. Ketchup, bread-
and-butter pickles that her Aunt Iris had made, and fresh
lettuce grown in their own garden were available too.
They'd had a warm spring and the tomato and pepper
plants that Daisy had planted were growing strong.

Daisy had brought home chocolate espresso cookies
that she'd made at the tea garden. By the time Jonas was
on his second one, he suggested, "I could make coffee to
go with these. I think I had enough tea this afternoon to
float in it."

Daisy laughed. "A cup of coffee does sound good."
She had one of those coffee makers that used pods because she drank more tea than coffee and rarely needed
more than one cup at a time.

"I can make three cups," Jazzi said. "I'll bring them
out then we can talk about colleges."

"Thank you, honey," Daisy said with a smile.

As Jazzi entered the house through the sliding glass
door, Jonas remarked, "My guess is that Jazzi's already
thinking about when she goes away to college. She's
going to miss the life she has now."

"I know I've been thinking about it a lot," Daisy admitted. "I'm certainly going to miss her."

"Let's sit on the glider," Jonas suggested.

Daisy and Jonas's romantic relationship had experienced a bumpy voyage. After a tempestuous few months, Jonas had created the glider for the two of them as an apology. The seats had heart-shaped backs, and they often sat on them, looking up at the stars and thinking about the future they could have. They sank down onto the glider now while the sun was dropping lower on the horizon. Orange and pink shot through the clouds.

As Jonas took Daisy's hand, she asked him, "Had you ever met Piper and Emory before today?"

"No, I hadn't. But I talked with Emory a while after they told us what happened with the clinic. I think he went at Hiram like that at the social because he feels guilty."

"Guilty? He didn't have anything to do with what happened at the clinic, did he?" Daisy asked, amazed.

"Oh, not guilty in that way. But Emory is the one who's holding them back from getting pregnant because of a low sperm count. That's why they went the *in vitro* route."

"That is so hard," Daisy said. "I researched it. It wouldn't have helped me and Ryan because I couldn't carry another child. But when we were considering adoption, we went to a couples' group. Many of them had considered *in vitro*, but it's so expensive. Not that adoption isn't, but one cycle of *in vitro* might not work."

"That's it exactly," Jonas said. "Emory and Piper used all of their savings and borrowed heavily from Piper's dad. They also took out a line of credit. Emory wants to become involved in the class action suit against the clinic to recoup their money. Piper doesn't think it's such a

great idea. So now on top of what happened, that's causing tension between them."

"I really liked Piper," Daisy said. "I was thinking
maybe I should invite her and Emory and Vi and Foster to
dinner. They're both young couples starting out in marriage. It could be advantageous for them to talk."

"It might be," Jonas agreed.

Daisy snuggled against Jonas's shoulder, happy where
she was . . . happy where they were in their relationship.
She and Jonas might have to have another discussion
sometime about whether he wanted a child of his own, or
if either of them wanted to consider adoption. That was a
whole universe that they hadn't taken seriously enough
yet.

For now, though, she was just happy to be sitting beside him, having him push the glider back and forth, hoping Piper and Emory would do whatever was best for
their future.

CHAPTER THREE

Daisy had just served tea and scones to a table of four women late Monday morning when the bell for the tea garden dinged and the front door opened. She was surprised to see Hiram Hershberger. Another gentleman was with him who was dressed in an expensive outfit for a summer day. The gray suit looked tailored to fit him. The white shirt seemed starched and the tie was expertly knotted.

When Daisy crossed to Hiram, he tipped his straw hat. "Good morning, Mrs. Swanson. I enjoyed your tea at the social gathering yesterday. At least it was social for a while. This is my friend Troy Richter."

Today Hiram was dressed in a short-sleeved aqua dress shirt, open at the collar. On top of that, he wore a chocolate colored vest that matched his slacks.

Hiram reached up to his hat and took it off.

"It's a pleasure to see you again," she said to Hiram. Then she turned to Troy Richter. "It's nice to meet you."

When Hiram leaned closer to her, she caught a whiff of strong cologne. In a conspiratorial voice, he said, "We'd like privacy if you can manage it . . . and definitely iced orange pekoe tea."

Daisy understood that the two men were going to discuss business. She wondered if Mr. Richter was a client of Hiram's. She wished she could ask Hiram a few questions about Eli Lapp, but that wouldn't be professional for either of them. Glancing over vacant tables, she led them into the spillover tearoom. Hiram scanned both rooms as if he was memorizing every detail.

Daisy and her Aunt Iris had bought the old Victorian after a bakery had existed on the first floor. From the start, they'd considered the fact that they wanted men to feel comfortable at the tea garden as well as women. They'd decorated the main tearoom with glass-top wood tables and mismatched antique oak hand-carved chairs. White and yellow bud vases with fresh lavender, in season now, adorned each table, and the walls had been painted light green. Daisy believed the color green promoted calming qualities, just as tea could.

Leading Hiram and Mr. Richter, she remembered when she and her aunt had planned the connecting room for spillover traffic. On specified days, she and her staff served afternoon tea with all its courses in that area. In her estimation, the spillover room reflected the best qualities of the Victorian with its bay window, window seats, crown molding, and diamond-cut glass windows. The walls in the room were the palest yellow and the tables were white. Each chair wore a cushion in blue, green, and yellow pinstripes. She motioned to a table for two in the corner near the window. At present, no one else occupied the room.

After the men were seated, Hiram, referring to his order for orange pekoe tea, told her, "I've appreciated orange pekoe ever since my visit to Sri Lanka. I found out there is no orange in orange pekoe tea. In fact, it's a grade of black tea."

"It is," Daisy confirmed. "The grading system for orange pekoe ranges from Orange Pekoe to Super Finest Tippy Golden Flowery Orange Pekoe."

"I learned that," Hiram acknowledged. "The leaf appearance determines the grade, right?"

"Yes, it does," Daisy said with a smile because Hiram was well informed. From what Daisy had heard yesterday, she surmised that Hiram Hershberger was never low key. He'd apparently experienced many travels, and he brandished his lifestyle now with flair in front of the community he'd abandoned. Apparently he was proud of what he'd accomplished and didn't intend to hide it, no matter who was watching.

"Would you like to see menus?" she asked both men.

"No need," Hiram told her as Troy Richter remained quiet. "I'm sure Troy trusts me when I say your baked goods are excellent. Bring him a selection, please. I'd like a cup of your cucumber avocado soup and those little chicken salad sandwiches if you have them. I'll sneak a cookie from Troy's selection."

"How about chocolate espresso cookies and mini lemon tarts?"

"That sounds perfect." Hiram winked at Troy as if to say, *I've got this covered.*

Troy Richter didn't look as if he were interested in what they were going to eat or drink. Daisy decided that wasn't *her* problem.

Richter, she thought to herself. *Richter*. She'd heard the name before, but she wasn't exactly sure where. She shouldn't even be trying to guess. Hiram's business was none of her concern.

However, as soon as she passed the sales counter in the main tearoom, Tessa, who was manning the sales desk, crooked her finger at Daisy.

Tessa Miller was Daisy's age. They'd gone to school together. Tessa lived on the second floor of the tea garden and was Daisy's best friend. She was a painter as well as Daisy's kitchen manager. Always dressing like an *artiste,* she wore colorful tops and skirts. Instead of a chef's coat, she wore a smock. Today it was patterned in lime green and yellow.

Tessa had French braided her caramel-colored hair to keep it in line, and her braid swung over her shoulder as she leaned toward Daisy. Her brown eyes were alight with curiosity. "Isn't that Troy Richter with Hiram Hershberger?"

"Do you know him?" Daisy kept her voice low. Tessa, along with everybody else in town it seemed, had heard what had happened yesterday at the social for the home-less shelter. She hadn't been there, but it appeared she knew Hiram and the man with him on sight.

"Troy Richter is the CEO of the Hope Clinic."

Whoa. That's where she'd heard the name. Hiram was

defending the clinic against a class action lawsuit. Had they come into the tea garden to discuss that? Wouldn't they meet in Hiram's office?

As if Tessa had read her thoughts, she said, "I understand Hiram often takes his clients to restaurants and coffee shops in York, Lancaster, and Philadelphia to discuss cases. As flamboyant as he is, I think he likes to be seen."

"He asked for a private table," Daisy remarked. "Maybe today he wants to be seen and not heard."

Tessa surreptitiously peeked into the spillover tearoom. "That's possible. Troy Richter looks as if he swallowed a strawberry whole," Tessa commented.

"I imagine the Hope Clinic has more than one problem," Daisy noted. "There could be a multitude of lawsuits, or a major class action suit." Daisy's attention suddenly swerved to the baked goods case and the order Hiram had requested. "Are you going back to the kitchen?"

"I am since that busload from this morning has departed. I was checking inventory. The case is almost empty. What do you need?"

She told Tessa what she'd promised the men.

"That's easy enough. I just made more of the chocolate espresso cookies. The tarts are in the walk-in. The cucumber soup is ready. I'll put together chicken salad and watercress sandwiches real quick."

"Sounds good. I'll watch the counter if you want to arrange the tier. They also ordered two orange pekoe iced teas."

"I'll have Cora Sue bring it all over."

"I'd like to take the tier to them myself," Daisy said.

Tessa's eyes sparkled with mischief. "You're just hoping you'll overhear something."

Daisy wagged her finger at Tessa.

Tessa ignored her and started toward the kitchen.

Five minutes later, Cora Sue had carried a tray with two iced teas, sugar syrup in a small crystal pitcher, cinnamon sticks lying across a cut-glass nappy, and a cup of cucumber soup, delivering it all with a flourish. When she stepped away and headed back toward the tearoom, Daisy carried the tiered plate of mini sandwich triangles, chocolate espresso cookies, and lemon tarts to the men's table.

Maybe Daisy had appeared more quickly than they expected because Hiram was tapping Troy Richter's arm saying, "The name of the tech who caused the accident will remain confidential. I promise you, no pressure put on me will induce me to reveal who was responsible. I'm steadfast. No one in my office will know the identity but me, mostly for the person's safety."

Troy responded in a morose tone, "Social media and the press are brutal. Nothing must get out."

They both looked up in surprise when Daisy set the tiered tray on the table. She didn't give any indication she'd overheard anything. She simply said, "Enjoy, gentlemen. Just let me know if you need anything else."

Then she retired from the room, leaving them in privacy once more.

When Daisy exited the kitchen an hour later to survey the tearoom, she was surprised to see Brielle Horn and her grandmother, Glorie Beck, sitting at a table for four in the center of the room. She was glad to see them. Brielle, a good friend of Jazzi's, had stayed with Daisy and Jazzi while her parents had been on a professional trip.

Brielle also helped serve at the tea garden this summer when a friend of Glorie's spent time with her . . . for Glorie's safety. Her arthritis inhibited her from doing activities she enjoyed. While Brielle had stayed with Daisy, Daisy had met Glorie, the seventeen-year-old's grandmother. She enjoyed the company of both, even though, at first, she hadn't been sure what to think of Brielle.

Approaching the table, Daisy could see that Brielle was keeping her hair short and spiked. Her natural black color made a contrast to her pink bangs. Her nose ring, eyebrow piercing, and Goth tattoos on her forearms had scared Daisy at first, if she was to be honest with herself. But she'd soon understood Brielle had to learn her own self-worth and how to make good decisions for her life. She was living with her grandmother now and they both looked happy as they sipped iced tea and munched on chocolate espresso cookies.

Glorie lived a somewhat plain life in a rural area of Willow Creek. Her curly, light-brown hair, streaked with gray, looked like a soft web around her face. Her uniform of sorts consisted of jeans and an oversized T-shirt. Today she wore a red one. Daisy had heard her claim many times that she didn't like fancy clothes.

Since everyone in the tearoom seemed content with what they were eating and drinking, Daisy looked around for her staff. Cora Sue stood at the sales counter ready to handle new customers. Foster, Vi's husband, was standing at the service cart glancing around, making sure everyone had what they needed. Since Daisy had just been in the kitchen, she knew everything was under control in there.

Foster gave her a thumbs-up sign and pointed to the table where Brielle and Glorie were seated. Daisy knew that meant he'd cover for her. She loved her son-in-law as if he were her own son. He was good for Vi and a caring dad with their son Sammy.

After she gave him a nod, she pulled out a chair and sat at Glorie and Brielle's table.

"What are you two up to?" Daisy asked, as she looked from Brielle to her grandmother.

"We just stopped in for a snack," Brielle answered, her gaze pointedly going to Glorie's cane which was propped against the table.

Glorie's arthritis bothered her daily. Brielle had moved in with her grandmother partly to assist her and to make her daily life a little easier. Brielle had a nurturing side, and Glorie brought it out.

Glorie finished a cookie and then met Daisy's gaze. "I'm not supposed to be eating sweets, you know. But a little chocolate never hurt anyone."

"She didn't put sugar in her tea, so she thinks she's entitled," Brielle commented wryly.

"We had to get out of my house," Glorie revealed.

"Why?" Daisy asked, genuinely puzzled.

"We didn't have to get out of your house." Brielle explained to Daisy, "Mom sent someone over to install a window air conditioner in my grandmother's bedroom. She's supposed to try it."

"It will give me all kinds of aches and pains, even worse than I already have," Glorie insisted.

"You haven't tried it yet," Brielle reminded her.

"I sit in air conditioning at the doctor's office. It gives me goose bumps."

Brielle's pierced eyebrow arched as she rolled her eyes. "Mom said if the air conditioner makes summer easier, then she'll have central air installed in the house. You won't have drafts then."

"That window unit is going to make too much noise and block the light from the window."

Brielle patted her grandmother's arm. "That's why you need to let Mom have central air installed. It's quiet, no drafts, and it simply runs like the heat."

Daisy watched the give-and-take between Glorie and Brielle. They were good for each other. The past was meeting the present, and granddaughter and grandmother were learning a different kind of compromise.

"I don't think the situation with the air conditioner is going to be settled today, is it?" Daisy asked, with a hint of a smile.

"I think she'll sleep better," Brielle said. "Once the temperature hits ninety or ninety-five, she'll be thankful for that air conditioner. The doctor told her she shouldn't be out in the heat when it gets too hot."

"I'm still going to watch over my garden," Glorie mumbled.

"Well, I'm going to fetch the produce and pull the weeds," Brielle assured her.

After they talked about Glorie's garden for a bit which was very similar to Daisy's, Daisy decided to change the subject. She said to Glorie, "You know a lot of people in this town."

"I sure do. When my husband and I had that produce stand out front of our property, you wouldn't believe all the people we talked to in a day. Not just the one season either. People came back, year after year."

"I'm looking for a little history," Daisy confided. "Did you hear what happened at the social for the homeless shelter?"

"I sure did hear." Glorie pushed her plate away from her. "Those protestors scared a whole group of folks."

"They did," Daisy agreed. Jumping to the question foremost in her mind, she asked, "Do you know the Lapp family?"

"I surely do. I even remember when Eli jumped the fence, and the rumors that swirled all over town."

Since that was a time before Daisy had returned to Willow Creek, she asked, "What rumors were those?"

"Eli's family was convinced that Hiram Hershberger was the main reason why Eli left the Amish community."

Daisy leaned closer to Glorie. "How could that be?"

Glorie put her hand to her forehead as if that might help her recall what had occurred. "Eli admired Hiram. From what I remember, Eli had lots of spirit and he wanted to make his own way in the world and expand his views."

"He wanted to continue his education?" Daisy knew that goal could be frowned on in the Amish community.

"Not so much that," Glorie said. "He wanted to get out of Willow Creek and do some traveling. From what I understand Hiram took in Eli when he left his community. Hiram funded a trip for Eli to go out West and to New York City so Eli could get a taste of the world. Eli had been in trouble when he was still in school as early as sixth grade, then seventh. Although I don't know the story behind it, he damaged some *Englischer*'s property and the man wanted to press charges. Hiram stepped in and saved Eli more than once. Many people in town could see that Eli wasn't happy being Amish. Only his family seemed shocked when he left."

Brielle had been listening intently. Now she asked, "Like my parents were shocked when I told them I wanted to live with you?"

"It was a little bit like that," Glorie agreed. "But much worse in Eli's case. His family cut him out of their lives."

Daisy thought about the Eli Lapp she had seen . . . with the camouflage inhalation mask, the hoodie, and the attitude. Would Eli have left the Amish if it hadn't been for Hiram Hershberger?

That was a question only Eli could answer.

Daisy had taken the day off on Wednesday. Their tea-room traffic in summer was much heavier at the end of the week and she liked to be at the Victorian then. She liked to cook at home, especially for friends and family. Jonas was coming to dinner along with Tessa and Trevor Lundquist. Fortunately Jazzi liked everyone's company too, so Daisy was really looking forward to the evening. Since the temperature outside had been around eighty all week, she'd decided they'd eat outside on her patio.

In preparation, she partially cooked chicken pieces in

the oven that Jonas would finish on the grill with a specific sauce they all liked. She'd found the recipe in an old
Fanny Farmer cookbook. Jonas had arrived first since he
was going to help her with the meal. The potato salad in
the refrigerator was ready along with pickled beets. Jazzi
had tossed a salad. Daisy had also made baked beans in
the slow cooker. Dessert would be chocolate cake with
peanut butter icing because she knew both Trevor and
Jonas liked it.

Trevor immediately went outside to help Jonas after he
and Tessa arrived.

Tessa asked, "What is it about men and grills?"

Daisy laughed.

Jazzi said, "I'm out of this conversation for a while.
I'll kick around a soccer ball outside unless you guys
need me."

After Jazzi went outside, Daisy and Tessa divided up
tasks. As Daisy quartered berries for fruit salad and Tessa
sliced tomatoes, Daisy said, "I read the article Trevor
wrote for the newspaper about the social on Sunday. He
summed it up the way it happened. He's getting good at
taking photos too. He captured good shots of the protestors."

"I saw the segment that played over and over again on
the local news." Tessa attractively arranged the tomato
slices on the plate. "The stations concentrated on that
more than they did the homeless shelter. It's a shame."

"I'm hoping Arden can generate good publicity for the
shelter. She says she can, but I don't know how much experience she's had."

"You don't know her background before she opened
Vinegar and Spice?" Tessa inquired.

"Not really. I think she was raised in Baltimore, but I don't know why she decided to come here and open a business."

"Why does anyone move to Willow Creek?" Tessa asked. "I think it's to escape."

"Or maybe to find a refuge," Daisy said. "That's why I returned with the girls."

"And I'm glad you did." Tessa's smile was wide.

Tessa's smile brought back all the experiences they'd shared, through middle school, through high school, through letters and email while Daisy had been in Florida starting her life. She and Tessa could read each other well. They always had been able to. That's why they had become best friends.

After they all gathered around the table outside, dished out helpings of chicken, potato salad, and other accompaniments, Jazzi said, "I made a list of the colleges I want to tour."

Trevor looked curious when he suggested, "Give me the list."

"I'm mostly interested in social work programs, so I'd like to tour Shippensburg, Penn State or a satellite campus, University of Pennsylvania, King's College, and maybe West Chester University."

"Wow," Trevor said. "I might have to help your mom at the tea garden if she takes off for all those visits."

Seeing Jazzi's face fall, Daisy realized her daughter obviously hadn't thought of that.

Jonas intervened. "The tea garden is a well-oiled machine. I'm sure your mom could take a few drives and it will manage to survive."

"I'm just kidding," Trevor said. "You should explore

as many colleges as you want. Make sure that's where you want to go. Even as important as exploring the campuses, you should talk to the students in the programs that you're interested in."

"But how do I do that?" Jazzi asked.

Putting her arm around her daughter's shoulders, Daisy gave her an idea. "I can contact Stella Cotton. She might know a way." Stella was the guidance counselor at Jazzi's high school, and she and Daisy were friends.

"There is something else you might want to think about." Tessa plucked a chicken wing from the platter onto her plate. "You're going to have to write an essay, probably more than one when you apply to these colleges. You need to really think about what you want to do in terms that you can explain. Why is social work important to you?"

"You all know the answer to that," Jazzi said. "Because I'm adopted . . . because I searched for my birth mother and found her. If I hadn't had Jonas's help and Mom's support, that could have gone south really fast."

"You need to put that personal connection in an essay," Tessa commented. "Whoever reads it needs to feel your passion and caring for the subject and why you think you'd be good at helping families."

Daisy nodded. "She's right."

"Most of the time," Trevor joked. "To my utter disappointment."

They all laughed.

"While Jazzi is searching out colleges, I'm going to be doing more freelancing." Trevor reached for the bowl of potato salad.

"What type of freelancing?" Jonas asked.

"Any kind I can think of," Trevor concluded. "I don't

know how long the newspaper is going to exist. You know how small-town newspapers are going out of business. Right now, I'm looking at a series of articles about small towns for a social influencer's blog. That might get me some notice to open up a network to submit articles to."

"Just what are you going to say about small towns?" Daisy wanted to know. Trevor could be acerbic and bluntly honest.

"Everything you already know," he explained offhandedly. "I think I might do the first article on gossip . . . the fact that it's the life of a small town."

"Trevor . . ." Daisy chided.

"I'm serious," he said with arched brows. "You know I'm right. Everyone's connected. News travels fast like a supersonic plane rather than a horse and buggy, though horses and buggies have something to do with it too. I think it will be an interesting article."

"It will probably hit raw nerves," Jonas noted, wrapping his hand around a glass of tea. "I know you'll put truth in the article that no one can deny. Gossip in small towns helps business. Recommendations circle around better than ads. I know that's the way I sell a lot of furniture. I had someone buy a hutch last week whose brother saw the piece and then he wanted bookshelves. A cousin told me yesterday that she was interested in a pedestal table. We might call it gossip, but it's more like a circular file system. The gossip acts like a hub and all the residents circulate around it."

"I might want to talk to you more about this," Trevor said. "*Before* I write the article."

Trevor's phone buzzed. When he took it from his pocket to check the screen, Tessa bumped his arm. He said offhandedly, "Daisy doesn't mind. She knows I have contacts."

"An important contact?" Tessa murmured.

"This one is," he said seriously.

"Take it," Daisy advised. "We don't mind."

Trevor answered the call and said tersely into the phone, "Give me what you've got." Daisy heard him say, "Thanks. I'll follow up, even if I have to go to the scene myself."

After Trevor ended the call, he set the phone on the table and just stared at it. Then he turned to the group. "Hiram Hershberger is dead."

CHAPTER FOUR

An hour and a half later, Trevor returned to Daisy's home with news of sorts. He lowered himself onto the sofa beside Tessa. "It's true. Hiram is dead."

"I just saw him on Monday. He looked healthy enough." Daisy was having trouble wrapping her mind around the news.

"When I got the phone call, my contact said it looked as if Hershberger died in his office from natural causes."

"I hear a *but* in your voice," Jonas noted.

"When I arrived at the scene, I found out from someone else that the cops think someone used a stun gun on Hershberger. There were burn marks on him."

"A taser or a stun gun?" Jonas asked.

"Not a taser. At least not that they can tell. We'll have to wait for the autopsy to know for sure. I can't imagine merely the stun gun would have killed him."

"Was there a sign of anything else around?" Daisy asked. She'd become used to examining details about crime scenes and asking questions about them.

"That's the thing, Daisy," Trevor said with warning chagrin. "There will probably be a cop at your door or one of the detectives."

When that news took Daisy's breath away, Tessa asked, "Whatever for?"

"A cup of tea sat on Hershberger's desk. One of those bags of tea like you sell with an orange pekoe label—it had the tea garden's logo on it—lay on the credenza beside an electric urn. At least that's what my person who saw the crime scene said."

"I'd like to know who this person is," Jonas murmured.

"A journalist never reveals his sources," Trevor returned, half-seriously and half-kidding.

"Just what I need, a detective at the door of the tea garden," Daisy murmured.

"You can always go down to the station," Trevor advised with a twinkle in his eye.

"That would look even worse," Daisy protested. "I can imagine customers watching me slide into a patrol car to go down to the police station."

"They probably just want to ask you about the tea. You served the same kind at the social," Trevor reminded her.

"I know I did. And when Hiram came with his friend Troy Richter to the tea garden, he bought some. I guess he liked it that much. Now I wish he'd simply bought it at the grocery store."

"Anything else we should know?" Jonas asked Trevor.

Trevor raked his fingers through his hair, seeming lost in the information he'd gathered. "Not particularly. Right now the police are canvassing the area for witnesses. You never know who might have been around when the mur . . ." Trevor cut off his word and inserted instead, "When the death happened."

Trevor had almost said *murder*.

"The rumors are going to fly around town quicker than a telephone wire can take them," Jonas said.

"I bet cell towers are pinging already," Trevor added.

"Are the police spreading the news about the stun gun into the public domain?" Jonas wanted to know.

"No, but *I* found out." Trevor shrugged. "Leaks are called leaks for a reason. But my guess is they might keep the autopsy results under wraps. I think they're going to try to rush that."

"If a stun gun was used," Daisy surmised, "they'll certainly be pulling in suspects."

Jonas's expression was pensive. "Maybe not suspects. But I expect they'll be bringing people in who knew Hiram, especially anyone he's spoken to in the last few days."

Tessa nudged Daisy's arm. "If you *do* talk to the police, make sure you tell them about Troy being at the tea garden with Hiram. That's one connection they should know about."

"Especially since Troy was one of his clients," Daisy concluded.

"That's pretty much public knowledge," Trevor said. "But do tell the police, Daisy. Did Hershberger and Richter look like they were arguing?"

After Daisy thought about the scene that day, she answered quickly. "No. Hiram seemed to be himself. Troy Richter looked very serious. But then he's the one who might have a class action suit filed against his company."

"The detectives will want to collect any information they can," Jonas said. "Did your contact say if the office looked as if it had been ransacked . . . as if someone was searching for something?"

"My person didn't say that, and I didn't ask. How could I have missed that? I'll try to find out, but I would think if file cabinets had been opened or anything looked disturbed, she might have told me that."

"She?" Jonas asked.

"I was just using a universal pronoun," Trevor retorted.

"I won't ask any more questions about that because I know you're serious about keeping your sources intact. But, Trevor, it isn't good if there *is* a leak. You're not going to print any of this, are you?"

"Of course not, not until I get an okay from one of the detectives. But I'll tell you, with the crime that's gone on here in the past few years, I might think about doing a crime blog or even a podcast. You know the kind. It keeps the public up-to-date with how the crime is being solved. I might even look up cold cases and go after those. That's quite popular now from what I hear."

"Do you want to be a crime reporter or a detective?" Tessa asked with a bit of humor.

Trevor leaned his shoulder against her. "Sometimes investigations lead to solving crimes. Maybe I could help with it like Daisy does. But I see my blog expanding into an area bigger than Willow Creek. It's something else I'll have to think about. I have to make a living, Tessa, if I want a life . . . if I want a stable job so I can settle down some day."

Daisy watched Tessa's eyes grow a little shiny. Had these two talked about having a life together? Stability would mean a lot to Tessa because of her background. Did Trevor know that?

She and Tessa would have to have a heart to heart sometime soon.

Trevor leaned back into the sofa cushion. "In the upcoming few days, I'm going to be watching the detectives, where they go, and who goes into the police station."

"And at night, I'll be typing up all your notes," Tessa said but not with any rancor.

"I use a digital recorder most of the time when I'm talking to people," he told Jonas and Daisy. "But in the evening, I have to put it all together somehow."

"He's a perfectionist," Tessa said. "He won't turn in an article until every word is exactly the way he wants it . . . until every word says exactly what it should."

Apparently Tessa had seen Trevor working. Apparently she'd been around when he pulled his thoughts together and wrote up his articles. That was news to Daisy, even though it shouldn't have been. Trevor's work was a big part of his life. But it obviously didn't bring in the income that he'd like. Trevor was smart. He'd figure it out, and Tessa would give him the chance to do that if she was serious about him.

"I think we all need another round of chocolate cake," Daisy decided.

"And black tea," Trevor said. "I need the caffeine if I'm going to be up tonight making lists of questions, as well as lists of people I want to talk to, and looking up all types of stun guns and what they do."

Jonas said pensively, almost to himself in rapid-fire order, "Stun guns are legal in Pennsylvania. And someone had to get close to Hiram to *use* a stun gun. A taser can be used from a distance. A stun gun immobilizes the victim. The thing is—there has to be a reason for that immobilization."

"I don't understand," Tessa said.

"I've been thinking about this while we've been talking," Jonas explained. "If someone had come to Hiram's office to rob him, Hiram could have used a stun gun on the thief. I can see two scenarios. Either someone took the stun gun from Hiram and used it on him, say in a struggle . . . or someone came in with the intent to use the stun gun on Hiram."

"But why?" Daisy asked.

Jonas stood. "Maybe the autopsy will tell us that. I think maybe we should get out that bottle of Wild Turkey bourbon Daisy has hidden in her cupboard and have it with the black tea. What do you think?"

Tessa raised her hand. "I'm the designated driver. Go ahead, Trevor, if you want to pour some in."

"Maybe just a tad," he said with a hint of a smile. "It'll settle me down before the caffeine stirs me up."

"I think even I could use a little bourbon in my tea," Daisy decided. "Chocolate cake and bourbon tea it is."

Daisy loved the scents of summer. In her backyard on Sunday, she could smell the first bloom of roses. Here in Pennsylvania the first blooms were often the best. Her Double Delight was fuchsia and white. Her yellow Peace rose was a wide bloom that created full beautiful bouquets. Chrysler Imperial roses manifested a deep red-fuchsia bloom, huge with the most wonderful scent that could fill the first floor of her house if she brought enough of them in. Roses did take a little care, but not usually this first bloom. When the weather became more humid, she would go out in the mornings and spray them with a baking soda and water solution. That would help keep away black spot.

What she liked most about summer was holding gatherings outside. On Friday she'd called Piper and asked if she and Emory wanted to come to dinner. Daisy had said she'd invite her daughter Vi and son-in-law Foster too. She thought the four would have a lot in common. They could keep the outing casual and barbecue hot dogs and hamburgers in the backyard.

At first Piper had been hesitant, but then she'd said, "I think it would do Emory and me good to talk with another couple."

"Would you like me to ask your father to join us?" Daisy had suggested in case Lawrence's presence would make the couple feel more comfortable.

"Don't take this the wrong way, but I'd rather if it was just us," Piper had pleaded. "Dad inserts his opinions and sometimes Emory sides with him. I'd like to just talk without all the tension."

"Do you mind if I invite Jonas?"

"Of course not. He and Emory seemed to connect. What can I bring?" Piper had asked.

"What would you *like* to bring? Anything goes with a picnic supper."

"I have a couscous salad recipe that would be good. Would you and Jonas like that?"

"We're open to anything. That sounds good. And you can teach me how to make it."

"It's easy. What time would you like us there?"

"Why don't you aim to arrive at five and we'll eat around six."

"Can I ask you something?" Piper inquired.

"Sure, you can." Daisy wondered why Piper didn't just wait until Sunday. But then she found out.

"You said you and your husband adopted Jazzi because you couldn't have more children. When you found out you couldn't have more kids, did that affect your marriage? I'm sorry if that's too personal to ask."

It didn't take much intuition to realize that Piper's subtext was that whatever was happening with her and Emory was affecting their marriage.

"Ryan and I were committed to each other," Daisy confided. "But we had rough times. He kept trying to convince me that Vi and I were enough, that we didn't have to have any more children. Yet when we first got married, we talked about having two or more kids. I didn't want him giving up something that he might resent in the future. He didn't want to push me into something I didn't want to do. I don't think he was really on board with adoption until we worked through it and decided we could love any child as much as we loved Violet. It would be a promise like our marriage vows were. So we decided to adopt."

"I see," Piper had said, but Daisy wasn't sure she really had seen.

"We had arguments, Piper. We had a lot of tension. But we didn't go to bed angry and we smiled at each other in the morning, for our own sakes as much as for Vi's."

"What you're telling me is that even when things look bad, you have to stay optimistic."

"Yes. And work out a plan that can suit you both."

Now Jonas broke in on Daisy's thoughts about her phone conversation with Piper. He exited the sliding glass doors that led to the patio from the kitchen, carrying a large tray with two platters. On one platter, hot dogs were stacked and the other held beef patties. He looked good today, but then she might be a bit biased. His black hair was blowing in the breeze. He wore a light-blue T-shirt that made his skin look even more tanned than usual. She knew he'd been working the last couple of weeks helping someone tear down a barn. The farmer had told Jonas if he helped in the project, Jonas could have any of the reclaimed wood to use on his own creations. That was exactly the type of thing Jonas liked to do. Today he was wearing black cargo shorts and natural leather sandals. To her relief, he was feeling more at home around her house, and she liked that he was.

As he headed toward the grill, Daisy did too.

"It's a shame Jazzi couldn't be here. She enjoys a picnic," Jonas commented.

"Jazzi told me she'd let the couples enjoy their time together . . . that she'd rather go swimming over at Stacy's. But I really don't think she wanted to feel like the odd girl out, or like Sammy's babysitter. She's working a lot this summer at the tea garden and babysitting. So I'm glad she could enjoy time with her friend today."

Jonas set the platters on the shelf beside the grill. "Has she seen Brielle much?"

"Not as much now that they're not in school. Only on days they work at the tea garden together. Brielle isn't working as much as I thought she might. I think she's afraid to leave her grandmother. She feels she's there to take care of Glorie and that's what she has to do. But I'm a little concerned about that. Brielle needs time to be a teenager as well as a caregiver. Still, I don't feel I can butt in. I think Glorie will come to realize the same thing."

Jonas opened the lid on the gas grill.

Daisy remembered she'd forgotten to carry out the vegetable kabobs."

However, before she took a step toward the kitchen, Foster, Vi, and Sammy burst through the door. Vi was carrying Sammy while Foster toted a play circle deck that would work well on the patio. Sammy could sit in it and play with the toys around the circle. It would keep him occupied some of the time.

Letting Vi and Foster settle Sammy while Jonas put the meat on the grill, Daisy waited inside for Piper and Emory. While she pulled dishes from the refrigerator and set them on the counter to take outside, she thought about what the young couple was going through. She was setting rolls in a basket with a napkin liner when the doorbell rang. She hurried to the door eagerly, ready to invite the couple inside. Between the time the doorbell rang and the time she got to the door, something must have transpired between the couple.

Piper was saying, "I don't want to think about using hormones again and going through another cycle. Your body doesn't get crazy with it. *Mine* does."

Emory snapped back, "But I have to live with you while you're being crazy."

They both blinked at Daisy as if they hadn't expected her to open the door so quickly.

"Come on in," Daisy said to break the tension. "As I told you, we're eating outside. Vi and Foster are already here. They're anxious to meet you."

"I'd be anxious too." Emory said the comment under his breath, but still Daisy heard it. So did Piper. She gave him a glaringly dark look.

If Daisy sliced her hand in the air between Piper and

Emory, she could probably have felt the tension gumming up the atmosphere. It was that thick. "Would you two like a few minutes to talk?"

"We've done enough talking," Emory said with a sigh.

Daisy heard a meow from the landing. Marjoram sat there, her golden eyes on Daisy as if asking what the ruckus was all about. Her sister Pepper pattered down the steps beside her and stared at the couple.

Looking pretty in a strawberry-patterned sundress, Piper's expression was a combination of frustrated and sad as she carried a bowl with a lid. Emory, who was wearing charcoal board shorts and a gray T-shirt had his fists balled on his hips.

As Piper went toward the stairs, Daisy took the bowl from her hands.

"Aren't you two adorable?" Piper exclaimed.

Hearing the caring in Piper's voice, Pepper came down two more steps. When Piper offered her hand, Pepper smelled it and then rubbed against it. Piper sank down on the step while rubbing the cat's neck.

Petting a cat was a good calming mechanism, Daisy knew.

"Emory," Daisy said. "Would you like a beer? There are bottles in the refrigerator. We didn't take the drinks outside yet. If you don't mind, you can gather sodas too and take them out to the table."

"I don't mind," he said, looking a little less like he wanted to bite somebody.

In the kitchen, Daisy motioned to the doors leading to the patio. "I'll be out in a couple of minutes. Piper can help me bring out the food." Since Piper seemed to enjoy petting the cats, Daisy went to the kitchen.

A few minutes later, Piper wandered out to the kitchen. She motioned to the sink. "Is it okay if I wash my hands here?"

"Of course. I'm glad you made friends with Pepper. She's friendlier than Marjoram. Marjoram takes a little while to get to know somebody before she allows petting."

"Pepper even laid on the step and let me rub her belly. Most cats won't let you do that, not without a few kicks and scratches."

Daisy tossed the salad she'd assembled. "You're familiar with cats?"

"I had them growing up." Piper turned on the spigot and used the foamy soap on the counter. "Mom and Dad still have two."

After she dried her hands on the towel, she said, "I'm sorry about that scene at the door. Emory and I seem to argue about everything now."

"It's a tense time for the two of you."

"It is, but I feel like Emory is making it worse," Piper insisted. "He's pushing to take some kind of action, and I just want to absorb what's happened and think about what I want to do next."

Adding a serving spoon to the salad bowl, Daisy asked, "What's he pushing for?"

"First of all, I've looked into adoption. That's as expensive as a round of *in vitro*. I don't want to go deeper in debt. And even if the Hope Clinic is willing to give us a round of *in vitro* without cost, I don't know if I want to go through that again."

"Is it a possibility that they'll do that?"

"That all depends if they want to settle." Piper fidgeted

with the belt on her sundress. She looked as if she wanted to say more.

Taking a guess, Daisy suggested, "You don't think Emory understands how difficult it is for you."

Piper sank down onto one of the island chairs. "I know he doesn't. No man can understand what hormones do to a woman, the lack of them or too many of them. But on top of that, Emory's talking about finding out the identity of the person who caused the refrigeration malfunction. He wants to sue them separately from the class action suit."

"Does he really?" Daisy asked gently. "Or is he just trying to find an outlet for his frustration and anger?"

"That's probably the case," Piper agreed. "Other than telling him to go to a batting cage to take out his frustrations, I don't know what to do with him." She stopped suddenly and looked outside to where Emory was talking with Jonas. She also saw Sammy in his play deck sitting on the patio. Violet was stooping over him showing him something there. Foster was making funny faces at him and the little boy giggled.

Piper said, "And Emory probably doesn't know what to do with me. We're a pair, aren't we?"

"You're going through a tough time. Maybe having tonight simply to talk and joke and smile will help. I'm sure Vi will understand whatever you're feeling. And Foster can talk to Emory. We'll have a good night."

Piper seemed to make up her mind. Her shoulders were straighter and her chin was higher when she suggested, "Let's carry this food outside and have a picnic."

Daisy picked up a couple of the dishes and followed Piper out the sliding screened door.

* * *

Later that night after all the company had left except Jonas, Daisy sat on the sofa beside him. Jazzi had come home and after chatting a bit, she'd gone upstairs to her room with the cats.

Jonas asked Daisy, "Do you think Piper and Emory's marriage is going to survive this?"

"I suppose it depends on how much they want to stay together."

"If they can make decisions together," Jonas added.

"Decisions about babies aren't easy." Daisy had often spoken to Jonas about what she and Ryan had gone through—the guilt, the worry, their attempts to try to forge a future.

"If only we all had crystal balls," she said.

"Or if we thought like the Amish that everything works according to God's plan and will work out in the end," Jonas reminded her.

"Do you believe that?" Daisy asked, looking up at him, hoping in their future.

"I'm still trying to decide," he answered. "How about you?"

"I don't believe that as intensely as the Amish do. I feel what we do ourselves has a lot to do with God's plan."

"You go to church every Sunday," Jonas said. "Do you mind if I ask what you pray for?"

She didn't hesitate to answer. "I pray that my family, all of it, will stay healthy and they can meet everything that comes their way with grace and fortitude. I know life isn't easy. It's been easier for me than a lot of other people. Working at the tea garden, I hear so many stories. I see what our elderly customers are going through. I understand when cancer hits one member of the family, it affects the whole family. Ryan's battle with it taught me that. I watch couples like Piper and Emory and Vi and Foster struggling, trying to make enough income to raise a family, attempting to make decisions that won't benefit just one of them, but the whole unit."

"You've taught your girls well." There was admiration in Jonas's voice.

"I've tried."

They were gazing into each other's eyes when Daisy's phone played its tuba sound. It was sitting on the coffee table, and Daisy spotted Trevor's picture come up on the screen.

"I can let it go to voice mail," she told Jonas.

"He might have found out more information about Hiram's death. If you want to take it, I'm okay with that."

She squeezed his hand. "You're as interested as I am."

He grimaced. "I'll never admit to that."

"Hi, Daisy," Trevor said when she answered.

"Did you find out anything?" She knew he'd tell her if he did. They had a sort of a deal that had originated with one of her first murder investigations.

"The police found a witness."

She jumped on that. "A witness who recognized who went into Hiram's office?"

"Not exactly. The witness saw someone come from Hiram's office wearing a hoodie with one of those pollution masks and a baseball cap under the hoodie."

"So the detectives really aren't any further ahead."

"You could look at it that way," Trevor decided. "I think they're talking again to all the protestors. But anybody could have bought one of those masks somewhere, and hoodies are available everywhere as are baseball caps," he said with a bit of cynicism.

"So what's the bottom line?" she wanted to know.

"The bottom line is that they're paying special attention to Eli Lapp."

CHAPTER FIVE

The following morning after Daisy had refreshed each bud vase with a pink rose on every table in the yellow tearoom, she received an unusual phone call from Brielle Horn's mom. "Can you make time to meet with me?" Nola asked.

Today Brielle had come to work as a server. Right now she was helping Jazzi brew tea.

This was an unusual request from Nola Horn. Daisy had had a few sessions with Brielle's mom, but not everyday contact. "Is there a problem with Brielle working today?" Brielle had told Daisy that Mrs. Green, Glorie's friend, would be staying with her grandmother.

"No, no problem. I know she's working at the tea garden today. That's why I'd like to request that you come to my house."

This sounded important . . . maybe to Brielle and maybe to her grandmother too.

Over her lunch break, Daisy told her staff she had to run an errand but she'd be back within the hour. She hoped that would be true. June days were busy with tourists and bus tours and she didn't want to let her staff down.

Daisy had never been to Brielle's true home. She'd heard a lot about it. She'd gotten the impression that it was a mansion of sorts with a maid's suite and so many rooms a girl could get lost in . . . and feel lonely in. The house was in the country, though much of Willow Creek could be considered rural and country.

Daisy drove to the address Nola had given her and pulled into the long driveway. The edifice had an impressive entrance with a huge double door and palladium windows that rose high into the second story under a gable. There were two sharp roof pitches, both with more decorative windows. The triple-car garage had its own peaked roof and was set sideways on the lot and attached to the house. The house was all brick and Daisy guessed it was at least five thousand square feet.

Daisy took the walkway around the garage to the front door and noticed the security lights set into the ground along the manicured landscaping. Decorative spiral pines stood on either side of the stately entrance.

She climbed the two steps and rang the doorbell. A gong reverberated inside.

Daisy had taken off her apron at the tea garden and was dressed as she always was for work. Today she wore a comfortable pair of yellow cotton slacks and a yellow-and-white pin-striped blouse with cap sleeves. She wasn't sure why she thought of her appearance now except that every time she'd seen Brielle's mother, Nola had been dressed to the hilt, including spiked heels and professional suits. However, now when the woman opened the door, she looked much different than she had the last time Daisy had seen her.

Nola was in her mid-forties but today she looked older. She was wearing wrinkled off-white yoga pants that were loose around her ankles. The full blouse she wore with it had been buttoned incorrectly. She was thin. Daisy had noticed that before and she'd thought of her as skinny. Instead of her brown hair caught in a perfect bun at the nape of her neck as Daisy had seen her in the past, the strands hung down loose and stringy. Her hazel eyes were red around the edges as was her small nose that looked as if it had been wiped many times. She was bare-footed too. Previously, Daisy had noticed Nola's shoes had red soles on them which meant a very high price. Now her toenails weren't even manicured nor were her fingernails.

Daisy was suddenly concerned about the woman. "Are you okay?"

Nola stepped back deeper into the two-story foyer. Right away Daisy noticed the cool air-conditioned temperature, the hardwood floors that gleamed, and the floor-to-ceiling windows that let in so much natural light.

"Come into the kitchen," Nola invited. "We can have a cup of tea if you'd like."

"That would be fine." Daisy followed Nola through the two-story great room where a three-sided glass fireplace shared its warmth with the great room and the kitchen. When Daisy looked up, she saw a second floor catwalk that led to the upstairs bedrooms. Columns held it up. The house was as quiet as a tomb . . . and cold as one too.

Her clogs echoed on the wood floors as she and Nola walked into the kitchen. Daisy looked around and thought what a joy it would be to cook here. There was a double oven, gas stove, and a huge island for plenty of prep space. The ceramic tile flooring was neutral as were the granite countertops. The backsplash looked like Carrara marble. White custom cabinets lined the walls. The black handles represented a newer trend in kitchen design. The eat-in area where Nola gestured for Daisy to sit had a view of rolling farmland and a forest of pines. Puffy white clouds swagged across the blue sky above the treetops. Although the rest of the house was in pristine condition as far as Daisy could see, papers of some sort were spread all over part of the prep counter near the stove.

Nola quickly pushed them all together into a pile as if she were ashamed to have them there.

After silently pulling a copper teapot from a cupboard and filling it with water from the pot filler over the stove, she set it on a burner. She flipped on the burner, then opened the glass-fronted cupboard and pulled out teacups and saucers translucent enough to see through. After she set them on the table, Daisy noted that they were Lenox, one of the vintage patterns from the nineteen seventies. It was beautiful off-white china with white and yellow flowers on the rim and platinum trim on the outside and center rims. The teacup had the flowers circling the cup with a platinum rim on that too. Brookdale had been one of those patterns that a woman might register for at a fine jewelry store. She knew because Rose Gallagher had taken her and her sister Camellia to flea markets and pointed out the fine china. The china displays had always fascinated her mom . . . and Daisy too.

Her mother used to say, "Someday your dad is going to buy me a set of this china." He hadn't bought her Brookdale but something similar. Daisy remembered her dad had bought her mom that china on their fifteenth anniversary and her mother had been proud. She used it now for family dinners. When Daisy needed extra china, Rose lent it to her. It was a mother-daughter thing.

"The china is beautiful," Daisy commented to at least start small talk.

"I bought it in a consignment shop when I was first married," Nola commented but her voice broke a bit.

They were quiet until the teapot whistled on the stove and Nola switched off the burner. Crossing to another cupboard, she pulled out a cut-glass dish with an assortment of teabags and brought them to the table. "I'm sorry I don't have brewed tea. I never take the time. My mother used to, though."

At that, Daisy thought Nola's eyes misted over. Mother-daughter relationships could be very complicated.

To cut the tension, Daisy said, "You have a favorite of mine—country peach."

"Do you take sugar? I'm sorry I don't have any cream or lemon."

"No need for those. The peach tea itself is fine."

Daisy dunked her teabag into her cup and pulled it up and down, hoping the process of brewing would help Nola relax.

Nola chose a tea bag labeled cranberry. As she dipped it, her tea turned a beautiful shade of pinkish red. She'd also brought teabag holders and now they both settled their teabags on them.

"It will need a minute until it cools down," Nola said. "I wouldn't want you to burn yourself."

"I won't. While it's cooling, why don't you tell me why you wanted to see me?"

"Elliott and I are getting a divorce."

Even though Brielle had suspected that might happen, Daisy hadn't known if it would. Both Nola and her husband were lawyers and they had a joint practice, besides having a marriage.

"It's been a long time coming." Nola stared into her cup as if she was looking into the past. "Brielle doesn't know yet. I don't want to lose her along with my husband. I'm not sure what to do."

"How can I help?" Daisy asked softly.

Nola picked up her teacup and held it with both hands. "I'd like you to make sure Brielle and Jazzi have plenty of time together so Brielle has somebody she can talk to. I'm open to her talking to you too because I'm afraid she won't discuss the divorce with me."

"You don't know that. Brielle is expressive. She doesn't usually hold back her feelings."

"She doesn't with *you*. She does with me and her dad. I have something else on my mind too. I want Brielle to go to college, but I'm afraid she's going to want to stay in Willow Creek with my mom. I can see no reason to keep this house unless my mother would move in with me. I've asked her before and she said she wouldn't. Do you have any advice? Brielle and my mom respect you, so I guess I do too."

Daisy took a tentative sip of her tea. "Have you asked your mom again to move in?"

"She doesn't know about this either."

Daisy wasn't sure she should give Nola any advice. This was her private business and Daisy had no business intruding. "Are you sure you want me to tell you what I think?"

Nola set her teacup on her saucer with a decided click. "I'd welcome advice from somebody other than my financial advisor."

Nola probably paid him well for his advice. "You can't make all the decisions on your own when they involve other people because you have no idea how they're feeling unless you ask them. Do you think this is the time to make big decisions . . . like selling the house?"

"Probably not. But financially I really don't have any choice."

After studying Nola with her woebegone expression, Daisy decided to tell her what she thought. "My advice, if I have any, is to spend time with both Brielle and Glorie. See them separately and together. That could give you all direction."

"Do you really think so?" Nola sounded as if she wanted to be pumped up with more hope.

"I do. I won't say anything to Brielle until you speak with her, I promise you that."

Nola picked up her teacup once more. "I can see why Brielle likes being with you and Jazzi. I wish I could have provided that for her."

"Maybe you still can. Don't jump to the biggest decision you have to make. Try making the small ones first."

"Thank you," Nola said.

"Anytime," Daisy agreed.

Nola even smiled a little. "Maybe you'll have to teach me how to brew a real cup of tea."

* * *

When Daisy walked into Jonas's store—Woods—after she left the tea garden for the day, she realized his shop was a bevy of activity. She would be attending a concert in the park with Jonas tonight. She'd stopped in to make plans . . . and merely because she wanted to see him.

Jonas's store carried handcrafted furniture that he and others in the area created. She felt the store was always perfectly arranged. Huge high cubicles lined one side. The star of each cubicle was a ladder-back chair, each in a different color or finish, from blue to yellow to green to cherry and walnut. She felt any piece in the store—pine, oak, or aspen and always finished with a glossy shine—would fit into any house or apartment. However today, along with the pedestal library tables, the armoires and highboys, other pieces of furniture were clustered around—islands of reclaimed wood with quartz tops, reclaimed wood bookcases, side tables in reclaimed wood, distressed with blue, green, or white paint.

The store was absolutely packed with furniture. Daisy suspected Jonas's workshop behind the store also held new islands, tables, and hutches. There had been so much interest in the reclaimed furniture pieces that Jonas had set into the front window over the past few months, that he and Elijah Beiler had decided to undertake a special event. It was going to be located in a barn on Elijah's property. Elijah was a farmer who also handcrafted furniture. When his boys could take over farming details, he helped Jonas in the store. Elijah Beiler was a kind man, Amish, and true to his beliefs. Jonas liked being around him and so did Daisy. She hoped this endeavor of theirs was going to be a success.

To her surprise, Eli Lapp was in the store, covering one of the granite-tops with bubble wrap. She imagined each piece of furniture had to be wrapped and handled carefully while it was moved to Elijah's barn. The barn hadn't been ready before now to house all the pieces. After all, Elijah ran a working farm. But now was the time to move tagged and priced furniture there.

She knew Jonas had said Eli apprenticed with him sometimes. She just hadn't expected to see him today.

Jonas wore black jeans, low boots, and a wine-colored Henley short-sleeved shirt. Even his neck looked strong. His black chest hair peeked out over the buttons of the Henley. His forehead was creased with lines as he spoke with Eli. She couldn't help but look him up and down and admire everything about Jonas. He must have felt her eyes on him because he turned, spotted her, and smiled.

She crossed the store to where he and Eli were working. Today Eli was dressed in a blue shirt and black broadcloth pants. No suspenders though.

After she said hello to Eli and he greeted her in return, she said, "Everything here is gorgeous. I could fill my house with these tables and chairs and hutches. In fact, Jazzi is looking for a bookcase for her room. She's tired of moving piles of books from one place on the floor to another."

Eli raised his head to look at her. "Jonas has bookshelves in the workroom. They're fine."

"I imagine they are. I'll check them out before I leave."

Jonas playfully bumped her arm with his. "If Jazzi needs a bookshelf, I can easily make her one. You don't have to buy it."

Eli stared at Jonas. "That's no way to make money."

"Maybe not," Jonas agreed. "But I like to give my work to the people I love."

Daisy had never heard Jonas use the love word in public before. Her heart skipped happy beats.

As if he seemed a bit embarrassed that he had said the word aloud, Jonas changed the subject. "Eli and I were just discussing why he's against the homeless shelter."

"I'd like to hear about that too," Daisy suggested.

After Eli wrapped packing tape around the bubble wrap, he straightened and studied her as if to see if she meant her comment.

He must have decided that she did because he said, "Even though I left the Amish community, I still share some of the beliefs I learned as a child."

"What beliefs?" Daisy asked, curious what this would have to do with the homeless shelter.

"I believe families in the community should help their own before they become homeless, like Hiram helped me."

In a sense, she agreed with Eli. Still, she asked, "What if the family doesn't help? What if banks won't extend the grace period for a mortgage when a person's out of work? What if employers lay off employees without notice? What if families are already strapped and can't provide for another person?"

Eli was already shaking his head. "There is always enough food for everyone if we share. There's enough room in the smallest house if someone stays in a sleeping bag overnight. This town spending so much money on a shelter is wasteful."

This was a con against the shelter that Daisy hadn't heard before. Curious, she asked, "Did Hiram agree with you?"

Eli's face darkened as he frowned. "No, he didn't."

Eli's protest against the shelter seemed flimsy to Daisy. There was so much more to it than offering someone a place to stay overnight. There could be counseling and job training as well as help to give people a new life. But Eli believed what he believed, and she couldn't argue with that.

Jonas rested his hands on the bubble-wrapped granite surface and leaned slightly on it to peer at Eli with more care. "I understand why you have the beliefs you do," Jonas said. "But why did you wear a mask to the protest?"

"I wore it and didn't want to take it off because I didn't want anyone taking my picture or putting me on the news."

Jonas exchanged a look with Daisy and Daisy could sense what he was thinking. Daisy knew the Amish forbade photography of individuals. Their objection was based on the second commandment coming from Exodus. *Thou shall not make unto thee any graven image or any likeness of anything that is in heaven above or that is in the earth beneath or that is in the water under the earth.* It was a basic tenet and apparently Eli still believed in that one too. His Amish upbringing had apparently had a deep and abiding influence on him.

She looked at Eli differently today than she had on the day of the social when he'd been dressed in a hoodie and a camouflage inhalation mask. She was reminded that outside appearances didn't always reveal the person inside. Though she knew Eli was under suspicion for Hiram's death, she didn't think this young man who cherished the beliefs of his Amish faith could have done anything like that.

Would the detectives agree with her?

* * *

Concerts in the park were something new the community had started this year. Music was supplied by local bands. Tonight, the Rockin' Aces were playing oldies but goodies.

Daisy and Jonas sat on a blanket on the grass. The scents of summer were all around them—pine, leafed-out trees, honeysuckle not so far away. The honeysuckle brought memories back to Daisy of the times with Rachel on her family farm. Honeysuckle had grown up along the house on a trellis and smelled wonderful. It also attracted bees, and Rachel and Daisy had done their best to stay away from them. Rachel's brothers not so much.

The band played on a small stage surrounded by a white picket fence. The town council had spent time arguing with citizens about the cost of bringing electricity to the stage. But without the speakers no one in the park would have been able to hear the music except for citizens who sat close to the stage.

As Jonas and Daisy listened to the band's version of *My Girl*, Jonas dropped his arm around Daisy's shoulders.

Not only did this music have a good beat and romantic lyrics, but the words meant something to Daisy. She often played the oldies station on her phone's radio app when she was cooking or gardening or cleaning.

Her reverie was interrupted when Trevor and Tessa arrived to join them. Trevor unfurled a blanket next to theirs. "I thought there'd be more people here," he said.

"I guess this music won't draw a crowd," Daisy said with a smile.

"Or everyone is just too busy to take the time and enjoy the music," Trevor suggested.

Tessa, who had seated herself on the other side of

Trevor, leaned across him to say to Daisy, "I like that out-fit. That violet color becomes you. Those earrings too. You don't get dressed up often enough."

Jonas eyed Tessa. "Are you saying I don't take her out on enough dates?"

"If the shoe fits . . ." Tessa teased, never one to mince words with either of them.

Instead of being insulted, Jonas laughed. "I'll keep that in mind. More dinner dates in expensive restaurants."

"You'll be able to afford it after that sale you and Elijah are going to have," Trevor said. "You ought to be auctioning off the furniture. You'd make more money."

"Ever the pragmatist." Tessa bumped Trevor's shoulder with her own.

After a pause, Trevor said, "I do come bearing news."

Suddenly all attention was riveted on him, and the music faded into the background.

"What?" Daisy asked.

"The autopsy on Hiram was completed. The coroner suspected something beyond the stun gun killed him. It did. Hiram was killed with an insulin overdose. The autopsy revealed two injection sites. Apparently the stun gun was used to immobilize him for the injections. The killer knew exactly what he or she was doing."

CHAPTER SIX

The next day, Daisy left the tea garden to do an errand. As she walked down the steps at the front of the Victorian, a horse and buggy clomped down Market Street. The sound was as native to Willow Creek as the view of farmland surrounding the town. This horse was a beauty—a sturdy sorrel. Daisy couldn't help her gaze from following it a bit as it clip-clopped along the street.

The door of the tea garden opened behind her. Daisy exchanged greetings with Fiona Wilson, a regular older customer.

Fiona said, "Just the sight of the tea garden when I approach it makes me smile."

Daisy turned back to the tea garden to see if she could view it as Fiona must. She studied the green Victorian with its white trim, gingerbread edging, and the covered porch. A rainbow of ceramic pots sat on the gray plank flooring. The pots contained herbs like lavender, sage, and chocolate mint. Pink and yellow petunias added their color as did perky marigolds in orange and yellow, as well as zinnias in red, pink, and white. Her parents had started them at their nursery, Gallagher's Garden Corner, in early spring.

Daisy was proud of the business she and her aunt had developed. Her Aunt Iris was a real tea aficionado. Daisy had always liked tea from an early age, and she brought her dietitian's background to the recipes they developed and created in the tea garden. All this characterized a business she loved. Looking at the Victorian made her feel happy too.

To Fiona, Daisy said, "I hope everyone who comes here feels as you do. I'm going to Vinegar and Spice. Are you walking that way?"

"No. I'm going in the other direction to visit my sister." She raised the bag she carried. "We'll be sharing soup."

After good-byes, Daisy turned back to the sidewalk along Market Street and started walking toward the shop where she could replenish tea garden supplies. She noticed Betty Furhman was still in her shop, Wisps and Wicks. She was rearranging candles in her front window. All of her stock was handmade with natural scents.

Farther down the block, Daisy passed an insurance office and a store that sold belts, purses, and travel bags.

The next storefront was her destination. She needed to add to her stock of vinegars, olive oils, and various spices. She wouldn't mind talking to Arden Botterill if she was still there rather than one of her clerks.

When Daisy opened the wood door with its plate glass panes, she spotted Arden at the counter. Today she wore a two-piece red dress. Her light-brown hair had a trendy cut, chin length and layered.

"Hi, there," Arden said with a bright smile. "Is this business or pleasure?"

"A little bit of both. Do you have an order sheet? I'll check off what I need for the tea garden. Then I also want to add to my home cupboard."

"Sure, I do," Arden said, leaning under the counter where she pulled out a page-length form listing all the vinegars and olive oils as well as spices that she carried.

"I checked with Tessa before I left, so I'm certain of what we need." Daisy quickly went down the list, filling in numbers for each item.

"Tessa usually does this, doesn't she?"

"She does. But I told her I was coming down here and would take care of it. We've had our hands full with tour buses this week. Business finally slowed down and Tessa decided to work in the kitchen while I came here."

"Actually baking or preparing dough?" Arden asked, knowing a bit about how the tea garden was run.

"A little of both. I think she was going to mix up a new salad for tomorrow. I came up with a recipe and she's going to try it out."

"What is it?"

"It's crunchy slaw. It has coleslaw and red cabbage, shaved almonds, sesame seeds, sunflower seeds, and ramen noodles."

"Wow! That sounds interesting and different. I might have to stop in to try it."

"I'll be using your rice vinegar for it and the toasted sesame oil. Do you have anything new for me to try?"

Arden motioned to the rows of vinegars and olive oils. Bread cubes were piled in lined baskets and toothpicks stood in a small glass at the ready to poke into the bread cubes. A special spout on the sample bottle dropped olive oil or vinegar onto the bread cubes.

"I have a new one that's a blood orange olive oil. Try that first," Arden suggested.

Daisy did and liked it.

"That's great if you stir it into vegetables to roast." Arden pointed to a jar on the spice shelf. "And then top it with this orange pepper, just enough to give it some zing. I tell mothers who come in they might get their kids to eat their veggies that way."

"I roast vegetables a lot," Daisy said. "That would be a nice change."

"I also have new chocolate vinegar. Try a taste of that."

Daisy tried a bread cube with a sample of the vinegar on it. "That's different. What do you use it in?"

"It might sound strange, but I mix it with a little of the Tuscan oil and rub my beef roast with it. I imagine you could use it with pork too."

Daisy gathered up her purchases. "Okay. That will do it for me personally today. The blood orange olive oil, the orange pepper seasoning, and the chocolate vinegar. I still have the Tuscan oil."

"Sold," Arden said cheerfully. "Come on over to the counter and I'll wrap these up."

"When will you have the other order ready? I can have one of my servers come down and pick it up."

Arden shrugged. "I'll text you. If Judy comes in this afternoon, I'll have her deliver it to you."

"That sounds good," Daisy agreed. "Will you be attending the memorial service for Hiram this evening?"

Arden shook her head. "No. I really didn't know him."

While Arden was wrapping Daisy's purchases in navy-blue tissue paper that would keep the bottles from bumping into each other, her eyes took on an excitement Daisy hadn't seen there before. She asked, "Did you see that the negative PR from the social actually paid off?"

Daisy had had her share of negative PR for the tea garden, once when a murder happened there, and another time when one of her customers had died.

Arden kept wrapping. "Two big donors stepped up for the homeless shelter. They think it's a good cause. I have a question for you."

"About the shelter?" Daisy asked. She really didn't know anything more than what the town council publicized.

"Not exactly. It's about Foster. I'm thinking about asking him to create the website for the fundraising, and I think the town council has decided on the name New Beginnings for the shelter."

New Beginnings. Daisy liked that, especially if the town could accomplish what it was endeavoring to do for the community.

"Do you think Foster can handle it with his other commitments?" Arden asked. "We'd pay him the going rate for website development."

Could money be the deciding factor? Daisy knew Vi and Foster needed a new car. She and Gavin had decided they'd helped the young couple enough and they had to solve their own problems. Extra money for developing the website might give them the opportunity to do that.

"Foster does have a lot on his plate, and it's important to him to find time to be at home with Sammy and Vi. But he could work on the website at home, or at school between breaks or wherever he is. So it might work out. But you'll have to ask him. If he can't handle the time commitment, I'm sure he'll tell you so."

On the other hand, might the temptation of earning money for a new car be the deciding factor?

That evening, Daisy and Jonas entered the fire company's social hall. The facility was always well used. Couples rented it for wedding receptions and it was also employed for community social gatherings in the spring, in the summer, at Thanksgiving and Christmas. It also doubled as a senior center, though not in an organized way. Seniors gravitated there during the day to play cards and bingo.

This weekend, it would house a potpie dinner during Carnival Days. Today, however, it had a different use. She and Jonas were attending the memorial service for Hiram Hershberger.

Daisy's gaze scanned the hall that was housing more people than she expected. Cafeteria tables lined the room and rows of chairs faced the podium.

Daisy and Jonas sat throughout the service as a minister spoke for about twenty minutes. Most of his information about Hiram had seemed generic and not as if he had known Hiram at all.

To Daisy's surprise, Marshall Thompson took a place at the podium. Daisy listened to Marshall as he spoke briefly about his association with Hiram—how Hiram was a good lawyer and was passionate about defending his clients.

After he'd finished and signaled an end to the service, Jonas leaned close to Daisy. "Marshall and other lawyers from Philadelphia went together to have this reception."

"Really?" she whispered.

"Hiram didn't have any family. Eli said he had talked to Marshall and that's how this gathering had been decided. I noticed Eli in the back row. I think he scooted out just now. He's probably the only person here who really cared about Hiram."

Those who had been listening to the eulogy were starting to disperse to the buffet line and the tables. The Women's Auxiliary, who often served in the social hall, had set out sandwiches, salads, and sheet cakes.

During the ensuing chatter, Daisy felt a tap on her shoulder. When she looked up, she saw Nola Horn. She'd spotted Nola's soon-to-be ex-husband when she'd first come in. But Elliott hadn't acknowledged Daisy. She'd nodded to him and he'd looked the other way. Divorce could be nasty in many ways.

"Hi, Nola," she said with a welcoming smile. "You knew Hiram?"

"Our paths crossed. I didn't know him well, but I felt it was appropriate to pay my respects. So did Elliott, but he hasn't acknowledged that I'm here in the same room as he is."

In Daisy's estimation, Nola looked hurt. Daisy couldn't exactly tell if Brielle's mother was relieved the marriage was ending or if she still loved her husband. But there was finality in Nola's voice when she said, "It's definitely over."

"I'm so sorry."

"I don't know if *sorry* is the way I'm feeling, certainly regretful. I have my most regrets about Brielle, and about my mother too."

"Relationships can be mended."

"You really believe that, don't you?"

"I do."

Jonas leaned close to Daisy and said, "I'll go grab us food and seats. Talk as long as you want."

After a sigh, Nola glanced at Jonas. "You two seem to have a good relationship. The fact that he'd think about you wanting to talk to me and going to get food to take care of you means something."

Daisy looked at Jonas's back as he walked toward the food table—his purposeful stride, his long legs, his broad shoulders. He looked as good in a suit as he did in jeans.

"Yes, his caring means a lot. He has a protective streak I sometimes fight against. But I love it. And I love him."

"You say that with such certainty."

"Isn't loving supposed to be that way?" Daisy asked, studying Nola and her lost expression.

"I don't know if it was ever that way between me and Elliott," Nola confided as she sank down in a chair beside Daisy. "We bonded over the law. We had late-night discussions about everything from state law to the Constitution. We thought those similar interests were all we needed. But then I had Brielle, and Elliott felt like my taking care of Brielle took away from us. So I interviewed housekeepers and I hired a nanny. And look what's happened."

People milled about but Daisy kept her focus on Nola, suspecting she was thinking about her relationships with Brielle and Glorie. "You can change whatever you do going forward."

"I really don't know how you can be so certain."

How much did Daisy want to share? Whatever might help Nola. "I can be certain because I had issues with my mother for years. I never really knew what the basic problem was. I knew she seemed to care more about my sister than me. I was always close to my dad and my Aunt

Iris. Then when my daughter had a baby and went through postpartum depression, I learned my mother had gone through it too. It was a secret she had kept for all those years. My mom's year of postpartum depression came between her and me because she didn't bond with me. It was much different years ago than it is now. Doctors can diagnose postpartum depression now and help. Women are more aware."

"So what's happening now between you and your mom?" Nola asked.

"We're rebuilding our relationship. We really are. We're closer than we've ever been. So you have to believe that that can happen with Brielle and your mother too."

Nola gazed at the empty podium and the rows of chairs. "Any advice on how to start talking to my mom and Brielle?"

"Be honest. Tell them both what you're feeling. Tell them what you want for the future for all of you. That's all you can do, Nola. The rest will be up to them."

Nola ducked her head for a moment, and Daisy wondered if the woman's eyes had grown misty. When Brielle's mother lifted her head, she looked at Daisy. Her voice was thick when she spoke. "Can we be friends?"

That surprised Daisy and she had hesitated a second simply because of her surprise.

Nola went on, "I don't have any women friends here. I've never had many women friends. Maybe I've always been too competitive. But I like the way you relate to the women around you. I just thought maybe—" She waved her hand to dismiss her words. "Forget I said anything."

"I won't forget, Nola," Daisy assured her. "I would never turn away a friend. Sure, we can be friends."

Nola's smile was weak but it was there. "Thank you.

Now I'd better return to my office. It's the only place I see Elliott these days. We're splitting up our files and accounts. Once it's done, I can really move on."

Standing, she gave Daisy a last wavering smile and then she left the social hall.

Watching her, Daisy noted that Nola hadn't even nodded to her ex-husband as she exited the building. He was speaking with two other suited men who were probably lawyers too. They all had that look, a look that Marshall Thompson, who was standing a few feet from Elliot and his group, wore often.

Marshall, who had been an acquaintance of Jonas's, had come to Daisy's and her aunt's aid when her aunt had been accused of murder. He had also helped a friend of Daisy's. Marshall was tall, about six-two. Thick snow-white hair made him more than handsome. His suits always fit impeccably. She was about to go over to him to say hello. However, when she was about three feet away from him and the two men he was speaking with, she stopped. She heard the words *Hope Clinic*. Since the men were standing near the table that held punch, she stopped there to ladle herself a cup.

One of the younger men with gelled hair and hipster glasses was telling Marshall, "Only the CEO and Hiram know who caused the incident at the clinic that destroyed the eggs and embryos. The CEO's not talking and now Hiram's dead."

Marshall asked, "Are you sure the CEO knows?"

The younger lawyer answered, "He flew out of the country. Everybody thinks he knows. Maybe he's denying it because he doesn't want to be in anybody's crosshairs."

"Crosshairs?" Marshall asked.

The other man looked grave. "Hiram's dead, isn't he? He took his information to his grave. That's a real definition of attorney-client privilege."

Though Daisy wanted to listen to more of the conversation, Lawrence Bishop hurried over to her. He was pale, his forehead creased with deep lines. He looked more upset than Daisy had ever seen him.

"What's wrong?" she asked him as he approached her.

"Piper just called me. The police called her . . . and Emory. The detective wants them to go down to the police station tomorrow."

"Did something happen?"

"It's all because of that news footage."

Daisy set down her punch cup and took Lawrence by the arm to a spot near the wall where no one was standing. "Slow down. What news footage?"

"You saw the argument Emory had with Hiram, didn't you?"

"Yes, I did."

Agitated, Lawrence hit his palm against the wall. "The TV camera caught it. The police were going over the footage and they saw Emory fighting with Hiram. Piper told me they also found out she was a client at the clinic, a client who was damaged by what happened. I said I'd go with Piper but she doesn't want me involved in this. She doesn't want the police to bring me into the equation too. There was only one thing I could think of to do to help them."

"What was that?"

His gaze was intent on hers. "I know you've helped with other murder investigations. Both of us were in the middle of the last one, weren't we?"

Knowing what was coming, she shook her head, her blond hair rippling against her cheek. "Lawrence, I really don't want to get involved in this one."

His voice was low and coaxing when he said, "I can understand that. But even if you don't get involved, you can still help. Can you give Piper, at least, pointers on how to handle the detectives? I don't want her and Emory to turn into suspects."

"They should be consulting a lawyer, Lawrence, not me."

"I told Piper I would pay for a lawyer. She refused. She said she and Emory have borrowed enough money from me and they don't want to take any more handouts. So the closest thing I thought to a lawyer was you. Piper's down the street working at the bike shop. They're open until late. Will you talk with her?"

After a few moments of consideration, Daisy gave in. "Do you mind if Jonas comes along? He has as much insight into this as I do, maybe even more."

"That's fine," Lawrence agreed. "I know you understand helping your kids. You've done a lot for Vi and Foster. I still think of Piper as my little girl even though I know she's not. Emory tries hard but I just don't think he always understands Piper. *I* do."

Daisy wondered if there was a rivalry between Emory and Lawrence, and if Piper had to choose her loyalty carefully. That wasn't a good situation to put her in. Daisy was grateful her dad had always supported her decisions but didn't hold her back. He let her make her own mistakes. That was an important part of learning to be an adult. She'd tried to do the same with Jazzi and Vi. She supposed she wouldn't know if she'd succeeded for another twenty years or so.

Since a light breeze blew and the sun cascaded down over the waterfall begonia flower pots that the town had hung on lamp posts, Daisy and Jonas strolled toward Wheels a short time later, enjoying the June weather. The bike shop had opened last fall on Sage Street which was in a section of Willow Creek that had begun to be revitalized. Old buildings had been given new facelifts that consisted of sandblasting, colorful siding, and black shutters. The black shutters were a theme the town council had decided would spruce up the whole town. Businesses had a choice, of course. But the town council believed the more shops that used the black shutters along with flowerpots in front of their shops, the more the shops would attract tourists. Daisy had to admit they were probably right.

Wheels had taken over a small warehouse on a corner. Large plate glass windows had been inserted into the storefront with black shutters on either side. The window displays were arranged with bicycles of every make and color. Daisy had no idea what the differences were between bicycles. She simply knew that they appeared sleek, much different from bikes she'd used as a kid. They also looked costly.

A row house stood next to the small warehouse corner shop and was fashioned in the same beige siding, black shutters, roof corbels, and narrow attic windows that were shuttered. Up a few steps, the front door was framed. The doorframe was an elliptical-style arch with keystones. The front door itself was painted bright blue. Daisy wondered if the shop owner lived there.

Daisy and Jonas stopped at one of the windows to peer inside. "Do you know anything about bicycles?" she asked.

"A little," he said. "When I was in Philly, I had a bike so I could get around faster sometimes in traffic."

When she glanced at him to see if he was telling the truth, he winked. "I rode trail bikes too. It's a great form of exercise. Mine wasn't nearly as expensive as any of these."

"How much do you think these cost?"

He pointed to a matte black bike in the center. "That one has a carbon steel frame and it looks stylish. It probably has mechanical front and rear disc brakes. My guess is that it would run around seven hundred bucks."

Daisy whistled. "You're kidding, right?"

He pointed to another one. "That's a Schwinn. It would probably come in around two hundred fifty dollars. It's a mountain bike."

To Daisy the gray bike Jonas had indicated looked sturdy, maybe what a boy might use. "I really like color on my bikes," Daisy commented, thinking that her comment sounded very girly.

Jonas just smiled and pointed. "There's one. That's a twenty-inch mountain bike for a girl."

Daisy studied the bike with its blue bars and another one that was a little larger with pink bars.

"Both of those probably come in around three hundred dollars," he said. "Of course, there are always used bikes for sale in the community paper."

"Or at an auction," Daisy mused.

Daisy and Jonas moved on to the second plate glass window. "That's probably more like what I would use to run errands around the tea garden."

Jonas laughed as he studied the bike. They were both peering at an Amish kick scooter foot bike with a basket.

It was a combination of bicycle and scooter, and many Amish women used them. The one they were staring at was hunter green.

"Even those are about three hundred dollars new," Jonas said.

Now that they were at the second window, Daisy could see Piper moving around inside the store. She had a cloth in her hand and was polishing one of the bikes.

Daisy motioned to the young woman. "I don't know what to tell her. I want to help Lawrence but I don't want her to get into trouble."

"Just tell her about your experiences. Speak the truth. I'll do the same. You've got this, Daisy."

Jonas's accepting expression coaxed Daisy to lean against him, look up at him, and touch his jaw. So much had changed between them within the last few months. She could feel it. She liked what she was feeling.

A buzzer sounded when they opened the door to the shop and Piper looked up. Her freckles were more noticeable today, maybe because she was so pale. Nervous about her appointment at the police station?

With a slight frown, Piper messed up her auburn bangs by sifting her fingers through them. "Dad texted me that you were coming. I've been shaking since I got the call. I'm scared to death I'm going to say or do something wrong."

Wanting to put Piper at ease, Daisy glanced around the shop. "Your dad said you were the manager here."

Piper looked confused for a moment at Daisy's change of subject. "I am, but I don't know what that has to do with—"

Jonas interrupted. "Piper, I think Daisy's trying to get

you to be a little more relaxed so that you can listen to what she's saying and maybe hear her better. If you're all tensed up and stressed out, the information she gives you could go right over your head."

Piper's gaze canvassed the shop. When she turned back to Daisy, she was close to tears. "I understand that. One of the reasons I bike is to release stress."

"So you don't just sell bikes, you also ride them?" Daisy asked with a smile. She felt maternal toward the young woman who wasn't much older than Vi.

Piper tapped the bike handles as if she loved thinking about cycling. "I ride at least twenty miles a day. It's great exercise, keeps me in shape, and I feel like I'm fly-ing away from all my problems."

Jonas nudged Daisy. "Maybe we should consider buy-ing bikes. It would be something fun to do. Jazzi might even enjoy it."

"It's something to think about," Daisy agreed.

The buzzer on the shop door sounded. They all looked toward the door.

An Amish woman came in. She was dressed like Daisy's friend Rachel Fisher. The strings on the woman's *kapp* swept down over her black apron and she wore a dress of dark violet. She even had blond hair like Rachel's that was pulled away from her face into a bun under her *kapp*.

The woman walked over to one of the Amish bike scooters and put her hand on the basket.

Piper raised her brows at Daisy and Jonas, and Daisy said, "Go ahead. We have time."

When Piper approached the woman she asked, "Are you interested in the bike scooter?"

"I am. I have saved my money a long time for this."

Piper began talking to the woman about the advantages of the bike scooter and its merits.

Jonas said to Daisy, "Piper loves what she's doing here. She'll be more relaxed now when we talk to her."

Daisy hoped that was so because whatever advice Daisy gave Piper might keep her from becoming one of the detectives' suspects.

CHAPTER SEVEN

Twenty minutes later Daisy, Jonas, and Piper sat in a circle of sorts near a stand of bicycles.

Piper looked anxious when she turned to Daisy. "What do I need to know? What does Emory need to know? Maybe I should write it all down." She was about to jump out of her chair to cross to the desk for pen and paper.

Daisy grabbed her arm. "Just sit and listen, Piper. Then if you want to write anything down, you can. But I'm not going to give you the top ten ways to talk to a detective." She kept her voice light, hoping Piper would relax again.

Piper ran her hand through her auburn hair and looked down at her lap. "Sometimes I feel a little crazy. So much is going on . . . so much has happened."

Daisy took Piper's hand. "There aren't any secrets about how to talk to the police. You only have to do one thing—tell them the truth."

Piper's gaze held uncertainty and fear. "What if I'm not sure what the truth is? I mean, not just for me but for Emory too?"

"The only way you're going to get into trouble," Daisy said, "is if you give them too much information and more than they need to know. Don't embellish *anything*."

Jonas nodded and added, "Listen to their questions. Only answer the question. Even if they remain silent. Don't jump into the silence. Don't add what you think they want to know. Don't add more than they ask."

"There is something important I'd like to know," Daisy said.

"What?"

"Do you have an alibi?"

Regretfully Piper shook her head. "And Emory doesn't either."

"He wasn't with you?" Jonas inquired.

Piper's face reddened enough that her freckles practically disappeared. "We had another disagreement about joining the class action suit. We argued about it. After he left our apartment, he didn't return until morning."

"Did he tell you where he went?" Jonas asked.

First Piper looked at Daisy and then at Jonas. "He told me that he drove to Philadelphia to talk to a lawyer that his dad knew. But the attorney wasn't there."

"And he didn't come home after that?" Daisy asked.

Again looking embarrassed, Piper answered, "Emory said he went to a bar in Kennett Square and he stayed until three A.M. Then he pulled into a public parking lot and slept until morning."

"Do you believe he's telling the truth?" Daisy asked, hoping Piper's belief in her husband wasn't shaken.

"When he did come home, I could smell the alcohol on him. And his clothes looked as if he'd slept in them."

Daisy exchanged a look with Jonas and she could almost read his mind. Neither Piper nor Emory had an alibi. That wouldn't bode well when they spoke to the police.

Obviously thinking the same thing she was, Jonas gave a nod.

Daisy directed Piper, "Now you can get that pen and paper. I'm going to give you the name of an attorney that you should call. His name's Marshall Thompson. Tell him we recommended him."

"But attorney fees . . ." Piper started.

"Marshall usually gives his consultation fee pro bono and then you only call him if you need him. I think you and Emory need him."

Daisy knew it was only a matter of time.

The next morning, in fact, Detective Rappaport opened the door to the tea garden and lumbered inside. He didn't take a table as he sometimes did but crossed to the sales counter. He was standing there when Daisy exited the kitchen to see if Cora Sue needed help serving. The detective's gaze settled on her.

"I know why you're here," Daisy said instead of her usual friendly greeting.

Morris Rappaport had thick blond hair with lots of gray strands that looked as if it had been trimmed recently. Grooves around his mouth sometimes made him look younger . . . but not today because he wasn't smiling. There were plenty of lines on his face and his light gray suit coat was already creased. He'd also loosened his navy tie and pulled it a few inches below his open white shirt collar. "You know what I'm here for?" he asked.

"Maybe because I have a new batch of whoopie pies with peanut butter filling. The word must have gotten around the station." Her attempt at levity fell flat.

He looked exasperated with her. "Daisy, I have to ask you a few questions."

Apparently he wasn't going to join her in a bit of friendly rapport. They had started out as adversaries a few years ago, but they'd come to respect each other. Today she wasn't sure the detective had time for respect.

Still she couldn't let him bully her. "We can go to my office to talk. I'll have Cora Sue bring us whoopie pies. What kind of tea do you want?"

"I didn't say I wanted tea," he grumbled.

Looking him straight in the eyes, she asked, "Do you want a glass of iced tea?"

"Yeah, that would be good," he admitted, giving in.

Daisy almost smiled. When Detective Morris Rappaport was argumentative like this, it usually meant his case wasn't going well.

After they were seated in her office and Cora Sue had brought in glasses of iced tea and a bone china plate with the detective's favorite dessert, Rappaport crossed his arms on Daisy's desk. She thought she'd let him have the chair at the desk if it made him feel in charge.

"*You* pick up things that other people don't pick up," he began. "I saw you on the TV tapes, more than simply the ones that aired. You were listening to conversations, looking all around, serving people food. I want you to start at the beginning and talk about *everything* you saw and heard that day."

She knew her eyes probably grew wide. "Everything?"

He sat back in her desk chair. "I'll sift out what I think all of it has to do with Hiram's murder. Now talk to me. Start to finish."

Daisy did. She was pretty sure she was boring him when she told him about setting up the canopies and Jonas helping her with that. He looked agitated, probably because he didn't hear anything clue-like in her recitations when she explained that she and Iris had carried food and supplies from their work van to the tables and made everything look spiffy.

"Spiffy?" he asked.

"I just wanted to see if you were awake."

"Go on," he growled.

"Lawrence Bishop wanted me to meet his daughter Piper and his son-in-law Emory."

"I know Bishop. He's involved in several community functions. Why did he want you to meet his daughter?"

"Piper and Emory had been hurt by what had happened at the Hope Clinic and he wanted me to talk to Piper, woman to woman."

"Not Emory?" Rappaport asked.

"I'm not sure, but Jonas was the one who connected with Emory while I talked with Piper."

"What exactly did you talk about?"

"I told Piper about my experience in adopting Jazzi. I could see Piper was torn up by what had happened at the clinic. After she walked away, Jonas and I were talking when, all of a sudden, we started hearing chanting. It was coming from the protestors as they began marching toward the tents. I think everyone there became a bit frazzled if not outright scared. Jonas dialed dispatch and eventually you all showed up. Eli called for Hiram. Your officers took Eli to the station. I guess Hiram was going to follow. Before he did, he and Emory got involved in a discussion."

"A discussion or an argument?" Rappaport questioned sternly. "I want to know exactly what he said. Don't fudge on me, Daisy. I know you have a steel-trap memory."

"I don't have to remember," she said acerbically. "It was recorded for posterity and televised. He told Hiram that he was a miserable man for defending the clinic."

"And?" Rappaport prompted, using his hands in a go-ahead motion that coaxed her to continue.

"And," she said hesitantly, "Emory said someone should make sure that Hiram *couldn't* defend the clinic."

"Well, at least I know you're reliable. The tape showed exactly what you've told me. Do you think Emory Wagner is a hothead?"

"I don't know him well enough to say that. But, detective, the Wagners are upset by what happened at the clinic. Any couple would be."

"So tell me exactly why Emory was so upset."

"Piper thinks Emory is thinking mostly about the expense for *in vitro*. That's a big part of it. But the experience they went through is what is so frustrating. They had hopes and dreams and all the emotions that come with having a family. Piper endured the hormone injections."

She studied the detective. "Do you have any idea what that's like?"

When he didn't comment, she went on. "I imagine she had mood swings, hot flashes, feeling not at all like herself." When Rappaport was still silent, Daisy revealed, "During the couple's next session with their doctor, the embryos were going to be implanted. They'd spent two years trying to get pregnant. They'd had tests. They borrowed money for *in vitro*. Overnight all of their plans and hopes were dashed. How do you think *you'd* feel about that?"

"I know *exactly* how I'd feel about that," Rappaport responded with a grave look. "That's why I asked you about Emory's fuse."

"All the other couples who lost embryos would be just as upset, Detective."

"Oh, I know that. And we *are* checking into other couples. But I wanted to get your take on this whole thing. I can't tell you everything I know, but I know you'll tell me whatever *you* know. Won't you?"

Daisy realized that Detective Rappaport was being careful because police policy was supposed to forbid having civilians help to solve cases. But she and Rappaport had found peace with each other. He told her as much as he could, and she helped him with whatever she found out.

Business out of the way, Rappaport picked up a whoopie pie and ate it within two big bites. Then he took a few swallows of iced tea. He smiled at her. "Super good as always. Better than donuts."

She shook her head at him.

"It's good to see Zeke and Jonas are friends again," Rappaport commented. "I know the whole thing was hard for you and Jonas, and you almost broke up because of it. But it all ended up good in the end, don't you think?"

The detective was right that she and Jonas had almost broken up over Jonas's beleaguered friendship with Zeke. Zeke Willet and Jonas had worked on the Philadelphia police force together. But circumstances involving Jonas's partner had decimated the men's friendship. However, in the spring, Jonas had jumped in front of a bullet for Zeke. Grateful, Zeke had realized that they were still friends.

"I'm glad to see you care about their friendship," she said to Rappaport. "I believe Jonas sees you as a father figure. Since Jonas's dad was killed in the line of duty, he missed a role model growing up." When Detective Rappaport had come to town, Jonas and he had bonded.

"I'm nobody's father figure," Rappaport snapped.

"Then maybe you're simply a good friend . . . to both me and Jonas."

Rappaport lifted another whoopie pie from the plate, gave her a look that said she might be right, then ate it quickly and licked his fingers.

The music store, Guitars and Vinyl, was just that . . . filled with plenty of guitars and lots of vinyl. On her break, Jazzi had convinced Daisy to come with her into the store. Vinyl records appeared to fascinate Jazzi. She'd even purchased a turntable and speakers with her own money and set it up in her bedroom.

Double doors led into the shop where it was divided into two. To the left any musician interested in a guitar could find a model or brand—old or new—to suit him. On the right side of the shop, vintage vinyl records that Daisy suspected had seen better days served as wall decorations under posters of the Beatles, the Dave Clark Five, Heart, the Bee Gees, and others who had made their music memorable on the vinyl records. In the main floor space on that side, bins and bins and bins labeled with artists or recording labels were lined up beside each other.

It didn't take long for Daisy to realize that Jazzi wasn't just interested in the vinyl records but in the young man behind the counter who was sorting inventory.

Daisy knew Ned Pachenko. She'd met him through her son-in-law Foster. She'd planned a musical tea at the tea garden especially for children and Ned had been the guitarist she'd hired. But Ned had caught the flu and Gavin had taken over for him. Foster's dad was a man of many talents.

Daisy saw Ned now and then when he came into the tea garden with Foster and Vi. The young man was in his early twenties and good-looking in a surfer kind of way. His hair was blond and curly and those curls dipped over the back neck of his Grateful Dead T-shirt.

Daisy wanted to ask Ned for a favor. But she'd wait until Jazzi did her thing.

Jazzi went up to Ned, told him what she was interested in, and he pointed her to a specific bin.

He wasn't ignoring Daisy, however. He asked, "Have you planned any more children's teas? Foster told me that was a onetime deal."

At the counter, she peered into the case that held vintage records worth more than those in the bins. "It went over really well, so I plan to do it again." She glanced up at him, seeing that he might be interested in providing the entertainment. "I'm not sure when . . . maybe in the fall as we're gearing up for the holidays. The truth is, I haven't had time to sit down and plan the calendar. But I did want to ask you if you're free for the Fourth of July. I'm having an outside tea garden event. Would you consider playing while my customers eat and drink tea?"

Ned grinned at her. "I'm free. That would be a great gig."

"I'll call you about it closer to the Fourth to discuss it," she assured him.

Jazzi glanced over her shoulder at Ned. "She hasn't had much time for events because she's been involved in a murder investigation again."

Ned blinked, apparently unsure what his response should be.

Daisy felt herself flush, but she couldn't chide Jazzi for telling the truth.

Finally, Ned gave a shrug, as if the news wasn't too strange. "Foster told me some of the things that have happened to you." He said to Jazzi, "I think your mom has a ton of courage."

"She does," Jazzi agreed, then delved into the bin with the records once more, as if Daisy's involvement in murder cases wasn't a big deal. Daisy took this opportunity to wander about the shop, listening in on Jazzi's conversation with Ned. She wasn't ashamed to admit she wanted to know what Jazzi's musical interests were . . . and if her daughter really did have a crush on this young musician. A crush was one thing, but real interest was another.

After Jazzi pulled a Gene Pitney album from the bin, she pointed over to the guitars. "Am I too old to learn to play a guitar?"

Ned vehemently shook his head. "You're never too old to learn. My own dad taught himself to play the piano by learning chords when he was fifty. Anything's possible."

Daisy appreciated that philosophy. She wondered if Jazzi was seriously thinking about learning how to play a guitar or if she was just making conversation.

When Jazzi moved to another bin, Ned approached Daisy. "Foster told me you were at that social thing when the protestors charged the tents."

Daisy stopped by a bin labeled UK 60S BANDS. "I was. I was glad Jazzi wasn't there. It was a bit terrifying."

"I can imagine. I saw it all unfold on the news."

Ned's body language told Daisy that he had more to say. So she waited.

He gazed out the front window for a few seconds then returned his focus to her. "A couple of the protestors came in here a few days ago."

Daisy gave him her full attention. "How did you know it was them?"

He put his hand to his chin and rubbed across it. "I saw TV footage when the protestors pulled off their masks. A clip of that was only shown on the late-night news."

Daisy had only watched those portions that had been most televised. She didn't remember seeing the protestors unmask themselves because she would have been interested in identifying them. "Did they talk about what had happened when they came into the store?"

"I overhear a lot just standing at the counter," Ned admitted.

"Anything important?" If Ned had learned facts new to the investigation, they could be important.

"For the most part it sounded like the protestors were just backing Eli."

"I don't understand. You mean because he doesn't believe the homeless shelter should go forward?"

"I'm not sure that's all there was to it. One of them said Eli wanted to preserve that particular chunk of land for himself. He was saving to buy it before the owner decided to donate it for the homeless shelter. The protestors were just backing him up."

Daisy understood the idea that land was important to the Amish for many reasons. They made a living farming it, though the plot for the homeless shelter wasn't large enough for that. Still, families handed property down to their children so they could live on it, farm it, or start other businesses. The land had to do with generations working the earth, raising food on it, making a life on it. Tradition and history had a lot to do with each family's idea of what their property meant to them.

"Did Eli want to build a house on it?"

"From what I understood, Eli is thinking about opening a buggy shop so the Amish don't have to travel to Bird in Hand or even farther afield."

A buggy shop? That didn't seem to go along with Eli leaving his district and his family for another type of life. It seemed odd to Daisy that Eli left his faith but yet in the discussion they'd had, he seemed to be leaning toward it again. Was he thinking about confessing before his bishop and congregation and once again returning to his roots?

It seemed that Eli was a lot more complicated than anybody knew. Had Hiram understood that? Did Eli's ambition have anything to do with Hiram's death?

CHAPTER EIGHT

When Brielle Horn came charging into the tea garden on Thursday morning, Daisy guessed the young woman thought she was late for her shift. She wasn't late. She was right on time. However, after a second look at Brielle, Daisy studied the expression on the teen's face. Brielle looked angry enough to bite the tail from a snake. Daisy didn't know where that comparison had come from.

Brielle slipped past the sales desk and into Daisy's office where a cubby was located for servers to store their backpacks. Brielle was down on the floor stuffing hers into the square when Daisy entered behind her.

Brielle didn't move. Daisy hadn't tried to keep quiet and she was sure Brielle could hear her. But Brielle remained still as if after she pushed her backpack into the cubbyhole, she'd become frozen.

"Briclle," Daisy said softly.

There was no response.

Daisy slowly walked up behind her. "Brielle?" she called again.

Brielle swiveled around, still in the hunkered down position. When she blew her pink bangs away from her eyes, Daisy could see the redness there and the evidence of tears. This girl wasn't angry . . . she was terribly sad.

Daisy stooped down to Brielle and held out her hand. "Come on, honey. Talk to me."

For a moment, Brielle still didn't move. Then she tilted down her head as if she didn't want Daisy to see her tears. Finally she took Daisy's hand and let Daisy help her up.

Daisy rolled her desk chair over to Brielle. She pulled the other wooden straight-back chair close to the office chair until her knees were almost touching Brielle's after the teen sat. "What's going on?" She asked the question though she thought she might know the answer.

The angry expression had returned to Brielle's face and she balled her hands into fists in her lap. "My mother and father had a meeting with me this morning."

Daisy understood that must have been an early meeting.

As if Brielle had read her thoughts, she explained, "Apparently Dad had to leave on a business trip. So over croissants, he told me that he and Mom are getting a divorce. They acted so stoic about it as if they were telling me their jobs were changing or something and we had to move to a different state. That I was used to. But a *divorce*?"

"Brielle, this didn't come as a complete surprise to you, did it?"

Daisy had reason to believe that it wasn't a surprise at all.

"I know when I came to stay with you and Jazzi in March and my parents were taking that trip, I was afraid they were thinking about splitting up. But then when I moved in with Grammy, I thought they'd have the house to themselves. They could forget about me and remember why they got married in the first place. They could fix things."

Daisy wasn't sure what to say to Brielle to help her process this. She knew Brielle thought her world was falling apart, and maybe it was.

"Do you think if I hadn't moved out, they'd still be together?" Brielle asked plaintively.

Daisy tapped Brielle's balled fist. "Honey, take three deep breaths for me. Please."

Brielle blinked as if she didn't understand what Daisy had said.

"Three deep breaths. Come on," Daisy encouraged. "You can't think straight if you're not pushing oxygen to your brain."

Because she looked puzzled, Brielle followed Daisy's directions. When she did, her hands relaxed, her shoulders sank down a little and she looked as if she might cry again.

Looking straight into Brielle's eyes, Daisy assured her, "This is *not* your fault."

"But I—"

"Brielle, listen to me. This situation, whatever it is, whether it results in divorce or not, is between your mom and your dad. Whether you stayed or went, whether you lived with your grandmother or came to live with me and Jazzi, whether you got a job or didn't, whether you stay in school or don't . . . none of that has anything to do with what's going on with your mom and dad. Couples have their stuff separate from their children. Sure, the kids are involved, but it starts with the parents."

"They acted like they didn't care about each other. They acted like they didn't care about *me*! They just had an announcement to make."

Like most parents, when Daisy had had Vi, she hadn't known how to parent, not in any book-learning way. She hadn't been very close to her mom then. Ryan's mom who had since died had told Daisy, "All you can do is love her to the best of your ability. Treat her like the beautiful little creature she is and she'll love you back." Vi did love her back and so did Jazzi. She'd treated them both with all the love in her heart and all the kindness she could ever gather. She'd also raised them with honesty and she believed that had a lot to do with everything else.

As honestly as she could, she said, "I don't know your dad. I've only had one conversation with him before you came to stay with me and Jazzi. But I've gotten to know your mom a little better. She *does* care about you. My guess is she's hurting as much as you are. You need to talk to her about what you're feeling and about what the future might bring for both of you."

"There's no need to talk about the future," Brielle said stubbornly. "I'm staying with Grammy and that's it. What does Mom care what I do? She's so busy working."

"Weren't your mom and dad partners in the law firm?"

As if Brielle hadn't thought about that, she nodded. "Yes, they were. I don't know what will happen now."

"I imagine it would be very difficult to work with someone who you're divorcing," Daisy offered. "So your mom isn't only losing her marriage, she's also losing a work partner. She probably has to make all kinds of decisions about her professional life. Did you think of that?"

"No," Brielle answered sullenly.

"The last time I spoke to your mom, I think she was worried about you and college. She'd like you to attend one."

"I can't."

"You're smart and you have decent grades. I'm sure there's something you want to do with your future. Why can't you think about college?"

"I can't think about it because I have to take care of Grammy. I'm not going to leave her on her own. Not now. Not ever."

That was the hurt little girl in Brielle talking. Yet Daisy knew Brielle's intellect and her creative side would want to expand her horizons. If she stayed with her grandmother out of loyalty, what would happen to the way she thought about family? Would it be good for her? Or would it be better if she and Nola Horn and Glorie Beck came up with a solution that would suit all of them?

Daisy was curious how all was going at Jonas's store as he and his friend Elijah readied for their special sale. She hadn't seen much of him since their visit to Wheels. As he finished furniture pieces, met with other crafters, and thought about the arrangement of furniture in Elijah's barn, he'd worked long hours. He'd shown her a floor plan and hoped to stick to it.

On her break she walked down to Woods, eager to see Jonas's smile . . . eager to see him. The furniture store was still busy with activity but not quite as busy as the other day when she'd stopped in.

Elijah Beiler noticed her and waved. The Amish wood-worker who sold furniture through Jonas's shop was dressed the way he always was—in black pants with sus-penders and a dark blue shirt. His beard signified that he was married.

She crossed to him where he was polishing a dark wood chest. "You need Jonas, ya?" he asked with a small grin.

"I'd like to talk to him to see how he's doing. Do you think you're ready for the sale?"

"Getting there. Certain sure we'll be ready by the weekend. Jonas is in the workroom with his friend Zeke."

Daisy wondered what *that* was about. Jonas and Zeke had started over as friends in recent months. But that thread between them might still be fragile.

"If they're too involved in conversation," she told Eli-jah, "I'll come back out here and look at all this beautiful furniture."

Going behind the sales counter, Daisy went to the door that led into Jonas's workshop. A ventilation fan was humming in the room but she could still slightly smell the scent of stain and wood and polish. Jonas and Zeke were standing near Jonas's office, a cubicle that hardly had room for a desk and one other person. She didn't know whether to join the men or not. Because of the sound of the fan, they hadn't heard her come in. She could simply leave again.

She studied their faces which were serious but not stony. When Jonas was angry or particularly tense, the scar along his cheek stood out much more. It didn't stand out now. He just looked as if he was listening intently to whatever Zeke had to say. Zeke's handsome face with his squarish jaw seemed questioning but not particularly perturbed. Both men's stances weren't relaxed but they weren't tense either.

Her curiosity won out. After all, Zeke was probably working on Hiram's murder investigation. That's what he and Jonas might be discussing. Jonas had left his old profession behind but he was still a detective at heart.

As she approached, the two men heard her and stopped talking. After greetings all around, Zeke said, "You must have mental telepathy."

"Why?" she asked innocently. "Are you two discussing something I'd be interested in?"

The two men exchanged a look.

Jonas explained, "Daisy just came by to ask me what time I'm taking her to dinner tonight." He winked at Daisy.

"You two don't believe in texting?" Zeke asked sarcastically.

"Face to face is much better," Jonas told him, hanging his arm around Daisy's shoulders.

Zeke rolled his eyes. "I might as well tell *you* what I was just telling Jonas. You'll question him until he spills it anyway."

Jonas just gave a little shrug as if that was normal in their relationship now.

Zeke grimaced. "I was just telling Jonas that the security guard at the Hope Clinic carries a stun gun."

"Do you think *he's* the one who used it on Hiram?" Daisy wanted to know.

Zeke leaned against the doorjamb and sighed. "That's what I was discussing with Jonas. It seems a little too obvious."

After studying Zeke's face, Daisy said, "But there's more to it than that, isn't there?"

Zeke shook his head. "Telepathic. I knew it. I asked the guard if he knew who was responsible for the clinic's mishap when all the eggs and embryos were destroyed. He insists he doesn't know."

"You don't believe him," Daisy suspected. "You think he's holding back something."

After a long look at Daisy, Zeke said, "Maybe we should have had *you* interrogate him. I still don't get why people talk to you so easily."

"Probably because she doesn't grill them to death," Jonas said. "She strikes up a conversation and they spill whatever they know. It's those blue eyes of hers."

Daisy batted her lashes at both of them. "Honestly, you two. I've been underestimated my whole life because of my blue eyes and blond hair. Don't you two do it too." A note of warning in her voice made them both smile.

"I wouldn't dream of it," Zeke told her seriously. "I know you're a force to be reckoned with. Jonas doesn't realize what he's getting himself into."

"Oh, I realize it," Jonas said. "That's why we make such a good couple."

Zeke looked from one of them to the other and nodded. "You know, when I think about all the suspects for this murder, I think mostly of all those couples who lost their chance to have children."

Both Jonas and Zeke knew what that felt like. Jonas had been dating his partner when he was a detective. She'd become pregnant with some manipulation on her part, having her IUD removed when Jonas didn't know about it. She'd wanted to have a family with him even though Jonas had been against having kids because his own dad, a law enforcement officer, had been killed in the line of duty. He hadn't wanted that to happen to a family of his.

Zeke had been friends with both Jonas and Brenda. One night, Brenda had betrayed Jonas with Zeke. The whole situation had ripped Jonas's and Zeke's friendship apart. When Brenda died, a baby had died too. Jonas and Zeke hadn't known which of them was the father, but they'd both felt the loss. Both men had grieved and felt torn up inside. So Daisy believed Zeke when he said he understood what the couples felt.

Jonas squeezed her shoulders tighter and she knew he did too.

"Do you really think that could be a motive for murder?" Daisy asked.

"You saw how Emory Wagner went after Hiram on the video," Zeke pointed out. "My guess is that his anger was more about losing the chance to be a dad than it was about a class action suit."

"Any luck tracing more witnesses who might have seen someone on the street after Hiram was murdered?"

"No more witnesses. We're going to lean harder on Eli Lapp."

With a quick look at Jonas, Daisy could see Jonas didn't like the idea.

Zeke took a deep breath and then blew it out. "I know you don't think he had anything to do with it, and maybe he didn't. But he could know something that could lead us to a clue. It's quite possible somebody wanted the name of the person who caused the clinic's problem."

"Hiram wasn't the only one who knew," Daisy said. "So did Troy Richter."

"Yes, well, it's public knowledge that Troy has been

out of town . . . out of the country actually. We did some checking. The day after you saw him with Hiram at the tea garden, Troy flew to the Grand Caymans. We're still waiting to talk to him."

"He wasn't here when Hiram was murdered?"

"Apparently not," Zeke stated as if he didn't like the idea. "We'll be questioning him further once he's back. But if Hiram was the only other person who knew and someone wanted revenge on the tech who caused the malfunction, then Hiram was the target."

"Do you think he gave up the information?" Jonas asked.

"I don't know. If he did, someone else could be in danger. If he didn't, Troy is probably fortunate to be away."

Zeke's attention swung back to Daisy. For a moment she thought he was going to lecture her again about not becoming involved. He'd done that before along with Detective Rappaport. However, this time he said, "I know you hear rumors at the tea garden. I know people can't keep their mouths shut no matter what secrets they're keeping. So if you hear anything, let me know."

"I will," Daisy promised. She meant it.

That evening, Daisy decided to take a drive and visit a friend to pick up fresh eggs. The drive to Rachel and Levi Fisher's farm always calmed her. This time of year, farms came alive in so many ways. She would spot a farmer with six mules tilling a field or women hanging laundry on wash lines that were strung from the house to the barn. Every sight helped her remember childhood days on the farm with Rachel.

Back then Rachel's parents had grown shrubs and

trees for Daisy's mom and dad to sell at Gallagher's Garden Corner. Daisy had spent many days with Rachel and had learned to admire the Amish family and their way of life. Her family and Rachel's had lived very differently. Rachel's family hadn't used electricity and they'd traveled in horse-drawn buggies. But both families' values had been very much alike—hard work, strong faith, and deep family bonds.

As she drove down the lane that led to the back of the Fishers' house, Daisy remembered sitting along the shore of the pond with Rachel, squishing their bare toes in the mud. She remembered high cornstalks and the hide-and-seek games they'd played within the rows. She recalled Rachel's brothers and their fondness for naughtiness and practical jokes. The farm had held wonders Daisy couldn't find in her own backyard—a snowy owl high in the barn eaves in winter, springtime kittens running amidst the hay bales in the barn, a springhouse where the family had kept watermelons, potatoes, and onions. Daisy had learned to ride a horse on that farm as well as drive a buggy. She hadn't done either in a very long time.

Daisy left her car in a gravel area meant for parking and took a huge indrawn breath of honeysuckle, trees that had blossomed, and grass that had recently been mowed. She heard hammering in the distance.

Levi's grandmother came to the door of the mudroom before Daisy could even knock. Mary was short and wore a dark purple dress today with a black apron. Her gray hair in a bun was defined by a white *kapp* and the strings floated behind her shoulders. Her face was wrinkled with her age and her smile. "Did you come for my wonderful *gut* shoofly pie? You are just in time for it."

"It's good to see you again, Mary. Actually I came for eggs."

"No reason why you can't enjoy shoofly pie before you leave with eggs, *ya*?"

Rachel came to the door to stand beside Mary. "Good to see you. I have your eggs ready, but like *Maam* says, you need to come in and have shoofly pie and tea. Ain't so?"

As Rachel drew her into the kitchen, Daisy relaxed into her memories of long ago. The kitchen smelled wonderful. The aroma of roast meat was still in the air as well the sweet sugary scent of pie. A breeze blew through the window above the sink. Daisy noticed a teakettle sitting on the gas stove. Rachel must have turned it on before she came out to greet Daisy.

Mary took teacups and saucers from the beautifully fashioned handmade hutch in the corner and set them on the table. Mary helped any way she could on the farm and did much of the cooking. But she also spelled Rachel at the shop now and then. Active, with sharpness and intelligence shining in her blue eyes, she didn't show her actual years.

"You heard the hammering outside?" she asked.

"I did. Is Levi working on Esther and Daniel's house?"

The construction was on Rachel's property. One of her daughters was getting married and her betrothed along with members of Rachel's family were building a house for them.

"Even Esther is helping them," Rachel said with a shake of her head. "She's always been such a tomboy, and there are special touches she wants in her house."

Daisy knew that didn't mean decorative touches. The Amish considered decorations prideful. But Daisy suspected a window over the kitchen sink would be one of the features that Esther desired in order to watch children out back in the future.

"The house will be well-built, that's certain sure," Mary said. "Levi knows how to handle wood just like your beau, Jonas."

Daisy smiled. Everyone in town seemed to know that she and Jonas were serious now. Much of what had happened between them had been very public. She found she didn't mind that at all.

"I hear Jonas and Elijah are going to have some sale. It's the talk of the town," Rachel said.

"I hope they do well for everyone's sake," Daisy said.

Rachel pulled out a chair and pointed to it. "Sit. Take the day off your feet."

Mary had already brought the shoofly pie to the table and scooped out a big slice for Daisy.

"You want my sweet tooth to grow, right?" Daisy asked the older woman.

Mary grinned. "I know how you like your sweets. You wouldn't bake them so *gut* if you didn't."

Rachel's youngest, Luke, who was eighteen now, hurried through the mudroom to the kitchen. His face was red under his black hat and he looked hot in his blue work shirt and black trousers. One suspender slipped crookedly over his shoulder.

When he rushed in, oblivious to Daisy, Rachel said, "We have company."

He stopped and turned and smiled at Daisy. "Hi! *Gut* to see you." Then he looked at his mother. "I just came in for a thermos of that lemonade. We're all terrible hot."

Rachel went to the counter to pick up a jug. "It's all made and ready for you. You only have another hour or so of daylight."

"Esther's a slave driver," he grumbled.

Rachel laughed. "Rather her than your *dat*." *Dat* was the Pennsylvania Dutch word for father.

Luke took another look at Daisy. "Are you going to help Eli so the law doesn't nab him?"

Mary warned, "Luke."

The Amish didn't want to become involved with any law enforcement or any government entity as far as that went. They wanted to stay off the grid as much as they could and Daisy had always understood that.

"I don't think Eli needs my help," Daisy said.

"One of those detectives, Zeke Willet, has questioned him three times. Word is—Eli's in big trouble. It's a shame this happened now."

Rachel and Mary looked as curious as Daisy was. So Daisy asked, "Why do you say that?"

"You know Eli's family shunned him."

Daisy nodded because Rachel had told her that.

Rachel interjected, "Luke, I hope you're not going to share gossip."

Daisy was well aware that gossiping was considered a sin with the Amish.

"No gossip." He looked toward Daisy once more. "You know his *familye* will accept him back if he repents."

If Eli repented and recommitted himself to his faith and community, his family would open their arms to him once more. "I understand that," Daisy acknowledged.

"It's a secret," Luke said with his voice lowered a little.

"If it's a secret, you shouldn't be talking about it," Rachel reminded him with a motherly glare.

"I know Daisy can keep a secret," Luke concluded with certainty.

Daisy held out her hand to Luke as if to stop him. "If you tell me something that has anything to do with the murder, I might have to let the police know."

"Nothing to do with the murder," Luke assured her. "It's just Eli and Miriam Yoder have been seeing each other secretly. He knows the Millers would be against it. But if he gets *gut* with God and the bishop again, he and Miriam should have a future."

Could Eli be thinking about rejoining the Amish community? If so, did that have anything to do with Hiram Hershberger's murder?

CHAPTER NINE

Daisy enjoyed serving the outside tables at the tea garden. The flagstone patio with its many colors of gray, green, taupe, tan, and dark brown lay under white tables with glass tops. The jaunty umbrellas bore yellow-and-white stripes in their canvas coverage. Alongside the building, Daisy had set pots with all kinds of herbs from ornamental oregano to pineapple sage to rosemary and lemongrass. In between those pots sat yard ornaments. Her favorite was a cat perched on top of books that were set upon a stone. The cat wore glasses.

She took a few deep breaths, inhaling the herbal scents. This would be a busy weekend. Her sister Camellia was visiting and staying with their parents. She'd arrived last night. Daisy wanted to stop in and see her at the nursery if she could manage a break between morning customers and afternoon tea service. She was hoping to convince

Camellia to join her and Jonas at the carnival tomorrow night. Her sister wouldn't enjoy the chicken potpie dinner—she vigilantly watched her calories, but she might like the music and other treats at the carnival. Daisy was hoping dinner at her parents' house on Sunday would be pleasant instead of contentious as Camellia's visits sometimes were.

This Friday morning as Daisy canvassed the patio to make sure everyone had been served to their liking, she spotted someone she had been looking for in particular—Marshall Thompson, the lawyer she'd consulted on many an occasion. He sat alone at a table, drinking iced tea. Her aunt had told her that he'd requested orange pekoe and he wanted to see Daisy when she was free. Knowing Marshall liked baked goods, she brought him a plate with an assortment of lemon tea cakes, chocolate espresso cookies, and a cinnamon scone. Today Marshall wasn't wearing his suit jacket. His white shirt was crisp, although he'd opened it at the collar. The morning was already warm. His office wasn't that far away and she assumed he'd walked. Although he was in his sixties, Marshall was fit and took care of himself.

He smiled at her as she approached him with the plate of cookies.

"How did you know I was ready for a second breakfast?" he asked in a joking manner.

"A little birdie told me you might enjoy them."

He laughed a deep chuckling sound and said, "Your aunt knows my tastes. I come in here often enough."

Daisy pulled out one of the white chairs around the table from him. "Did you stop in for a good start to your day?"

"Maybe that and a little conversation."

She eyed him speculatively. "Should I guess what that conversation would be about?"

"It's about Hiram, of course."

"You're the only one who spoke at the memorial service who knew him. I was glad you did that. It's a shame Eli didn't speak as well."

Taking a lemon tea cake from the crystal dish, Marshall held it. "I think Eli Lapp was afraid he'd say something he shouldn't, something that might embarrass him or Hiram or maybe the Amish community. Right now, I think that boy is trying to get back into his family and doesn't want to set anybody's teeth on edge."

"I believe that might be true," Daisy said without giving anything away. After all, the fact that Eli was dating Miriam Yoder *was* a secret. Still, in Willow Creek, secrets didn't stay secrets very long.

Marshall ate the cookie and smiled. "I think the class action suit against the clinic is going forward."

"Do you know the lawyer who is taking it on?" Daisy asked.

"Someone from Philadelphia. On the other hand, I've heard that many of the clinic's clients want to sue the person responsible for the mishap. The problem is—nobody knows who that person is."

"I understand Troy Richter is out of town," she commented, simply wanting to see what Marshall's response would be.

"Not just out of town. He's out of the country."

"And Hiram was the only other one who knew who caused the malfunction?"

"Supposedly, but that's hard to believe. Accidents like that don't happen in a vacuum. There had to be somebody else around when it occurred."

Turning the information she'd learned over in her mind, she offered, "You don't think it could have been a real accident like the refrigeration unit malfunctioned or there was an electrical surge or something? I don't know how those things work."

After Marshall took a swallow of iced tea, he shook his head. "Not from what I understand. Someone made a mistake with the temperature setting. Someone is responsible. But I'm not sure that someone had anything to do with Hiram getting killed."

"I don't understand."

"Take this class action suit, for example." He picked up the scone and waved it at her. "Everybody's discussing Emory Wagner's argument with Hiram, and the fact that he had a motive."

"Hiram was defending the clinic that destroyed Emory's dreams," she reminded Marshall.

"That could be true," the lawyer agreed. "But on the other hand, think of all the clients Hiram has had over the years. He's won lawsuits and he's lost them. He's drawn up wills, living wills, durable powers of attorney, maybe against relatives' wishes. I remember a client he took on who had a DUI. Hiram somehow got him off on a technicality. He's protected one heir against another in a contested will. The list goes on and on."

"Are you saying the police are never going to solve this?"

"I'm saying that unless they find very able-bodied clues, unless something particular leads them in one main direction, they're going to be floundering. You know what happens when they flounder and the mayor comes down hard on the chief of police."

She considered the chief of police and how he thought.

He had a gruff no-nonsense, get-it-done attitude. "I know what happens. They focus on one main suspect who has a motive, means, and opportunity."

"Exactly."

"And why are you telling me all this?" she asked, concerned about his answer.

Marshall finished his scone. After he swallowed, he took another long swig of his iced tea. "Let's just say I'd like to see this one solved. The right way. Hiram and I weren't friends, but we were working colleagues. We respected each other. We even knew a little bit about each other's lives."

Marshall was a compassionate, understanding lawyer. She'd seen that aspect of his personality many times. "I can understand that. If anything happened to anyone I worked with, I'd want to see the culprit caught. But what does that have to do with me?"

"Oh, Daisy," he said with a crooked smile. "When I work, I sit in my office most of the day and don't see anyone but my receptionist. I go to court now and then but I'm like a hunter with one objective in mind. I do my job. I do my part, and then I go back to my office where I work some more."

"And you do very fine work," Daisy pointed out.

He nodded in recognition of her compliment. "Thank you. The point I'm trying to make is the fact that I don't see or talk to many people. I have clients and they are my focus. However, *you* are different."

Daisy took a deep breath, suspecting where this was headed. "Different how?" she asked warily.

"Your tea garden is one of the centers of Willow Creek for gossip and chatter. Everybody knows that. You go from table to table serving, listening, watching."

"Not on purpose," she mumbled.

He chuckled. "Certainly, it's on purpose. You come to work each day with a sunny disposition intending to make people's lives better with your baked goods, with your tea, and with your personality. You choose servers and helpers who do the same thing. All in all, it makes for lively conversation, confidences exchanged, and secrets exposed. I've sat in your tearoom and listened to all of that. So I know it's true."

"You think I'll hear something important."

"Of course, I do, because you *always* do. You run down a lead better than any detective I know."

That was a compliment she'd never intended to earn. "You do realize I don't intend to put my life in danger again. That's happened too many times. I have too much to live for—daughters, a grandchild, and somebody I care about very much."

"So *don't* put your life in danger. *Don't* track down a lead. But *do* listen, use your radar, pick up those bits of conversation that could be meaningful and important. I know you can do this, Daisy. You've done it many times before. All I'm saying is pay attention to every scrap of information, and then hand it over to whatever detective you trust the most who will do the best thing with it."

"I trust both Detective Rappaport and Zeke Willet."

"There you go. All you have to do is convince them that what you tell them is important enough to pay attention to. That's all I'm asking."

She narrowed her eyes at him. "You make finding Hiram's killer sound very simple."

"Not at all. But I'm counting on you to pick up a few of the most important puzzle pieces, and then hand them over to a detective so he can solve the crime."

After Daisy studied Marshall for a good long moment, she shook her head. She studied him again and he tilted his head with a supplicant expression.

"All right," she said in acquiescence. "For you, I will listen. I will watch and I'll use my intuition. But that's it. You might have to step in and press a detective to get done what you think needs to be done. Is it a deal?"

Marshall extended his hand to her. "It's a deal."

She shook his hand, knowing she was probably committing to more than she wanted to.

Daisy didn't know what to expect when she walked into Gallagher's Garden Corner after formal tea service that afternoon. Since she and Camellia didn't always get along well, Daisy was a bit anxious as she stopped in at the nursery to say hello to her. Supposedly Camellia was helping her mom and dad today.

In mid-June Gallagher's Garden Corner was as busy as busy could be. Not only residents of Willow Creek bought flowers here. Her parents had such a nice selection of flowers, bushes, and trees that surrounding communities came to the Garden Corner so residents could fill their gardens and pathways with beautiful posies. Annuals like petunias, geraniums, zinnias, and snapdragons rose from six-packs on tables both outside and inside the facility. Customers also wandered in and out of the greenhouses.

Daisy found her mom and Camellia watering plants in one of those greenhouses. Camellia had always cared about hair, makeup, and the latest styles while Daisy had been more of a tomboy. Daisy noticed, however, that Camellia was letting her brunette bob that had always been in a chic shorter cut, grow out more. Now it reached her shoulders. She was wearing white jeans and a celery-colored crop top. The outfit was more appropriate for a day of sailing than a day working with plants and potting soil.

Daisy had always felt that her mom favored Camellia. For years she hadn't known why she'd felt that way. Finally her mom had come to terms with the postpartum depression she'd experienced the first year after Daisy was born. She'd confided that she and Daisy had never bonded well. Daisy's dad and her Aunt Iris had taken over and cared for Daisy. During that eventful year, the groundwork had been laid for future turmoil.

Now that Daisy understood what had happened, she and her mother were coming to a better understanding. Her mother was supportive and tried to reach out to her so they could cement the relationship that had now become one of understanding and trust. Daisy didn't know, however, if Camellia knew the whole story about their mom, her postpartum depression, and the distance she'd always felt with Daisy because of it.

Camellia had never been married. She had majored in marketing and had PR skills up the kazoo, but she never seemed to solidly fit into a relationship. Three months was about how long she dated one man.

Although they were very different, Daisy loved her sister and wished they were closer. Last Thanksgiving, when Camellia had visited, she'd been dating. Robert had come along with her, and Daisy wondered if he was along now.

After a hug and a kiss on the cheek, Daisy asked her sister, "Did Robert come with you?"

As soon as the question sailed out of Daisy's mouth,

she saw her mom, who was standing behind Camellia, shake her head. That meant Daisy shouldn't have asked.

Camellia looked up at her, her brown eyes narrowing. "We broke up. Didn't Mom tell you?"

Daisy shook her head as her mother came up to stand beside Camellia. To Camellia, Rose said, "I didn't know if you wanted me to tell everyone."

"I don't care," Camellia responded with an off-handed shrug. "We weren't suited for each other. It just took six months to figure that out."

Daisy said sincerely, "I'm sorry."

Camellia blew off her sympathy. "No reason to be sorry. I meet a lot of men in my profession. Someday I'll check all the boxes on a man and we'll click."

Daisy wasn't so sure about that. Camellia was beautiful, no doubt. But she wasn't the easiest woman to get to know. She portrayed a strong exterior but Daisy knew her sister was vulnerable underneath. You didn't grow up with someone without knowing that.

Their conversation drifted in less personal directions for a few minutes, Camellia explaining she had to be in New York by Monday evening. She also mentioned that she was thinking about buying an RV, taking vacation time, and traveling a bit.

That was a huge surprise. Camellia was not the camping type. But an RV with running water and electricity you could plug into, let alone a TV hanging on the wall, would be something Camellia might contemplate.

A woman in jeans, a gray T-shirt, and well-worn sneakers came into the greenhouse and motioned to Daisy's mom. She called, "Rose, I need your opinion about something. My azalea bushes didn't winter well. I was thinking about pulling them out and just putting in forsythia instead."

"I'm coming, Pearl. I don't know if you want forsythia in place of azaleas. Let's go look at what other offerings we have."

Daisy's mom gave her a look that asked if she and Camellia would be all right together.

Daisy nodded. "We're good. I'm going to pick out marigolds to take home to put in the garden. The bunnies might stay away from my plants that way."

Camellia asked, "Marigolds are those little yellow flowers with brown centers, right? They're not very pretty."

"They can be," Daisy said lightly. "And in the garden, it's the smell that keeps the bunnies at bay. But I like to put them in pots with my other flowers too. Do you want to help me pick some out?"

"Sure," Camellia said. But she didn't look particularly enthusiastic about the idea.

They went to the table with many varieties of marigolds. Camellia pointed to yellow ones that looked more like little daises. "Those are pretty."

"They show up well in pots, too. I'll take a flat of them along with some of those vanilla puffy ones."

"Vanilla?"

"That's what they're called because they're almost white."

Camellia shook her head. "I never paid attention when Mom planted all those flowers in the yard. But you did."

"I did, and I still enjoy gardening."

Camellia went to fetch one of the carts used to transport flowers to the checkout desk. Daisy laid two flats of marigolds on the cart.

Camellia looked out over the expanse of tables with flowers as well as standing balls of bushes and trees. "Every time I've come here lately, one thought keeps running around in my head."

As far as Daisy knew, Camellia hadn't been at the Garden Corner since last summer when she'd visited for a weekend. Nevertheless, she listened.

"Mom and Dad should be thinking about retiring, not selling more bushes and flowers. Dad shouldn't be lifting all those plants and Mom shouldn't either. I saw him this morning carting a tree ball. A tree ball! He's too old for that."

Daisy wasn't exactly sure what to say. She knew her dad had considered selling the nursery but had decided against it. Daisy posed a question. "How would you feel if Mom and Dad went to work out at a gym every morning?"

"That would be fine. There would be trainers there to tell them what they could do and what they couldn't do."

An argument with Camellia was not something Daisy wanted to tackle today. Yet she felt she needed to defend their parents' choices. "Don't you think years of experience tell Mom and Dad what they can and can't do? Dad knows his back gives him trouble now and then. When it does, he has Cliff handle the tree balls." Cliff had been working beside her dad for the last few years. He was a family man in his forties who seemed to enjoy the nursery as much as her father.

"You merely see what you want to see," Camellia said. "When I'm here, I have a better perspective."

"When you're here, you don't realize what happens on a day-to-day basis. You don't realize how happy the nursery makes Mom and Dad."

In spite of herself, Daisy could feel a real argument coming on. She could be patient with Camellia for a certain amount of time, but Cammie in the end always had a way of pushing her buttons.

A woman Daisy didn't recognize was peering over the boxes and trays of plants. Daisy was about to move so she could round the table when the woman, who was nicely dressed in a pale blue pair of slacks and a T-shirt, asked her, "You're Daisy Swanson, aren't you?"

As Camellia looked on curiously, Daisy admitted that yes, that's who she was.

The woman extended her hand. "I'm Marla Diffendorff. I recognized you from the news clip."

"You mean the social gathering for the homeless shelter? I served tea and goodies from Daisy's Tea Garden."

"Yes, you did. But your photo has been in the newspaper before too—interviews with that reporter Trevor Lundquist after a murder has been solved."

"Once or twice," Daisy acknowledged, fudging a bit.

"Are you looking into Hiram's unexpected death?"

If most people had asked, Daisy would have said *no* she wasn't and turned away. But there was something in this woman's expression, in her sparkling hazel eyes, that told Daisy she was invested in Daisy's answer.

Instead of answering, Daisy asked, "Did you know Hiram?"

Marla ducked her head for a moment and then raised her chin. Her eyes were moist. "I dated him about a year ago. A rumor is making the rounds that an overdose of insulin might have been what killed him. I know for sure that it would have."

"I don't understand," Daisy said. She knew a high dose of insulin could kill anybody.

"Hiram had problems with hypoglycemia. If anybody knew that, Hiram's death could have been premeditated."

As Daisy thought about it, she knew that Marla was correct. If the killer knew hypoglycemia plagued Hiram, he or she would have known the insulin would surely kill him.

"Have you spoken to the police about this?"

Marla shook her head. "I didn't know if I should. I didn't know if they'd just laugh at me. You know, ex-girlfriend thinks she has some information that could matter. I certainly don't want to be in the spotlight."

"You really need to tell the police about this," Daisy insisted. "If you don't want to go in personally, call the main number and ask for Zeke Willet. I know he'll be interested in hearing what you have to say. He'll take down the information and do what he should with it."

"You're sure about that?"

"I'm sure. This could be important information to the investigation."

Marla reached out and squeezed Daisy's arm. "Thank you. I'm so glad I saw you here today. Your encouragement was just what I needed."

After Marla picked up a flat of marigolds, she waved good-bye and went toward the checkout desk.

Already Daisy could see Camellia's disapproving frown. "You're not going to get involved in another investigation, are you?"

Daisy picked up a flat of the French vanilla marigolds and put them on her cart. Then she looked up at her sister. "No, I am not going to get involved."

As she wheeled the cart to the checkout counter, she wondered if she'd just lied to her sister.

* * *

On Saturday morning, Daisy felt disappointment as she baked brownies with Tessa in the tea garden kitchen. She told Tessa, "Camellia doesn't want to meet me and Jonas at the carnival. She said she just wants to spend her time with Mom and Dad."

"Maybe she does," Tessa advised.

"Maybe. But I wanted her to get to know Jonas better without tons of family around."

"There will be time for that," Tessa said with confidence that made Daisy smile.

Cora Sue, with her bottle-red topknot bobbing, hurried into the kitchen. "Marshall Thompson is here. He ordered chocolate espresso cookies and orange pekoe tea. I served him but he said he'd like to talk to you. I'll tell him you'll be out."

It was unusual for Marshall to stop in at the tea garden two days in a row. He sat in the spillover tearoom with its window seat. Cora Sue had given him the table by the diamond-cut glass window.

Marshall was usually very staid and well groomed. But right now, he had chocolate espresso cookie crumbs around his mouth. Daisy couldn't help but smile.

"My weakness for these must show." He picked up his napkin and wiped his lips.

"I'm glad you like the cookies. Jonas does too."

"Chocolate and coffee. What's not to like? Do you have time to join me?"

Everything seemed calm for the moment. She pulled out a chair and sat across from him. "Did my cookies bring you back so soon?"

"Your cookies *could* do that, and maybe your tea too. But I wanted to let you in on what happened."

She was all ears and Marshall could see that.

Reaching for his glass of iced tea, he took a few swallows and set it back down. "Troy Richter called me."

"Is he back?"

"No, he's not. That in itself is cause for concern. He's still in the Cayman Islands."

Daisy was almost literally on the edge of her seat. "So what did he want?"

"He's trying to convince me to take over the defense of the clinic."

"Seriously? Defense against the class action suit?"

"Whatever suits develop. He heard about the Philadelphia lawyer the clients of the clinic hired. The truth is I don't *want* to take on the Hope Clinic as a client. I believe Hiram was killed for a reason and it has something to do with that clinic. I don't want to touch it with the proverbial ten-foot pole."

"What did you tell Troy?"

"I told him the truth—the clinic needs to settle."

"That would mean a sum of money for each of the clients who lost embryos or eggs."

"Exactly. As well as the *in vitro* process funds themselves. Those people deserve to have their money back for a process that didn't happen." Marshall's gaze held an understanding of what had happened to the couples as well as the clinic's responsibility in the matter. He picked up another cookie and swallowed it in three bites.

It looked to Daisy as if he were stress eating. That surprised her. "How did Troy respond?"

"He said he doesn't want to settle. If he refunds *in vitro* fees and gives free services, the clinic can't afford that. It will have to close."

"So what's his plan? Drag this out in court for years?

That would cost him too." Daisy could see there were no good solutions for the clinic but there were ethical ones.

"I pointed that out but he had a solution."

"I can't imagine what *that* would be."

"As far as he's concerned, he wants to put all the blame on the tech in charge when it happened. He wants to let his clients go after that person. Apparently that's what Hiram was going to do."

"That's a terrible idea!"

"That's what I told him. Then I finally got the truth out of him."

Just thinking about that vulnerable tech upset Daisy. "What truth was that?"

"He's still away because he's afraid the person who went after Hiram will come after him. After all, he knows who the tech was who caused the accident."

"Do the police know? Whoever that tech is could also be the one who killed Hiram."

"Troy said he's keeping his mouth shut."

If Troy stayed away and the police didn't know who caused the accident, would they ever be able to solve the question of who killed Hiram Hershberger?

CHAPTER TEN

After they parked, Daisy and Jonas held hands as they headed for the firehouse social hall on Saturday evening. This time of year, carnivals were a big part of summer fun in the area. The firehouse's social hall would be serving a chicken potpie dinner to make money for the volunteer fire company. To the rear of the building where there was a plot of land, a carnival was set up that also brought in much needed funds. For entertainment, the carnival organizers had erected a Ferris wheel as well as children's rides—cars that ran around in a circle on a track and ladybugs that did the same. There were two rides for the older kids—a spin-and-turn that shook them up and then turned them in a circle, and swings that flew higher than any swing should.

Interspersed among the rides were stands—the usual

ones with stacked bowling pins and softballs to try to knock them over as well as ducks that swam around in a ring with numbers on the bottom that signified what prize the entrant would receive. There was a shooting range, a pretend one of course, where shooters could knock down targets that would give them points, again all adding up to a prize. Food trucks and booths sold corn dogs, burgers, fries, cotton candy, and funnel cakes, as well as taffy apples and caramel corn.

Before they explored the carnival, Daisy and Jonas had decided to enjoy the potpie dinner. As they stepped inside, he leaned into her shoulder. "This dinner won't be as good as yours or your mom's."

She poked him. "You thought you had to say that, right?"

He gave her one of those innocent boyish looks. "Of course not. I meant it."

Daisy's Aunt Iris was a member of the Women's Auxiliary. They were the group who'd be making and serving the chicken potpie. After Daisy and Jonas followed the buffet line to the cafeteria-style meal, they ran their trays along the track in front of the serving pans. Daisy could see her aunt was busy at the stove where large pots of boiling broth cooked the doughy potpie squares. She didn't bother her.

Along with the chicken potpie which was square flat pieces of dough covered in gravy with bits of chicken and potatoes, they were served rolls and coleslaw, the creamy kind. Desserts in the form of apple cobbler, chocolate sheet cake, and shoofly pie with a sweet gooey filling topped with crumble were among the offerings at the end of the serving line.

Jonas led Daisy to a table where they were the sole oc-
cupants. "I thought you might want a quiet dinner since
you're around people all day," he said when she gave him
a questioning look.

"You could be right about that. Sometimes I think my
ears are going to explode with all the chatter when we're
constantly busy. But I'm grateful for all the tourists who
stop in."

After they ate in silence for a few moments, Jonas
asked, "What's Jazzi doing tonight?"

"She's coming to the carnival but she wanted to attend
by herself. She's actually been asking me for the car more
often. She left before we did so I take it she was going to
Stacy's and they were coming together."

"She's growing up fast."

"Too fast. I'm going to really miss her next year when
she goes to college."

"Is that all that's bothering you?"

Something she loved about Jonas was that he could
read her so well without her saying a word. "It isn't just
Jazzi leaving for college that makes me happy and sad all
at the same time. It's that after she does, everything is
going to change."

"Change can be good," he reminded her.

"Yes, well, remind me of that when I'm sitting alone in
the house with the cats and Jazzi's gone."

He swung his arm around her shoulder. "Maybe we
can change *that*."

Daisy wondered what Jonas meant by that, but before
she could ask, her aunt approached their table.

Iris slid onto the bench beside Daisy. "I wanted to
say hi."

"You looked busy in there . . . and hot. The air conditioning doesn't do much good when you're standing in front of a boiling pot."

Iris nodded, sweat still beading on her brow. "I did need a break from the stove, but I also wanted to talk to you."

Daisy had just spent the morning with her aunt at the tea garden before Iris had left to start helping with preparations for dinner here. She wasn't quite sure what this talk was going to be about. "Has something come up I should know about?"

"Well . . ." her aunt drawled.

Jonas peeked around Daisy to check out her aunt. "Are you going to get Daisy involved in something?"

"I might," Iris admitted. "The question is, should I?"

"You can't tease us like that, and then not tell us," Daisy warned her. "Come on, spill it. What do you have to tell me?"

Iris leaned a little closer to Daisy and beckoned Jonas to lean in too. "There's a security guard at the Hope Clinic."

Daisy caught on right away. "Is this the guard who supposedly carries a stun gun?"

"It is. His wife is also a member of the Women's Auxiliary. Mavis is inside dishing out the coleslaw."

Daisy had gone through the line quickly with Jonas and couldn't remember who was dishing out the cabbage salad. "What about her?" Daisy asked.

"I spoke with her before we started cooking this afternoon. I told her that you sometimes look into murders and things like that."

"Things like that?" Jonas questioned with raised brows.

Iris waved her hand at him dismissively. "You know what I mean."

"And?" Daisy prompted.

Iris crossed her arms on the table. "She says she'd be willing to talk with you."

Daisy was a little confused. "Did she talk to the police?"

"No, they only questioned her husband. They didn't talk with her."

After Daisy thought about it for a moment, she turned to Jonas. "Wouldn't you say that this has to be a sign?"

His frown and the expression in his green eyes said that he didn't want her to get involved. Yet if she wanted to, it was her decision to make. He answered with, "It's a sign all right. It's a sign that Iris knows you too well."

Daisy touched his jaw and tapped it with her finger. He understood that she appreciated his respect for her and her decisions. Then she turned back to her aunt. "Does she want to talk to me tonight?"

"Oh, no," Iris said with a firm shake of her head. Then she put a slip of paper on Daisy's tray next to her plate of potpie. "Here is Mavis's number. When you make up your mind what you want to do, you can call her. I also gave Mavis your number. So if she calls you, that's just another serendipitous sign, right?"

"Right," Daisy agreed.

However, one look at Jonas's face said he might not agree with that conclusion.

After finishing their potpie dinners and slices of shoofly pie with whipped cream on top, Daisy and Jonas walked through the barkers along the midway at the carnival. Many of them were people they knew from Willow Creek. They stopped often and talked much. The community gathered here to have a night of relaxation, treats, and to watch their kids have fun. A country band began playing at the back of the lot, and residents had set up lawn chairs or stood around enjoying funnel cakes, corn dogs, and French fries.

Suddenly Daisy caught Jonas's arm. "Look over there."

Over there Daisy had spotted her daughter Jazzi. Tonight the teen wore clunky jeweled sandals, blue-patterned shorts, and a navy crop top. Her black hair flowed long and straight over her shoulders and down her back. Daisy believed her daughter was beautiful. Tonight, however, it wasn't her appearance that she was watching.

Jonas leaned his shoulder against hers. "Who is he?"

"I think he was president of the junior class."

"Does that mean she has good taste?" he teased.

The young man was tall and lanky. His dark brown hair fell over his brow and looked as if it might have been gelled back at the start of the evening. Dusk was falling now and Daisy didn't know how long Jazzi had been at the carnival.

"I think his name's Mark," Daisy told Jonas. "Mark Constantine."

"He looks as if he's keeping a respectful distance."

Daisy watched the couple more closely. "His hand's almost touching hers."

"But he didn't take hold of her hand *yet*."

Daisy could tell Jonas was trying to keep his amusement at her reaction in check. "I suppose that's a good sign," Daisy agreed.

Jonas nudged her shoulder. "A good sign for Jazzi or a good sign for *you*?"

"I'm acting like an overprotective mother, aren't I?"

"Is this the first boy she's dated?"

"This might not be a date," Daisy protested.

Daisy watched as Mark's hand curled around Jazzi's.

"It looks like a date to me," Jonas observed.

She took her gaze from the young couple and eyed Jonas. "You think I'm being silly."

He shook his head and turned serious. "I think you're being a mom."

"I have questions."

"If we run into them, you *are* going to chill and act matter-of-fact, aren't you?"

There was levity in Jonas's question, but she knew it carried advice too. "At least she drove herself here tonight," Daisy muttered.

Jonas took hold of Daisy's hand and pulled her toward the Ferris wheel. "Come on. *We're* going to have some fun. Any questions you have, you're going to save until later, right?"

Jonas was moving away from Jazzi so fast that Daisy only had time to say, "If I ask them then."

He pulled her up the platform to wait for one of the cars on the Ferris wheel.

"Do you think this is safe?" she asked him. "They take these rides apart . . ."

Jonas gently pulled her down onto the swinging seat. The operator of the ride attached the bar in front of them.

Jonas turned his face to hers, studying her. "Safe. You're going to ask me if this is *safe* after you've faced off with murderers?"

"Shhhh," Daisy said, putting two fingers playfully over Jonas's lips. He kissed them and grinned at her.

The Ferris wheel started turning.

They were almost to the top when Daisy said to him, "I'm thinking about calling the security guard's wife."

Suddenly they were at the top of the Ferris wheel and it stopped. Jonas blew out a frustrated breath, turned toward her, and kissed her.

She forgot about murderers, security guards . . . and even Jazzi.

When Daisy took her break on Monday, she thought about her sister returning to New York today. Yesterday at dinner at their parents' house, Camellia was mostly interested in their Aunt Iris and Vi. She hadn't exactly ignored Daisy and Jonas but . . .

Daisy shook off thoughts of Camellia and crossed the street, walked a few shops down, and then opened the door into Quilts and Notions, Rachel Fisher's shop. As soon as she did, a comforting feeling fell over her. The shop brought back memories of Rachel's family home when they were both just girls. The shop also signified to Daisy the best Willow Creek had to offer in patterns, materials, and above all, quilts. It was a bright store where quilts hung from high racks. The patterns were varied. One resembled her own Sunshine and Shadow quilt that covered her bed at home. Others were the Tumbling Blocks pattern, various Crazy Quilts, and a Wedding Ring Quilt. She studied that one for a long time. She hadn't thought about wedding rings in a few years.

Quilted potholders in colors from purple to hunter

green to yellow and black fanned out on two shelves beside placemats that were also handcrafted. Another area of the shop held bolts of cloth in the colors many Amish women used—violet, hunter green, navy blue, light blue, and even aqua, to patterns that the *Englischers* in Willow Creek purchased—flowers, squares, plaids, and prints of all sizes and shapes. A corner rack that spun around held books about the history of Lancaster County and quilts, pattern books, crochet directions, and knitting patterns.

Rachel stood near the quilt rack shelving buttons on a side stand. When she saw Daisy, she said, *"Wilcom! Wie discht du heit?"*

Rachel sometimes used Pennsylvania Dutch with Daisy because she knew Daisy understood a bit of it, especially when it translated to "How are you today?"

"I'm fine," Daisy responded.

"Did you come to visit or do you need something?"

Daisy stood close to Rachel and lowered her voice. "Jazzi was with a boy at the carnival."

"I see," Rachel said, obviously trying to hide a smile. She set the bin of buttons she was carrying onto the floor. "That shook you up a bit, ain't so?"

"Yes, it shook me up. I'm trying to get used to the idea that Jazzi's going away to college next year. I really don't want to add her dating this year into that mix."

"She has to date to find her *lieb,* ya?"

"She's too young to find her love." As soon as Daisy said it, she knew what Rachel was thinking. "I know your daughter isn't much older and she's getting married. I watched Vi get married young. That wasn't what I expected for her. I want to see Jazzi capture her dreams."

"What if her dream is having a home and family like her sister . . . like you?"

Daisy sighed and leaned against the shelves. "I know I have to let her make her own decisions."

"Ya," Rachel said, sort of as a prompt.

"She knows I'll support whatever she decides to do."

Rachel nodded. "She does."

"So why do I feel as if I'm not giving her enough guidance? Why do I feel that her growing up and moving on is a sad thing not a happy thing?" Her voice became thick as she asked the question.

"Because you're her *mudder* and you're going to miss her. You can't put your feelings on hold and pretend. It's just like when Jeremiah was courting our Esther. I didn't think he was right for her. In fact, I was sure of it. But she had to figure that out for herself and she did. And now she's going to be happy with Daniel. She figured it out and your Jazzi will too."

Daisy's shoulders relaxed and her chest tightness loosened. "You always make me feel better."

"That's what friends are for. You help me too."

Another reason why Daisy had visited Rachel lay heavily on her mind. "Maybe you can help me in another way. Jonas won't really tell me if he agrees with what I want to do."

Rachel cocked her head, the narrow ribbon of her *kapp* flurrying in front of her. "Does this have something to do with Hiram?"

"You're too perceptive."

"I've been your friend since we were *kinner*."

The fact that they'd shared thoughts and feelings since they were children mattered. "Aunt Iris gave me the number for the security guard's wife."

"The security guard at the Hope Clinic?" Rachel inquired. "Do you think she knows something?"

"I don't know. The police only spoke to her husband so I'd like to talk with her. Bad idea or worse idea?"

The lines around Rachel's eyes crinkled deeper. "You wouldn't have brought it up unless you thought it was a good idea. Something I found out might help you decide."

"What did you find out?"

"Levi heard that Eli inherited part of Hiram's estate. The rest of it went to our district's medical fund."

Daisy knew that the Amish didn't have insurance, another way they stayed off the grid and away from any type of government or English control. Each district funded an account that would cover community members' medical bills. They held a mud sale each year, a type of auction that helped add money to that fund.

"It's a wonderful *gut* thing that Hiram left that to us. No one would have expected that. But for Eli, that might not be such *gut* news."

Daisy thought about the repercussions of that inheritance. "This means that Eli is even more a suspect. It means he could have had a motive."

"Are there other suspects?" Rachel asked.

"Emory Wagner is one because he fought with Hiram at the social. There are other couples who lost embryos who I'm sure are grieving and are angry."

"Do you think Eli had anything to do with it?" Rachel asked, worried.

"Jonas doesn't think so. But he might not know about this latest news. When I talked with Eli, I didn't get a sense that he could hurt anybody. Even though he left the faith, I think those values have stayed with him." She thought about the fact that he was dating Miriam and he could be returning to his faith.

Rachel tenderly touched Daisy's arm. "You said Jonas isn't certain whether you should call the security guard's wife."

"He's not," Daisy responded with a sigh.

"So let me ask you this. What would Vi say if you told her you want to question this woman?"

"She'd probably tell me not to get involved."

Rachel continued, "What would your mother say?"

Daisy wrinkled her nose. "Probably the same."

After a pause, Rachel asked, "And what would Jazzi say?"

"She'd probably say to do it."

In the silent pause after that answer, Daisy could hear the women who were looking at fabric and talking about what they would be sewing. The scent of fabric and rose petal sachets easily wafted to her.

After about a minute, Rachel asked, "So are you ready to make the decision?"

Just then a customer at the other side of the store called to Rachel. Rachel waved to her client and said, "*Ich bin om cooma.*"

Daisy knew that phrase too. Rachel had told her customer that she was coming.

"Go on," Daisy encouraged her. "After considering everything we've talked about, I'm not ready to make a decision. I'll know when and if it's right to make the call."

Rachel patted Daisy's arm again, then hurried to take care of her customer.

Daisy was about to look around for new placemats when her phone played its tuba sound. Quickly taking it out of her pocket, she saw Jonas was calling. She answered, "Hi, there."

"Are you at the tea garden?" he asked.

There was no urgency in his voice so she guessed this was a social call. "I'm on my break. I'm at Rachel's shop."

"I have a question for you. How would you like to meet me after work? There's something I'd like to show you."

"Sure, I can meet you. Jazzi's babysitting today instead of working at the tea garden. She dropped me off this morning and she borrowed my car. I can drive my work van wherever you want me to meet you. Where are we going?"

"I'll give you the address. You'll be surprised," Jonas said.

Daisy didn't know how much she was going to like this surprise. Though with Jonas, it could only be good.

In early evening, Daisy parked next to Jonas's SUV in the gravel lot at . . . the animal shelter! She remembered the article about Four Paws Animal Shelter that had appeared in the *Willow Creek Messenger.* She looked over the building that had once been an old school house. The shelter had been the dream of a farm family who lived in Willow Creek. Noah Langston and his sister Serena had grown up on a farm taking care of all the animals there. Their dream had had to wait until they were old enough and knowledgeable enough to pull together their resources and establish Four Paws.

Recalling other details, Daisy remembered that Noah was a veterinarian and Serena had earned a business degree. She and Noah had given up their former lives to establish the shelter that was a nonprofit, no-kill shelter that relied on donations and fundraising events. They'd purchased the old property with the schoolhouse for a song because the building had been falling apart and the town wanted to rid itself of it. It looked like a schoolhouse you might see in pioneer photos of olden days out on the prairie.

The building had an open front porch with two steps up to it and pillars holding up the roof. Daisy imagined it might have once been white clapboard but the structure was now sided in red. A cupola was perched on top of the gabled roof over the front porch. The red siding made the building stand out which is what the brother and sister had intended. Noah and Serena wanted to make sure everyone knew about the shelter and took it seriously. In the past year, they'd added an additional room as well as dog runs out back. Trevor had written a follow-up article about that.

The large black door was decorated with four huge white paw prints. Daisy opened the door and stepped inside into the modern era. Gray laminate flooring looked durable and easy to keep clean. The counter in the front room looked sturdy with a glazed butcher-block top. A young woman sat behind the desk and Daisy thought she recognized Serena from a photo in the newspaper. She wore her brown hair in a distinct braided corona design. A black standard poodle was stretched beside her chair.

At the counter, Daisy smiled at Serena and the poodle. "I'm Daisy Swanson. Jonas Groft asked me to meet him here."

Serena smiled back. "I'm Serena Langston."

"I hear you do wonderful work here."

Serena's green eyes sparkled. "We try. Our work is only as good as our volunteers, and the people who adopt. I know exactly where Jonas is. Come on. Follow me."

Daisy followed Serena and her dog companion through a door that led into the new part of the building. On either side of the hallway were Plexiglas rooms with crates. Daisy imagined volunteers spent time with the canines housed there.

"Fortunately we had an adoption fair last week and many of our dogs were adopted."

Daisy noticed a few as they passed the crates but didn't spend long looking because she knew she'd want to take them all home.

"You don't have any cats that I can see."

"We're hoping to add a cat room within the next year or so. It depends on how our funds hold up."

Serena led Daisy out a back door to the dog run area.

Daisy spotted Jonas in one of the runs with what looked like a golden retriever.

Serena opened the door for Daisy to enter the run then said, "I'll be inside if the two of you need me."

Jonas stood at the far end of the run with the dog and waved at her. She saw the genuine smile on his face and knew what was probably happening. She was about to walk toward him when he held up his hand for her to stop.

"Stay there and call Felix to you."

So the dog had a name and Jonas already trusted the canine enough to share him with someone else. She called, "Felix. Come."

Felix, his silky creamy fur rustling as he ran to her, was a handsome dog. His ears waved and his tail pushed the air back and forth.

At the end of the run, his front paws stopped him as his brown eyes looked her over. Instinctively, she stooped to him and let him smell her hands. His tail swooped back and forth as he intently sniffed.

"You probably smell food and kitties on me," she said to him.

He kept sniffing up to her wrist. Then he tilted his head and rubbed it against her fingers.

Walking toward her, Jonas decided, "You passed inspection."

She scratched Felix behind his ears, and he seemed to enjoy the affection. "Serena said there was an adoption fair here last week. I guess Felix wasn't adopted?"

"Felix's owner just brought him in a couple of days ago. She moved into an assisted living facility and she had to give him up."

At that news, Daisy petted his flanks. He kept bumping against her as if he wanted more.

Crouching down with her, Jonas studied the two of them together. "Felix is about five years old and has had training by the woman's son."

"He didn't want Felix?"

"He lives in Mechanicsburg and already has three dogs. He didn't feel he could handle another one."

Daisy looked into Felix's eyes. "You like attention, don't you?"

He bumped against her again as if he'd understood what she said.

She laughed as she rubbed her fingers through his silky, golden-white fur. "You're a handsome boy. You look as if you've just had a bath."

"The volunteers groomed him this morning." Jonas's gaze hadn't left her and Felix.

Now Felix moved his attention from Daisy to Jonas. He stretched out his front paws, his rear up in the air, and then he sat at Jonas's feet. Jonas laid his hand quietly on the dog's head.

"You've decided, haven't you?" she asked Jonas.

When Jonas nodded, Daisy knew he'd found a new friend.

CHAPTER ELEVEN

The pet store on the outskirts of Lancaster called Fur and Feathers welcomed canine clients. Since Jonas had submitted forms the week before he'd decided to adopt Felix—Four Paws did background checks on applicants—it didn't take long to finish same-day paperwork. Afterward, Jonas needed pet supplies. The fact that they could all go into the store together was a bonus.

Felix stayed by Jonas's side throughout the store. Obviously, he'd been trained well to heel. Daisy looked over the dog beds—Felix would need a large one—while Jonas chose a collar and a lead. Jonas added a toy to the cart. Daisy did too and they grinned at each other. A large bag of dog food went into the cart next along with cans of wet food. Dishes to eat and drink out of were next.

Jonas said to Daisy, "Do you think I should buy two dog beds—one for downstairs and one for upstairs?

"That depends. Are you going to let Felix sit on the furniture?"

"It's going to be his house as well as mine," Jonas answered practically.

It was a good thing that Daisy and Jonas felt the same way about pets.

"It might be a good idea to have a bed for upstairs and downstairs. And you know what else? One of those self-warming pads would be good. In the winter, you can put it in one of the beds. Jazzi laid one on the chair in her room. Both cats like to sleep on it when it's cold outside.

"You have the best ideas."

"I try," she said, hooking her arm through his while Felix walked next to her.

After Jonas charged the supplies, they went outside to his SUV. They climbed inside with Felix in the back seat. However, he poked his head up between their seats, looking first at Jonas and then at Daisy.

Gently she said to him, "You're going home with *him*." She pointed to Jonas.

Jonas pointed to her. "But you're going to be seeing her a lot."

Felix didn't seem to mind. His brown eyes appeared to glow with the knowledge that he was going home with someone.

Jonas was about to start the vehicle when his phone buzzed. He took it from the console and gave a shrug when Daisy looked curiously at him.

"Hello," he said. "This is Jonas Groft."

"Hello, Mr. Groft. My name is Adele Gunnarsen. I was Felix's mamma."

The woman was speaking loud enough that Daisy could hear her. Still, Jonas said into the phone, "If you don't mind, I'm going to put you on speaker. I have someone else here who would like to hear what you have to say."

Adele's voice was a little shaky when she said, "I don't mind at all. The volunteer at the shelter gave me your number. That's not always kosher, but she and I are friends. She kept her eye on Felix for me."

"I'm so glad to hear he came from a loving home," Jonas said.

"He did. I don't want to hold you up now, but sometime I can tell you my story. I'm at Whispering Willows Assisted Living facility. I have a favor to ask you."

"Of course," Jonas agreed.

"Whispering Willows allows pets to visit. I would love to see Felix now and then, if you're so inclined."

"I think that would be a good idea," Jonas told her. "Visits to you will help transition Felix into my care. You could tell me all of his idiosyncrasies. Maybe I should ask straight out—does he chew up shoes?"

Adele gave a little laugh. "Not shoes, exactly. But my husband Horace had a pair of slippers that Felix liked to drag around. In fact, I still have them. I forgot to send them along with him."

"I'm sure Felix would like to have them," Jonas gently assured her.

"I was afraid you'd mind if I called you."

"Not at all."

"The fact that you are willing to talk to me means that you are going to provide Felix with a home that he's going to like."

"I hope that's true."

"There's one more thing I'd like to tell you."

Daisy listened and watched Jonas while he waited.

"Felix's name means happy and fortunate," Adele explained. "He was the best dog in the world and I hope he'll bring you much happiness."

After Jonas ended the call, he and Daisy looked at each other. Jonas's eyes were misty, as well as hers. She knew that visiting Adele Gunnarsen was going to be high on Jonas's priority list.

Lunch with her mom was something Daisy tried to do at least once a month. Even though it was difficult sometimes for her mom to get away from Gallagher's Garden Corner, she did because she knew she and Daisy needed to mend a relationship that had been broken for a long, long time. Now they'd found their way back to each other. Time together was important.

While Daisy waited for her mom, she made a decision. Taking the slip of paper out of her pocket, she called the security guard's wife. She held her breath.

When Mavis answered, Daisy introduced herself and explained, "I know your husband spoke to the police. But I thought there might be some detail you could tell me that they missed."

Mavis said, "I'm *so* glad you called. I didn't know if I should really call you. My husband has been working at the clinic since it first opened. My son's on the waiting list for work there, too. But now since this happened, they might not hire any longer. I hear you own a tea garden. How nice. Tell me about it."

Daisy did. A little. Then she asked, "Does your husband bring his stun gun home with him?"

Without hesitating, Mavis responded in a high voice, "Oh, no! Never. He has to hand it in when his shift ends.

You know he gets really tired now when he puts in twelve-hour days. I hate when he works nights." Mavis continued on, telling Daisy all about that.

That's when Daisy realized Mavis simply needed someone to talk to . . . someone to give her a little attention.

Mavis was a dead end.

Shortly after Daisy ended the call, she met her mom in front of the diner's main entrance. Sarah Jane's sported huge hex signs of birds on the front wall and a hex sign with hearts on the other side of the door. The diner wasn't busy around one-thirty, the best time for privacy. Sarah Jane, who was behind the counter, spotted them and smiled.

Sarah Jane was often cook as well as hostess. She had help, of course, but she liked to control everything about her diner. Her strawberry-blond curls fell over her forehead and around her ears. They tousled a bit when she walked. She was rounded and a little overweight but she had lots of energy. She catered to the elder population of Willow Creek by running coupons in the newspaper and online for everyone over sixty. Today she was wearing her blue gingham apron and fuchsia-and-green sneakers.

To Daisy and her mom, Sarah Jane said, "I have the booth in the back where you like to sit."

Daisy's mom smiled. "Perfect."

Her mother was wearing her bright pink lipstick today, and her ash-blond hair looked as if it had just been permed. It curled close to her head and didn't move much when she walked.

Sarah Jane herself rather than one of her waitstaff led them to the back booth and laid a menu on either side when they sat. "Susie will be here shortly to take your order. The meatloaf's especially good today from what I hear."

As Sarah Jane walked away, Rose leaned across the table and said to Daisy in a low voice, "I can't eat meat-loaf and mashed potatoes for lunch. That's too heavy. I'd fall asleep as soon as I went back to the nursery."

"Get whatever you want, Mom. Sarah Jane's suggestions usually roll off her tongue because they're the special of the day."

"Her chicken salad is delicious," Rose said. "I think I'm just going to have the chicken salad in the tomato, you know, cut like a flower? She puts hard-boiled eggs around it. That should be perfect."

Although Daisy was listening to her mom, she was distracted. The two men seated in the booth behind them were having a heated discussion. One of the men was Lawrence Bishop. The other was Daniel Copeland, a good-looking man in his mid-thirties. Likewise, he was a member of the town council. He had rusty brown hair, a patrician nose, and a very firm jaw. She knew lots of women in Willow Creek thought he was handsome and quite a find because he was the assistant manager of the Willow Creek Community Bank.

Glancing at the menu, she couldn't help but hear the raised voices behind her. At first trying to ignore them, she said to her mother, "I think I'll order the tuna melt with a side of slaw."

"When you were little, you loved when I made tuna melts. It was one of those economical meals that didn't take long to fix. In fact, that might have been the first thing I taught you to cook."

"We made them in a toaster oven," Daisy said with a laugh. "We toasted the bread, laid the cheese on the toast, and let it melt for a few seconds. Then we added the tuna and the top piece of toast. But I also made a mess. The tuna would fall off the grate down into the tray."

"You can't learn to cook without making a mess," her mother said. "And you've turned into a fine cook."

"I had a good teacher."

"I think you learned more from your Aunt Iris than me," her mother said honestly. "You and I didn't spend enough time in the kitchen together."

Daisy realized her mother still felt sad and guilty about that because she'd given a lot more attention to Camellia than to Daisy.

"You taught me about flowers and plants, though. We spent time in the garden together."

Susie came to take their order. After they'd given it, Daisy noticed the men in the booth behind her had lowered their voices. Maybe they'd realized they were loud.

Suddenly, however, Lawrence who was sitting directly in back of Daisy, raised his voice again. With some heat, he said, "Troy should find a lawyer for the clinic who's willing to settle fairly. Somehow Hiram turned into a shark of a lawyer and that's not what the community needed."

Daniel's voice rose to match Lawrence's. "Troy has every right to protect his business, and that's what Hiram was going to do. When the clients signed their contracts, they must have read the clause that clearly stated outcomes weren't guaranteed. You need to get off your high horse and remember that clinic is running a business."

With that, Daisy heard shuffling behind her. She couldn't help but look over her shoulder. Daniel was leaving the booth and striding down the aisle to the door. Lawrence stood too. Even from the side, Daisy could see that he was red in the face and angrier than she had ever seen him as he strode to the front of the diner.

Her mother asked, "Wasn't that Lawrence Bishop, the teacher at the high school?"

"Yes, and the other man was Daniel Copeland."

"The loan manager at the bank?" her mother asked. "I hear he's a force to be reckoned with. Very strict about to whom he'll give a loan and to whom he won't."

Daisy confided, "Lawrence isn't usually that stirred up. But this isn't a good time for him and his family. His daughter Piper and her husband Emory were clients of the Hope Clinic."

"They were trying to have a baby?" her mom asked.

Daisy nodded.

"I don't know what I think about having a baby that way," her mother mused. "Too much involvement with the hands of man. But I'm certainly not judging a couple who want to bring a beautiful new life into the world. I suspect they're very upset at what happened."

"They are, and Lawrence is too on their behalf. On top of that, the police questioned Piper and Emory about Hiram Hershberger."

"Gossip has been running rampant about that at the nursery. It's all because of that TV crew and how they taped Emory Wagner Jr. arguing with the lawyer."

Daisy hadn't realized that Emory was a *junior*. But that made sense because many fathers and sons in the area had the same names.

"That's true," Daisy agreed. "If it weren't for what the TV station televised, I don't know if Piper and Emory would stand out for the police. There are many other couples who were affected."

"I think the clinic should settle with them and not run this through the courts," her mother offered.

"I don't know what will happen. I heard Troy Richter's out of the country. My guess is he doesn't want to answer a lot of questions right now." Daisy had been confiding more in her mother, and Rose seemed to appreciate that.

"He'll have to answer questions eventually," her mother said with an expression that Daisy had seen many times before. "Consequences follow actions."

Her mother had repeated that phrase often over Daisy's childhood. And she believed her mother was correct in that assessment. However, what Daisy was most worried about, at the moment, was Lawrence's expression as he left. Who knew he could get that angry? Just how angry might he have been if he'd confronted Hiram?

When Vi entered the tea garden with a friend late in the day, Daisy remembered the conversation she'd had with her older daughter last night. After she'd spent time with Jonas and Felix, she'd stopped in at Vi's where she'd peeked in on a sleeping Sammy. Vi had said, "There's a woman in my mommy group, Ramona Lowell, who doesn't have many complimentary things to say about the Hope Clinic."

"What are her complaints against the clinic?" Daisy had asked.

During her pregnancy, Vi had foregone having her brown hair highlighted but now with her postpartum depression a distant memory, she cared about her appearance again. The highlights and natural makeup were part

of her new persona. "I don't know what her complaints
are but that's why I think you should talk to her. Ramona
has one child and would have been going through *in vitro*
to try and have another if this thing hadn't happened at
the clinic."

"So Ramona is home with her child?"

"Most of the time. I think she transcribes manuscripts
for a writer to bring in extra money."

"Why don't you bring her into the tea garden late in
the day tomorrow? I'll probably have lunch with your
grandmother around one-thirty. Maybe if you come in
around four?"

"I'll see if she's free," Vi had said.

Apparently Ramona had been free. Vi had come inside
first, her friend following her. They were talking and
laughing so Daisy knew that's who it was. Ramona was
tall and slender with short blond hair in a pixie cut and
long bangs. She was wearing jeans and a bateau-neck
slouchy top in peach with three-quarter-length sleeves.
Her nose turned up at the end and her mouth was wide
with a smile.

Daisy waved Vi to the spillover tearoom where only a
few guests still sat drinking tea and enjoying baked goods.
Vi chose a table near the diamond-cut windows. The bay
window looked out onto the street where Daisy noticed a
courting buggy with a chestnut horse clopping by.

When she stopped at the table, Vi made introductions.

"I've heard a lot about you," Ramona said right away.
"We talk about a lot of things in the mommy group, and
our own moms are certainly one of those things."

"Uh oh." Daisy held her hand over her heart. "I don't
think I want to know about those conversations."

"All good," Ramona assured her. "Vi told us how you helped her after the baby was born, finding all the right help for her. So many people don't know anything about postpartum depression. I'm glad you did."

"My aunt was the first person who clued me in," Daisy explained. "After that I looked up everything I could find on it. I tried to hit it from all angles—a medical doctor, the mommy group, nutrition, and vitamins."

"In my case it all worked together," Vi agreed. "But I don't know if I could have helped myself. That's why the mommy group is so good. Everything we share helps all of us."

"What can I get you to drink and eat?" Daisy asked.

"I saw on your sales board over the counter when I came in that orange pekoe is the special this month. Can I have orange pekoe tea unsweetened and iced?"

"Sure you can. How about scones, whoopie pies, or cookies? They're on the house."

Immediately Ramona shook her head. "No, I watch my carbs. But I did see cabbage sausage soup on your menu. Could I have a small cup of that?"

"Certainly. Vi, how about you?"

"The same iced tea and corn chowder for me."

Daisy went to the kitchen herself and brought out what the young women had ordered. After she set a tray on the table, she spooned honey into her cup of hot orange pekoe tea. As they ate and sipped, Daisy let the relaxed atmosphere continue at the table.

After she stirred her tea a second time, she commented, "Vi doesn't usually tell me about specific conversations in your mommy group. But I have a friend whose daughter had her dreams smashed by what happened at the Hope Clinic. Does that ever come up in your conversations? I don't want to know any confidences. But I'd like to understand in general how the clinic operates."

"I'm not sure that's something I should talk about," Ramona said, a little shyly.

"I don't want to make you uncomfortable," Daisy assured her.

"I haven't mentioned this at our mommy group," Vi said. "But my mom has helped the police department gather facts about their cases."

"What kind of cases?" Ramona asked.

"Murder cases," Vi said.

At first Ramona looked astonished, then she responded, "You're serious, aren't you?"

"I am. When she talks to people, sometimes she can find out things the police can't. I already told her that some folks weren't pleased with the way the clinic operates."

Ramona hesitated, but then she said, "I don't think I'm talking out of school to tell you that the clinic's success rate isn't all that great. Not when you consider other clinics across the country. The Hope Clinic advertises that it's one of the top clinics, but I looked up the others and that claim is not true."

"Maybe they have a good PR department," Daisy said, thinking about Camellia and her work. She'd often told Daisy that you could spin any fact to make it look better. Could that be true about the clinic? "I'm sure I can find easy documentation about that. Is there anything else?"

Ramona took a spoonful of her soup, wiped her mouth, and set down the spoon. "I haven't had as much to do with the clinic as some. My husband and I just started the process. But not everyone at the clinic is committed to their work. Some of their people have a nonchalant attitude as if what they're doing doesn't matter or isn't as important as it should be."

"Do you have any specific names?"

Ramona studied Daisy but then shook her head. "I don't think I want to give you those."

Daisy could understand that. Her apron had a big daisy logo on it and two large pockets. In one pocket, she always carried coupons for the tea garden as well as some of her own business cards. They both came in handy. The other pocket held her order pad for extensive orders.

Now she slipped her hand behind her phone in her pocket and pulled out one of her business cards. She slid it across the table to Ramona. "There is my card. My cell number is on there too. If you feel there's anything else you want to tell me, just give me a call."

"You're trying to find out who killed Hiram Hershberger?" Ramona asked.

"*I'm* not trying to find out. The police are. But I don't think they have any good leads. There are so many suspects, and that friend I mentioned is one of them. So if I find anything out that I feel could lead them in a particular direction, I'll consult with them and tell them."

Ramona checked with Vi. "This isn't something you've talked about in the mommy group."

"That's because, for the most part, I don't want Mom involved in it. My sister Jazzi has an opposite outlook. Let's just say she's more adventurous than I am."

Ramona gave Daisy a wink. "I have heard the name Jazzi brought up once or twice."

Daisy laughed. "I just bet you have."

That evening, Daisy, Jonas, and Jazzi enjoyed salmon kabobs on the grill. They sat on the patio at the picnic table talking about their day. Jonas had brought Felix over to meet Jazzi, and Jazzi seemed entranced by the dog. He even sat by her while they ate, maybe hoping to earn a tidbit from her plate. Even when she didn't give it, he sat at her feet. Daisy had peeked under the table more than once and he'd seemed quite content.

After they'd finished dinner, however, he went around to Jonas's side of the table and sat looking up at him as if he were waiting for something.

"What's that about?" Daisy asked Jonas. "Does he think he's going to get an apple dumpling for dessert?"

Jonas chuckled. "No. Last night after supper I took him outside to play fetch for a while. I think he's asking me to do that." Jonas took a ball from his pocket. "And I think he's smart enough to know this was in my pocket."

"I'll play with him," Jazzi said. "We can have a good run together."

"You're sure you don't have something else you want to do?"

"Maybe I can work off the apple dumpling before I eat it," Jazzi said, taking the ball from Jonas. She stood at the edge of the patio and called, "Come, Felix."

Felix didn't even hesitate to run to Jazzi. She led him deeper into the yard and then threw the ball for him to chase. He streaked after it, his tail flying. It didn't take him long to find it and he ran back to her and dropped it at her feet.

"You're good at this," she said. "Let's do it again." She picked up the ball and tossed it in a different direction. Felix ran after it, through grass and dandelions, stopping only when he found it with his nose.

"I think they're going to be friends," Jonas said.

"I think so too. Are we going to have him meet Marjoram and Pepper tonight?"

Jonas shook his head. "I don't think so. Let's wait on that. I don't want to overload him with too much excitement at one time."

Even though they were sitting on the patio at the back of the house, Daisy could hear tires on gravel at the garage. Not long after, her phone made a *ding-dong* sound. That was the front-door camera app telling her she had a visitor.

After she peered at the screen, she said, "It's Piper! I'll go inside and see what she wants."

Daisy went through the sliding glass doors off her kitchen, passed the dining room table into the living room and stood at the front door. When she opened it, Piper was looking down at her white espadrilles. She was wearing white slacks and a red T-shirt. Her hair was caught back in a ponytail.

Piper said, "I saw another car parked down there." She waved toward the garage. "Am I intruding on something?"

"That's Jonas's SUV. He's out back with Jazzi and his dog. He brought Felix over to explore the property and run out some energy."

"I'm sorry I just dropped by," Piper started again.

Daisy cut her off. "It's fine, Piper. Come on in. We're about to have apple dumplings and there are plenty."

"I don't usually eat desserts," Piper said. "I wanted to talk to Jazzi if she's here."

That was a surprise. "You want to speak with Jazzi?"

"I do. I'd like to talk to her honestly about adoption. I'm trying to get a good sense of it, and I'd like to ask someone who was actually adopted. I thought about Jazzi. Do you think she'd mind talking to me?"

"I don't think she'd mind. She's quite open with her feelings about it, and with her search for her birth mother. Why don't we go out and ask her?"

As they crossed through the kitchen, Daisy said, "I was talking to someone about the attitude of the nurses and the techs at the Hope Clinic. What did you think about them?"

Piper shrugged. "I didn't think about them much, really. Some were cool. Some were business-like. Others were just busily efficient. I imagine you know how staff can be. Everybody has a different personality. They all wore smiles. Some techs meant their smiles, and some didn't."

"Did that effect how you felt about what you were doing?"

Again Piper shrugged. "No, not really. I like the doctor I was working with." She looked pained as she blew out a breath. "Every time I talk about the clinic these days, my stomach forms knots."

"Grief over what happened?" Daisy asked.

"I feel like crying most days. My dad and Emory are consulting with a lawyer in Philadelphia about suing the individual responsible for the malfunction. That's how they're handling what happened. The two of them have concluded that in class action suits, it's the lawyer who makes all the money. I don't know if they're taking my feelings into consideration at all."

Daisy knew when a family was involved in grief and loss, each person handled it differently. "What are your feelings about a lawsuit?"

"I think we should go into mediation that will lead to a settlement. That's the kind of lawyer I want to hire. But Emory and Dad are much more forceful about their opinions."

Daisy remembered Lawrence and Daniel's argument at Sarah Jane's Diner. Lawrence had certainly been forceful then.

After Daisy and Piper exited the kitchen onto the patio, Daisy called Jazzi over. Daisy explained, "Piper has questions about adoption. Would you be willing to answer them?"

"Sure." She looked at her mom. "Are you and Jonas going to stay out here?"

Daisy glanced at Jonas who was rubbing Felix's head and scratching him around the ears. "Yes, we'll stay out here and play with Felix."

Jazzi said to Piper, "Why don't we go into the living room and talk. I can tell you anything you want to know."

After about fifteen minutes of playing with Felix, Daisy went inside and took the apple dumplings out of the oven where she'd kept them warm. Looking in on Jazzi and Piper, she pointed to the hot tray. Jazzi and Piper both shook their heads. She carried the dumplings outside to Jonas and set the tray on the table. She'd brought along a small pitcher of maple syrup to pour over them.

"Those look delicious," Jonas said.

"I don't make them very often, and I'm not sure why.

Probably the calories. Somehow I tell myself if I have a small slice of apple pie, I'm not getting as many calories as I would in one of these."

Jonas took a dog treat from the pouch on his belt because Felix was eyeing the dumplings. Jonas pointed to the dumplings. "Good for human. Not good for dog." Then he held up the dog biscuit. "Good for dog. Not good for human. Sit."

Felix sat and Jonas let him take the biscuit from his hand.

"Adele's son certainly trained Felix well," Daisy noted.

"Felix knows the basic commands," Jonas agreed. "Other than that, he and I seem to have an intuition on what we need and when we need it."

"That's a good thing."

Jonas took his fork and sliced first into the pastry shell covering on the soft-baked apple, and then down into the apple itself. He took the bottle of real maple syrup and poured it over the dumpling. When he took a bite, he closed his eyes for a moment. "This is so good, Daisy. You should really open a tea garden."

She swatted his arm.

He kissed her with maple syrup on his lips.

As they were both enjoying their apple dumplings, Daisy's phone played its tuba sound. She lifted it from the table and studied the screen. "It's Trevor."

Jonas waved his hand at her. "Go ahead. I have my mouth full of apple dumpling."

With a roll of her eyes, she answered the call. "Hi, Trevor. Do you need something?"

"I'm not sure," he said. "I have news for you."

"What kind of news? Nothing's happened to Tessa, has it?"

"No. Tessa's fine and so am I. I found out that one of the techs from the clinic, Thelma Bartik, has disappeared. She's not answering her phone and she isn't at her house."

"Is that odd?"

Trevor's voice was tempered. "It's very odd. Even worse than that, her neighbors haven't seen her for two days."

Daisy's stomach clenched at that news even though she didn't know the person he was speaking about. But anyone missing for two days wasn't just a glitch. A person missing for two days could most likely have something to do with a murder.

CHAPTER TWELVE

The following morning at the tea garden, Daisy asked Tessa, "I have an appointment at ten. Can you cover for me?"

They were in the kitchen baking scones and cookies for the morning crowd. Tessa peeked into the oven and straightened up again. "Sure, I can. How long do you think you'll be?"

"I'm not sure. Probably no more than an hour."

Tessa was wearing a fuchsia smock today. Her caramel-colored hair was French braided. Her eyes narrowed as she looked Daisy up and down. "Is anything wrong? Are you feeling okay?"

Daisy poked one of her hands into the pocket of her apron, not knowing what she wanted to say. After all, this was Tessa—her best friend. Since the security guard's wife was a dead end, she'd decided to do something else to further the investigation, at least for now. "You know Trevor called me last night?"

"Yes, we were together when he did. One of the techs from the clinic disappeared. Her neighbors hadn't seen her for two days. Does that have something to do with you?"

"In a way it does. Piper and Emory Wagner are suspects in Hiram's murder. So is Eli Lapp. Jonas has a fondness for him."

"Does that mean you're going to do some investigating?" Tessa had lowered her voice so Eva, who was washing teapots at the sink, wouldn't overhear.

"I think it's time I do something that the detectives can't."

The buzzer went off on one of ovens.

Tessa held up her finger for Daisy to wait a minute. She removed a tray of snickerdoodles and set them on a rack on the counter. Then she went back to standing at the oven with Daisy. "And just what can *you* do that they can't?"

"I'm a woman," she said simply.

Tessa shook her head, still not understanding.

"I've decided to go undercover. Early this morning, I called and made an appointment at the Hope Clinic. They fit me in at ten. Let's face it. They're not getting a lot of clients right now."

"What are you going to tell them?"

"I'm going to tell them I'm thinking about having children, but my age is a problem."

"Women are having kids at forty."

"Right, a lot of them with *in vitro* help."

When Tessa cocked her head, her braid flipped along her smocked sleeve. Her voice lowered even more. "Are you thinking about having children?"

"You know I can't have kids. That's why we adopted Jazzi. When I had a miscarriage a year after we had Violet, it caused a uterine tear. It was highly unlikely then that I would carry a baby to term, and I imagine the same would be true today."

"But?" Tessa prompted, still in that low voice.

Daisy glanced at Eva, not wanting her to think they were talking behind her back, even though they were. The water was running and Eva was concerned with the bone china teapot she was washing out.

"I could freeze my eggs. Jonas and I have talked about it a little, but not seriously. If I froze my eggs, I'd have to use a surrogate. Jonas has as much as said adoption is always on the table."

"So this little jaunt you're going on really *is* under-cover."

When Daisy showed up in the waiting room of the clinic five minutes before her appointment time, she scanned the room and almost whistled. Everything was sleek and modern, rather than simply utilitarian. The sign above the registration desk, in bronze metal lettering, read THE HOPE CLINIC. The wall under the sign was painted light gray. Stainless-steel cabinets with a counter ran across the length of that wall. The countertop there looked like marble but it was probably a form of quartz. The counter, about six feet removed from the stainless-steel cupboards, housed a receptionist and a desk with a computer inlaid underneath. The receptionist's counter there again looked like quartz but Daisy supposed it could be granite with gray, black, and white marbling.

Daisy noticed the front of the receptionist's desk was inlaid glass tile in colors of gray, white, and taupe. The luxury vinyl tile on the floor again had a porcelain-like look to it but could withstand wear and tear of clients coming and going. The six chairs scattered in the area appeared to be black leather, not vinyl. Chrome coffee tables were glass-topped and devoid of any magazines.

When Daisy walked up to the counter, the receptionist looked up and smiled. Daisy said, "I'm Daisy Swanson. I have an appointment at ten."

The receptionist checked the list on a paper to the side of her computer. "I see that you do. Let me get you checked in."

She asked for Daisy's address as well as her birth date. She was ready to hand Daisy a clipboard.

Daisy knew what those papers would ask her—medical conditions, prescriptions she took, etc., etc.

To avoid all that, she told the receptionist, whose name tag said BARBARA, "I'm just here for a tour today. If I seriously decide to do something, I'll fill out all your paperwork then."

The receptionist didn't look happy at that news. Barbara said, "That's not how we operate here."

Daisy returned, "If you want me to take the tour, that's how *I* operate."

Apparently weighing what she should do and say, Barbara finally advised Daisy, "Why don't you have a seat. I'll buzz someone for your tour."

Crossing the reception area, Daisy sat on one of the leather chairs. Barbara had a muted conversation over her phone with someone. Shortly after, a woman appeared in a doorway that led inside the clinic itself. She was short, rotund, with black hair that was cropped and parted severely to the right. Her red cat-eye glasses made her face look even rounder. She was wearing black slacks and a loose pale green blouse with HOPE CLINIC embroidered over the pocket. Her multi-colored beaded lanyard held her name tag and probably a security card. Her name was Maya Neuman.

She called softly, "Daisy Swanson?"

Daisy stood and approached her. After Daisy knew she had this appointment this morning, she'd dressed a little differently than she usually did for work. She was wearing a tailored light-blue sheath with cap sleeves. It was a dress she sometimes wore to church with white chunky beads and a matching bracelet. She'd wanted to look upscale for this appointment. She was glad she'd taken the time to do that because Maya looked her up and down and then smiled as if she approved.

Daisy felt a sick feeling in her stomach, suspecting everything this clinic did was based on money. She hoped not. Bringing children into the world needed to come from kindness and compassion, not monetary gain.

Daisy followed Maya into an office where Maya educated Daisy on freezing embryos, *in vitro* fertilization, and how the clinic operated.

Knowing she had to be engaged in the conversation, Daisy said, "I'm interested in having my eggs frozen. Then once I'm married, if I'd like to have children, it would be a possibility." She told Maya about her own situation and about not being able to carry a child to term.

Maya insisted, "Our fertility specialists here would evaluate you and give you an honest appraisal of what can be done, including finding a surrogate and the legal ramifications of that."

"If I wanted to delve into all that," Daisy responded, "I'd bring my fiancé with me. I just wanted to come for a preliminary tour and see how I feel about the clinic."

Maya didn't seem too happy with that news, but she kept smiling. "Come on. I'll show you around."

As they walked, Daisy realized she'd used the term *fiancé* for Jonas. She found she liked the idea of being engaged to him. Did he feel that way too? The facilities in the main section of the clinic were fairly mundane until Maya and Daisy came to a closed door with a small square glass window. There was a key pad on the door and Daisy imagined Maya's security card would open it.

Maya pointed through the window. "That's where the magic happens. I can't take you on a tour inside there. Everything must remain sterile. I hope you understand."

Daisy was about to answer when Maya's phone buzzed. At least that's what Daisy thought it was.

She was proved correct when Maya pulled a phone from her pocket.

"I'm needed in one of the exam rooms," she told Daisy. "But I'll be right back." Maya disappeared down a hall.

Daisy stood there waiting, taking in everything she could.

Suddenly the door she was standing in front of opened, and a woman in blue scrubs came out. She studied Daisy with questions in her eyes.

Daisy said lamely, "I'm just taking a tour."

The tech smiled. "You're going to try *in vitro*?"

"Possibly. I'm curious about something."

"What?"

The young woman looked to be in her twenties. She was wearing a blue scrub cap but blonde strands peeked out underneath it. She didn't wear makeup and she was very attractive. Daisy wondered if she was a nurse or an LPN. She decided to do a little poking. After all, that's why she was here and she didn't have much time.

"I had this appointment and I wasn't sure I should come."

"Why not?" the young woman asked.

"There's been a lot of bad publicity about the Hope Clinic. The latest rumors concern the disappearance of one of your techs . . . Thelma Bartik."

The woman in front of her glanced through the window in the door, then she looked around the room as if she were expecting someone to barge in suddenly. "I can't talk about that," she said in a low voice. "I really can't."

She scurried off down the hall that Maya had disappeared into.

Maya reappeared seconds later. Maya said, "Something has come up, and I think our tour is going to have to end. Why don't you make an appointment with the receptionist to start testing?"

"That sounds like a good idea. Thanks very much for your time today."

Maya smiled. "That's what we're here for." Then she hurriedly walked her out to the reception area again.

The receptionist targeted Daisy with her gaze. "Shall I schedule you for another appointment?"

"I'm going to have to consult my calendar at home," Daisy said. "But I'll give you a call."

Before the receptionist could make any other comments or ask more questions, Daisy hurried out the door.

Outside, she decided to reconnoiter a bit. Going around the side of the building, she saw a janitor dragging a trash bag out to the dumpster. She knew sometimes those who seemed faceless learned the most about the facility where they worked. She went up to the man who was stocky and short, wearing gray overalls and a gray shirt. He was almost bald with steel-colored hair growing above his ears and in a thin row across the back of his head.

After he tossed the black bag into the dumpster, Daisy said, "Hello. Can I talk to you?"

After the man turned toward her, she could see he had a stubby nose, a high forehead, and bushy silver brows. His jowls wiggled as he asked, "Pardon me?"

Daisy looked around to see if anybody else was in the vicinity. No one was. "My name is Daisy Swanson. I'm looking into Thelma Bartik's disappearance. Do you think you can help?"

The name tag on his shirt read CLETUS SIMPSON.

Cletus's mouth opened into a round O as if he were stymied for words.

"Did you know Thelma?" she asked.

"I knew her," he mumbled.

"Can you tell me if she was the tech who caused the accident that destroyed eggs and embryos?"

Cletus took a step back from her. "I ain't saying nothin'. I don't know nothin'."

Looking him straight in the eyes, she suggested, "Cletus, I think you might know more than anybody else in that clinic."

"I don't," he maintained stubbornly.

Daisy sensed she couldn't push any further. He would just go inside and shut the door. So she did the only thing she could do. Opening her purse, she took out a business card that she'd prepared in case she needed it.

She held it out to Cletus. "I own Daisy's Tea Garden. The police have their eye on friends of mine and think they're involved in Hiram Hershberger's death. But I think his death might have something to do with this clinic. If you remember anything, or if you know anything else, especially about Thelma, give me a call, okay?"

He stared at her business card as if it might bite him. Then he quickly took it and stuffed it into his pants pocket.

Without another word, he hurried inside and closed the steel door.

Daisy wasn't sure if her appointment had been a waste of time . . . or if it would eventually provide clues.

Did dogs really hate cats?

This was the night that Daisy and Jonas were going to find out.

She and Jonas were together in the way that was only going to get more serious. He was a doggie parent now and that meant Felix would be welcome in her house. She really didn't want to close Marjoram and Pepper upstairs in one of the bedrooms when Felix and Jonas were over. They didn't like closed doors and neither did she. But . . .

Jonas kept Felix on a lead as they stepped over the threshold into Daisy's house. Daisy wasn't sure what would happen if Jonas didn't hold onto Felix.

However, once inside, Felix just sat and looked up at Jonas as if asking what happened next.

"Should we let him sniff around?" Jonas asked.

"It's really Marjoram and Pepper's domain, so they should be the ones to decide where he goes and what happens."

Jonas stared into Felix's shiny brown eyes. "The women rule the roost here, bud."

As if Felix understood what Jonas was saying, he plopped onto the floor and waited.

Jonas slipped the lead off his collar. "Are you sure you don't want to pen up Pepper and Marjoram and let him smell at them under the door or something. Isn't that what all the experts suggest?"

"We could do it that way," Daisy agreed. "Or . . ." She waved at the stairway.

Marjoram and Pepper had stopped on the landing and were peering through the slats. Marjoram gave a sharp meow as if she'd just seen Felix. Pepper, who always listened to her sister, ran back up the stairs as if to get Jazzi. Daisy could hear Jazzi, who had been warned about this meeting, come out of her bedroom.

"Come on, Pepper," the teen said conversationally. "Let's go downstairs and see what's happening. I think we have a new visitor."

The two feline sisters stayed on the landing while Jazzi descended the rest of the stairs. She motioned to Felix. "Don't you want to meet him?"

Felix's tail was swishing quickly back and forth. His nose was in the air even though all four paws were stationery.

"I don't know, Daisy," Jonas said. "Maybe I should take him back outside."

She laid a hand on his arm. "Let's see if they can settle their relationships without our barging in. I'm going to go over to the staircase so Marjoram and Pepper know they have another ally."

"Four against two? Do you think that's fair?" Jonas asked, amusement in his voice.

"You two are big enough to hold your own," Daisy teased.

As Daisy reached the staircase, silence prevailed. Everyone was frozen in place.

Marjoram was the first one to budge. After all, she liked Jonas, and she was the more curious of the two cats.

"Go to it," Jazzi said. "You're more ferocious than he is."

Marjoram glanced at Daisy and then Jazzi as if their coaxing helped. She drew herself up tall and pranced down the rest of the stairs. After she leapt off the bottom step, she slowly crossed two feet toward Felix, then arched her back, hissed, and straightened her tail until it arrowed straight up in the air.

"Oh, this is going well," Jonas muttered. "Felix, stay."

Felix's tail swished faster. He inched forward.

"Release him from his command," Daisy offered.

Jonas eyed her as if she were crazy.

"Really, Jonas," she coaxed.

Jonas reached down and patted Felix on the head and made an up gesture with his hand. "Okay, boy. Let's see what happens."

Pepper slowly came down the stairs behind her sister. She hissed too, her tail a black fluffed wand.

Whether Felix was used to cats or not, Daisy didn't

know. Nevertheless, he seemed to be because he ignored the cats, padded over to the coffee table and spread out on the rug.

Daisy couldn't help but laugh.

Pepper and Marjoram ran back up the stairs.

"You're retreating," Jazzi accused them. "Come on back down. He won't hurt you. I can tell. He's a good boy."

Her calming voice must have calmed them. They didn't go the whole way to the top of the stairs but returned to the slats and peered down at Felix who seemed to be very much at home.

"Maybe they'll live upstairs now," Jazzi offered, half-teasing, half-serious.

Daisy went over to the sofa and sat. She motioned to Jonas to come join her. With eyebrows arched, his jaw tense, he did. Felix got to his feet, went to Daisy, and let her scratch behind his ears.

The felines had come down to the landing once more, but they couldn't quite see Felix where he sat with Daisy at the sofa.

They ventured down two more steps.

"They're coming," Jonas told her.

"Good." Daisy continued to pet Felix. Jazzi stayed with Marjoram and Pepper. It wasn't long before Marjoram jumped up on the back of the sofa and peered down at Felix.

Daisy said conversationally, "You'll like him once you get to know him." She took her hand from Felix and offered it to Marjoram's nose.

The cat smelled it, raised her head and looked at Daisy as if to say, "You've got to be kidding." She jumped down on the sofa beside Daisy and hissed again at Felix but didn't arch her back this time.

Felix appeared to be immune to cat noises. He took a step toward where Marjoram was sitting on the sofa and put his nose down right at her feet. Marjoram narrowed her golden eyes at Daisy then shifted her focus to the dog.

Felix made a little huffing sound and Marjoram shrank back. But when he didn't move closer, just kept his nose there, the feline sat on the sofa, tucked her paws under her, and stared at him.

Jonas studied them both. "I should snap a picture but I'm afraid they'll move."

Daisy shrugged. "One down and one to go."

Daisy was intrigued by barns—old ones, new ones, red ones, gray ones. In Lancaster County, many barns sported hex signs on their gables. Sometimes a clothesline was attached from the roof of the barn to the house.

The barn she entered Saturday morning had a stone base and white clapboard sides reaching to a high slate-colored roof. Today the loft hatch was open. A breeze blew through it making dust motes dance. The windows around the barn were high, and the stalls that usually housed horses were empty.

Jonas and Elijah Beiler would be holding their sale here. They were talking to a few men who Daisy guessed had brought wood furniture to sell today.

Instead of tagging Jonas right away, she moved around the barn, examining a roll-top desk, a secretary with a drop-down shelf, cedar chests that were often called hope chests. She stopped before a beautiful one with a mosaic wood inlaid lid. The wood had been sanded and coated to a beautiful shine, the colors ranging from blond to chestnut to walnut to mahogany.

She was about to open it, knowing she'd smell cedar inside, when she spotted Eli Lapp and another man over by the side door of the barn. She thought she recognized the fellow with him as another one of the protestors. She did raise the lid to the cedar chest then, hoping it would partially hide her so Eli wouldn't catch her peeking at him. The scent of cedar surrounded her and she looked down into the chest. It had a beautifully crafted interior.

Moments later, her gaze rose to Eli again who was so busy with the other man that he didn't notice her at all. She saw Eli's fellow protestor hand him an envelope. Eli opened the white flap and took out the bills that were inside, counting them. She couldn't tell the denominations but he seemed satisfied with what he'd received.

Just what was Eli involved in?

The protestor who looked to be around Eli's age tipped his straw hat to Eli, gave a roguish grin, and then circulated in the barn as if he were looking for something in particular. Daisy guessed he wasn't.

She'd lowered the lid to the chest when she spotted Eli slip out the barn door. On a whim she decided to follow him.

Eli quickly walked away from the barn and any traffic around it. His boots scattered gravel as he headed for the large chicken coop. Daisy didn't believe he was going to collect eggs.

She slowed down at the building about as big as a two-car garage. Chickens squawked from the other side. Keeping her back to the building, she sidestepped around the exterior. At the corner, she stopped. When she peered around the side, she spotted Eli talking with a young Amish woman. Miriam Yoder? Both of them looked happy as he showed her the envelope and the money inside. After he did, he folded the envelope and pushed it into his jeans pocket. With a huge grin, he took Miriam into his arms, hugged her, and then kissed her.

From Daisy's vantage point, they looked like a young couple in love.

Trying not to make any noise, she returned the way she'd come. Inside the barn once more, she waited by the door.

From across the room, Jonas spied her and beckoned to her. But she held up her hand with one finger as if to say, *Give me a minute.*

He nodded and returned to attaching prices on the pieces of furniture.

It wasn't long until Daisy saw Eli as he hurried back to the barn. He nodded to her and was going to pass her when she said, "Can I talk to you for a minute?"

Eli studied her impassively but didn't move away.

Instead of revealing her knowledge of his meeting with the woman who must be Miriam, she pounced on the other activity she'd seen. "What's going on?" she asked him. Sometimes an open-ended question like that produced more information.

This time it didn't. He said, "I don't know what you're talking about."

"I saw money exchange hands between you and that protestor."

With a scowl he reminded her, "I was one of those protestors too." There was more belligerence in his tone than she'd expected to hear.

So she asked him again, "What's going on, Eli?"

Her low question didn't prompt information. Instead he turned his back on her, headed back outside, and threw over his shoulder, "It's none of your business."

Maybe it wasn't, she thought as she watched him walk away. But that exchange of money could be the business of the police.

CHAPTER THIRTEEN

When Daisy finally approached Jonas, he was talking to Zeke Willet. As soon as he spotted her, however, he stopped talking, turned, and embraced her. Then he gave her a resounding kiss. Neither of them cared who was watching.

The kiss might have gone a little longer than it should have because Zeke tapped Jonas's shoulder. "We were talking, remember? I know your brain's probably a little foggy . . ." He trailed off and grinned.

Jonas had the grace to flush. He said to Zeke, "I haven't seen Daisy since Felix met the cats."

Zeke scrunched up his face as if that wasn't the subject he'd expected to talk about. Keeping with the levity of it though, he asked, "How did *that* go?"

"At first Jonas was worried," Daisy told him.

Jonas waffled his hand back and forth. "Dogs and cats don't always mix. At first there was a lot of hissing."

"But after they all got used to each other, they got along." Daisy's voice was light, keeping with the moment.

"I suppose then there's hope for humans," Zeke commented wryly.

Daisy laughed. There was definitely hope for humans. After Marjoram had decided Felix was an okay dog, Pepper had jumped on the bandwagon. In fact, Pepper had ended up sleeping near one of Felix's paws while Jonas and Daisy and Jazzi sat on the sofa and watched a movie. Daisy had felt as if she'd like many more nights like that one.

Before any of them could comment further, Lawrence Bishop came hurrying toward them. "I'm glad I caught all of you together," he said.

"Has something happened with Piper or Emory?" Daisy asked.

"No. The town council just had an emergency meeting. We've chosen the man who will head up the fundraising for the shelter."

"Who is it?" Zeke asked.

"His name is Dalton Ames. He's from Harrisburg and he's supposed to be good."

"Supposed to be?" Jonas inquired.

"That's just it," Lawrence said. "That's why I'm glad I ran into you three."

Daisy could feel an "uh oh" forming in her subconscious.

"The other members of the council were impressed

with his résumé. But I want to know his ethics. After all, think about Hiram."

"I don't understand," Daisy said. "How does this compare?"

Lawrence glanced at Zeke. "I want you to do a background check on Dalton Ames."

Zeke shrugged. "I'm not sure I have cause to do that."

"I want you to think about something," Lawrence said. "Look at what happened to Hiram. I heard about cases he took that filched income from the elderly or made him consider his fees above the right thing to do. What if this fundraiser isn't honest? What if Ames has ulterior motives? He's from a big city and we're a small town. Maybe he thinks he can put one over on us. I need you to do a deep background check. Find out what he's been involved in . . . if any of it has been nefarious. If he's been fundraising for charities, just what did he do for them? Do they have good things to say about him?"

"Certainly he had recommendations and references on his résumé," Zeke said.

"Oh, he did. But I know how that goes," Lawrence protested. "Just think about the letters that high school students have us write to recommend them for college. They only go to the teachers who had positive interaction with them. They're certainly not going to go to someone who didn't. I want to know if there were any complaints against this man and, if so, what they were. Doesn't that merely make good sense?"

Jonas nodded. "I suppose it does. But how is the rest of the town council going to feel if you do this?"

"They don't have to know, not unless Zeke finds something that I need to share with them. Isn't that the point of the background check?"

Zeke still looked troubled. "Mr. Bishop, it sounds more like you need a private investigator to do this. I'm not sure I can dig like you want. I can find out the obvious—if Ames has a record, if he has any warrants against him, maybe even charities he worked for. But after that"—Zeke shook his head—"I have a murder investigation to deal with."

Lawrence rubbed his chin and then the back of his neck. "I do understand that. Can you at least do the preliminary check for me? I'll find someone to do the rest."

Daisy was hung up on something Lawrence had said. She asked him, "Are you saying there are clients or maybe people Hiram brought suits against who would kill him?"

"Take any lawsuit," Lawrence exclaimed with a lift of his hand. "Someone has to be on the losing end. Hiram has been practicing law for a long time. Cases mount up and so do enemies."

"Then this murder might never be solved," she concluded not for the first time.

Bristling, Zeke contradicted her. "Wait a minute. I'm not going to stop until I find out who murdered Hiram."

"I suppose you have a suspect list?" Daisy asked.

"We do," Zeke said warily.

"Maybe you should find out how many of those suspects use insulin," she offered.

"HIPAA regulations make it tough to learn medical information."

"If you're questioning suspects, you can probably find out from them. Anyone who's innocent won't even know why you're asking."

After Zeke thought about it, he shook his head. "It

would almost be easier to track down the people who knew Hiram was hypoglycemic."

Daisy agreed with that. "Maybe it would be, but that could be harder to find out."

Zeke arched his brows. "I have my methods."

What Zeke was telling her was that he wouldn't quit until he got his man or woman. She hoped that would be true.

Vi had invited Piper to lunch at her apartment on Sunday after church and she wanted Daisy to join them. Daisy was happy to do that. She always loved spending time with Vi and Sammy, and she thought she could learn more from Piper about what was going on with Emory too. She scolded herself for even thinking about that but there it was. She couldn't hide the fact that she was getting involved in the investigation. So far, however, she hadn't really learned anything that she could tell Zeke.

At eight months old, Sammy was doing more than growing. He was busy as long as he was awake. He'd learned to crawl and that meant exploring as much as he could wherever he could. Of course, he was also putting anything and everything into his mouth. That was a constant concern of Vi's. She had toys in the refrigerator that she used for that purpose because he was also teething. But as soon as they hit the floor, she was there picking them up and washing them.

Daisy couldn't remember if she'd been that compulsive about it, but she appreciated the way Vi was mothering and how much she loved Sammy.

Vi had been breastfeeding when Daisy arrived at her apartment, climbing the stairs and opening the baby gate at the top of them. Since the floor above her detached garage hadn't been finished when her barn was renovated to be her home with the girls, she'd decided to finish it into a small apartment for Vi and Foster. That had always been her plan so she'd have added income or for the purpose of one of her daughters living there if they decided to stay in Willow Creek. Especially since Sammy had been born right here in this apartment, the space already held memories. However, Vi and Foster were decidedly tight on space. The living room and kitchen were one room. Instead of leaving space for a nursery, they'd decided to make one big bedroom that had a connecting bath with a sink, commode, and walk-in shower. They put up a screen for privacy between the crib and the couple's bedroom space. They'd furnished it with mostly thrift store furnishings that Gavin had helped with. It was a cozy little place and it looked as if Vi had straightened it up before Piper had arrived. No toys were strewn about.

Piper was sitting on the small sofa next to Vi, watching her nurse the baby. She seemed taken with the union between mom and son and totally absorbed with it. Was she thinking about a time when she'd have her own baby at her breast?

Vi called to Daisy, "Hi, Mom. I'm hoping he takes a little nap after I feed him. He's been crawling around here like one of those sweeper robots all morning. I might have to get him knee pads at this rate."

Both Piper and Daisy laughed. Daisy commented, "That's what overalls are for."

She noticed that Sammy was wearing a jean set that Vi had bought at A Penny Saved, the clothing store that helped anyone on a budget. The little blue striped T-shirt he was wearing under the coveralls was one Daisy had bought for him. His feet were bare because he wouldn't keep on socks or shoes. As soon as Vi put them on, he grabbed them off. Yes, and into his mouth with them too.

"I've never seen anyone breastfeed before," Piper said, almost reverently.

Vi looked up at Daisy. "I asked if she wanted me to cover up but she said no."

"It's so natural," Piper said, her voice soft. "Vi told me she would never breastfeed without covering herself in public and I understand that. But I want to know about it because I want to do it someday." She stopped to give it thought. "If we adopt, I guess that won't be possible."

Daisy came to sit on a small chair that Jazzi and Vi had upholstered themselves. The small geometrical patterns on the material were in various shades of blue and violet with a taupe background.

Daisy sat with the chair facing toward the sofa and laid her purse on the coffee table. "I bottle fed Jazzi," she told Piper. "No, it's not the same experience but it's special too. Whenever I held her in my arms and fed her, we grew closer. I know my husband felt the same way." She remembered taking turns with Ryan when Jazzi was up in the middle of the night.

"I don't know how Emory will take to fathering," Piper admitted honestly.

Vi, who had told Piper all about her postpartum depression, elaborated, "I'm not sure anyone knows how they'll take to parenting until it actually happens. Suddenly you have a responsibility for a child twenty-four hours a day for the rest of your life. You think you know what that's going to feel like, but I don't think you do . . . not until you have that baby in your arms . . . not until you give birth and realize you're on your own with this child. I think that's one of the reasons I wanted to have my baby here at the apartment with a midwife. Still, look what happened. My body turned on me in a way, and I had to get it lined up with my thoughts. I needed help to do that. There *is* help with everything. That's why I still belong to my mommy group."

Daisy asked Piper, "Have you attended any groups for parents who want to adopt?"

"No, we haven't. But that's because we still haven't made a decision."

Sammy had stopped suckling and Vi's son was looking up at her. His eyes drifted shut. "Maybe if you joined one," Vi interjected, "that would help you and Emory make your decision."

Piper looked especially young today. She was wearing shorts, a pink tank, and she'd fashioned her hair on top of her head in a messy bun. Her freckles were evident and she looked like a young woman in her teens rather than in her twenties.

Vi rubbed her hand across Sammy's brow. "He's fallen asleep."

Daisy asked, "Can I tuck him in?"

Vi gave her a knowing smile. "Of course, you can. I'll set out lunch while you're doing that. I made chicken salad. We can have sandwiches or scoops of salad on lettuce. I went to the bakery this morning and brought home croissants."

"That sounds good," Piper said. "My stomach's been tied in knots ever since this whole thing happened with the clinic. I'm actually hungry today."

"Mom brought over blueberry coffee cake for dessert

last night, so we can have that too. I might even bring out carrot sticks to make the whole thing healthy. Sliced tomatoes too."

Daisy loved the time she spent with Sammy whether she was playing with him, rocking him, or tucking him in for a nap. There was a rocker near his crib and she sat in it and rocked him for a few minutes. She knew it would take at least that long for Vi and Piper to set up the table. His cute little round face reminded her of Vi when she was a baby. He hadn't had his first haircut yet, and his brown hair curled a bit over his ears and down his neck. He was so cute Daisy wanted to hug him all day long.

When Daisy finally did lay Sammy in his crib, she knew the baby monitor would be recording everything he did. Vi had a wireless monitor set up in the kitchen and it blinked whenever Sammy moved.

After Daisy kissed the little guy's cheek, she returned to the living room. The table Vi and Foster used in the kitchen was small. They used folding chairs around it to have more room to maneuver. Daisy noticed the glasses of iced tea were already poured and dishes, silverware, and napkins laid out. Vi had left the sliced tomatoes and carrots on the counter because there simply wasn't room on the table. She'd lined a basket with a napkin and the croissants rested in there. The chicken salad was mounded in another bowl. She'd also opened a bag of potato chips and poured those into a serving dish.

She asked Daisy, "Still asleep?"

"He must have tired himself out."

"He was going strong when I arrived," Piper said. "I didn't know babies could crawl that fast."

"I think he's almost as fast as Marjoram and Pepper

when they dart across the room. Just wait until he's walking," Daisy warned.

The conversation around the table was light as the women talked about their lives.

Vi was still complaining about the motor scooter that Foster had bought because one of their cars had broken down. "We're saving every penny we can," she said. "Soon we're going to have to start paying Mom rent."

"Vi, I don't want you to worry about that."

"We made a deal, Mom. You had this apartment finished for us. You said you'd give it to us rent-free for a year. A year will soon be up and we want to pay."

"We'll talk about it," Daisy said. "We can always use a sliding scale."

Vi rolled her eyes.

Piper tried to suppress a smile. "You sound just like my dad, Mrs. Swanson. All my life he's wanted to protect me. When I married Emory, I think Dad thought he could release that responsibility into Emory's hands. But I don't believe he's ever done that. He's as protective now as he was before, maybe in a different way."

"My dad's always been supportive and protective," Daisy admitted. "But when I moved away for all those years, he really had no choice but to back off. Since I returned to Willow Creek, he's protective but at a distance. I like that."

"Does he worry when you're involved in murder investigations?"

"I don't tell him every detail," Daisy confided. "If he does worry, he hides it as much as possible."

A shadow seemed to cross Piper's pretty face. "I don't

know if the police still suspect me and Emory, or if they've moved on. Everything you told me was helpful when they questioned me. I don't think I was as nervous as Emory because of talking with you."

"I'm glad I helped." Daisy took a bite of the croissant loaded with chicken salad. Some of the chicken salad fell onto her plate and she wiped her mouth with her napkin.

"I heard a rumor," Piper said, "and I wondered if it was true."

"What's the rumor?" Vi asked.

"I heard that Hiram Hershberger died of an overdose of insulin. Is that true?"

Should Daisy say anything or shouldn't she? The bigger question was why was Piper bringing it up? Daisy decided to circle around Piper's question. "I'm not sure the police have all the autopsy results in yet. Why do you ask?"

"If it was insulin, it seems there could be a lot of suspects."

Vi tag-teamed with Daisy. "Why do you say that?"

"Taking insulin for diabetes is more common than it used to be," Piper mused. "Isn't it?"

Daisy's background as a nutritionist kicked in. "I think many more people are diagnosed early with diabetes now so they can protect themselves for the future. Diet is a big part of that, and there are medications besides insulin that help. I've never seen the statistics on the breakdown for the patients who use insulin."

"I think everybody knows someone who does," Piper said.

Daisy and Vi exchanged a look.

Vi inquired, "Do you know someone?"

"I do. Emory's mother is a diabetic who uses insulin."

Daisy felt as if a clue had dropped into her lap. She wondered if Zeke knew that. She also guessed that if Zeke did know that, Piper and Emory would even be more likely suspects.

Daisy was pinching herbs from the pots on the tea garden patio to use in her recipes when Foster came to talk to her Monday morning. She knew he wasn't serving out on the patio today so it was unusual to see him there. From his expression, she suspected he hadn't come out on the patio to refresh iced tea glasses.

"Is something wrong?" There could be a situation inside that she needed to take care of. But after all, Tessa was inside and so was Iris.

"There's someone here to see you—Miriam Yoder. She told me she didn't want to attract any attention but she wondered if she could talk with you."

"I suppose that means she doesn't want to sit at a table inside?" Daisy asked. Miriam was conscious of appearances. Apparently she didn't want many people knowing she was at the tea garden.

"Does she want me to come inside?" Daisy asked. "We could go to my office."

"I suggested that," Foster said. "But she asked if she could come out here."

Customers were enjoying tea and baked goods at a few of the outside tables. But she and Miriam could take a walk down by the creek. "Tell her to come on out." Daisy laid the herbs that she had gathered on the rim of one of the pots.

Foster stayed where he was and motioned to the person inside.

Miriam came out and crossed to Daisy. "I hope you don't mind," she said shyly.

Foster made his exit.

"I don't mind. Come on. Walk with me through the yard down to the creek. We can talk there."

Miriam seemed grateful for the idea as she said, *"Danke"* and they crossed the parking lot to take the walkway through the flower beds.

Daisy glanced at Miriam, a beautiful young woman probably in her late teens. Her light-brown hair was pulled back into the requisite bun. Her heart-shaped *kapp* was set high on her head. Today she'd worn a pale blue dress under her apron.

Daisy led Miriam down the stepping-stones until they were far away from the outside customers. Miriam walked gracefully beside Daisy.

"I guess you wonder why I'm here," Miriam murmured.

"Yes, I do. But take your time." Daisy knew for Miriam to come talk to her, her concerns had to be about something important.

"Me and Eli, well, we're in *lieb*."

"Love is a very wonderful thing, isn't it?" Daisy asked.

Miriam's eyes shone when she turned toward Daisy. "It is. But my *familye* doesn't know. They would think I'm *ab im kopp*."

Daisy knew that meant something in Pennsylvania Dutch like *crazy*. "They think you're crazy because Eli left the faith?"

"Ya. But Eli is going to fix that. I came to you because I don't know who else to talk to. Rachel told me I could trust you."

"Trust me with your secret?"

"Ya. But also—the police called Eli to their building. I'm afraid if they do it again, they're not going to let him go. I'm afraid he'll be charged with Hiram's murder."

"Are you sure he didn't do it?" Daisy thought broadsiding Miriam might bring out the truth.

Miriam swung around to Daisy, totally outraged. "Of course, he didn't do it! He has decided to confess his sins, return to his faith, and live in the Amish life. He can't do that with this hanging over his head. What should he do?"

Daisy wasn't sure why Rachel had sent Miriam to her. Maybe simply for common sense advice. "I'm not a lawyer so the advice I'm going to give you has nothing to do with the law or what the police might do. But I think Eli should tell the truth."

"He has," Miriam insisted.

"Has he?" Daisy asked pointedly. "Do you know *everything* about his life?"

Miriam looked totally perplexed.

"At the furniture sale, I saw Eli taking money in an envelope from another protestor. Do you know what that's about? Has he been honest about whatever *that* is?"

"He tells me much. He's been taking as many jobs as he can to open a business and give us a future," Miriam said with certainty.

"Do you believe it's honest work?"

"I do. Especially now. Yes, he deals with *Englischers,* but they're not bad, ain't so?"

"That depends. I know Amish women often take a back seat to the man they love. If you want to spend your life with him, maybe you should ask him tough questions."

"I can't believe he'd lie to me."

"There are lies by omission. When I asked Eli why money was exchanged, he wouldn't tell me. To me that meant he was hiding something. Do you think he'll hide it from you too?"

Miriam stared out over the creek. They could hear the burbling of it as it wandered over stones near the shore and flowed silently through the center . . . the deep part of the creek. Daisy knew its depth there was about ten feet. She could also hear a mockingbird in a tall silver maple tree as well as the chatter of squirrels.

When Miriam reverted to Pennsylvania Dutch again, Daisy knew she was upset. Miriam said, "*Wu schmoke is, is aa feier.*"

Daisy knew that saying well. *Where there is smoke, there is fire.*

Miriam's pale cheeks reddened and her chin lifted. "I'll find out what he's keeping from me, I promise you that."

"The two of you together should decide what you should tell the police if Eli needs to tell them anything more. Remember that hiding it could push him into even more trouble."

"Thank you for talking to me, Mrs. Swanson. You have really helped. *Gott segen eich.*"

Miriam had just said, *God bless you*. Daisy hoped they would all be blessed with the truth . . . and soon.

CHAPTER FOURTEEN

That evening Daisy was tilling the soil around the rosemary, marjoram, and lemon balm, along with the tomato plants in her garden, when she heard laughter along the side of the house. In the early evening, she expected Vi but she didn't expect to see Ramona. She had a little boy with her who was about three, and Vi carried Sammy in her arms.

Daisy waved to the two young women and motioned for them to come into the yard. "Just in time for me to take a break. Hi, Ramona. How are you? And who is this?"

"This is Petey." Ramona tousled her little boy's blond hair.

Sammy reached out to Daisy, both arms extended, his fingers wiggling.

"We're having a play date," Vi said. "We just decided to go for a walk and we ended up here."

"I have cookies and iced tea in the refrigerator. Are you interested?" she asked them both as she snuggled Sammy.

Petey looked up at Daisy with a grin. "Cook-ee."

Daisy motioned them to the glider and chairs. "Go ahead and sit on the patio. I'll go inside and get the tea and cookies."

Today Ramona was wearing a white tank top and navy-blue shorts. She swooped up her little boy whose hand she'd been holding. "Jim and I try to keep him on a healthy diet," she admitted. "But you know how that is."

"I certainly do. Is chocolate chip okay? They don't have nuts."

"That sounds good," Ramona agreed.

"I bet Petey might like the glider," Daisy suggested. "Sammy does." She handed Sammy back to Vi. His face scrunched up in a frown and he looked as if he was going to cry.

Daisy ran her hand lovingly over his cheek. "I'll be right back." She pointed to the glider. "Swing, back and forth." She motioned with her hand and a smile appeared on his face again.

She'd found her grandson was fairly easy to distract. Generally, he was a happy boy and didn't often have sad times. But she imagined he could be getting tired at this time of day.

"We had supper at my place," Vi said. "I made macaroni and cheese and they seemed to like that."

"Always." Daisy remembered her girls' tastes. "You and Jazzi wanted mac and cheese every time you could have it."

Swiftly Vi took Sammy over to the glider and sat with him on her lap. Since Ramona was thin, it was easy for Petey to slip in between her and Vi.

Ramona lifted her hand and brushed her long bangs across her forehead. "It's nice to get out. Jim really helps me with Petey, but he has things he likes to do too when he gets home from work."

"Speaking of male counterparts," Vi said. "Where's Jonas? I thought he might be here with you. Where's Jazzi?"

"Jazzi's babysitting tonight. I have to pick her up around nine."

"She couldn't convince you to let her have your car?" Vi asked.

"Not tonight. I had a couple of errands to run after work, so I dropped her off and I'll pick her up."

Ten minutes later, Daisy came outside with the tray and set it on the table. Vi, Ramona, and the children moved over there. Sammy sat on Vi's lap happily munching on bits of cookie that she fed him. Petey sat at the table with a small glass of milk that Daisy had provided and his cookie, taking small bites as he nibbled at it. He smiled at her with crumbs all around his mouth.

"What was Jonas doing tonight?" Vi asked. "You never answered me."

"He was delivering furniture from the sale."

"I heard about that sale," Ramona said. "I bet they did well."

"Only a few pieces didn't sell," Daisy said. "I think everyone was pleased. They're planning to do it again next spring or summer."

"Jim stopped in at the barn for a bit. He liked a tea cart and a set of TV tables, but we're watching every penny now. If the clinic doesn't settle with us soon, I don't know what we're going to do."

"Your funds were tied up for *in vitro*?" Daisy asked.

"Not just our savings, but we took out a loan too. And the bank isn't putting a hold on paying it back. I thought they might, given the situation. Hiram Hershberger defending a class action suit rather than settling certainly didn't help because we knew that would take months if not years. The bank knew all about it when we discussed it with them. Daniel Copeland told us another lawyer was going to pick up the defense."

"I did hear they were trying to find someone," Daisy acknowledged.

"There are plenty of lawyer sharks who would probably be willing to go at it. Even if they do, Mr. Copeland told us the clients in a class action suit usually don't make out real well. It's the lawyers who do."

Daisy heard the disdain for lawyers in Ramona's voice, and, in this case, she didn't blame her.

"Maybe Troy Richter will decide to settle," Daisy offered. "The expense of going to court for a long time can't be good for him either."

"I heard the rumor that he's out of the country," Ramona said. "Sure, he can just go flying off to an island somewhere, lie on a beach, and drink a piña colada while we're back here wondering how we're going to pay our bills."

As Ramona's voice had gone up, Petey looked up at his mom as if he were worried about her. She saw the look on his face and she brushed a few crumbs from his chin. She admitted, "I keep everything bottled up most of the time. The nice thing about girl talk is that I don't have to then."

"I know what you mean," Vi said. "I can talk to Mom and she mostly understands." Vi looked at her mother and winked. "But sometimes I think it's hard for her to remember what it was like when she was first married."

Daisy balled up a paper napkin and tossed it at Vi. "I can remember very well. I remember how much fun it was going home to my new husband at night . . . how we couldn't wait to see each other. Your dad wasn't a romantic, but he'd make a meal for me when I was tired, or he'd watch a rom-com with me when I knew he'd rather be watching a thriller. I specifically remember how ecstatic we were when *you* were born." She looked down at Petey and then at Sammy. "I have a baby book where I recorded every stage of your development as well as Jazzi's. I kept locks of hair, first teeth . . ." She trailed off.

Vi laughed. "All right. I get the idea. You remember. But you and Aunt Iris and Gram are a lot older than I am, even if you do remember. Things are different now."

"They are," Daisy agreed. "But you can talk to Jazzi too."

"I can," Vi admitted. "But she has a teen's concerns. She has butterflies over a boy looking at her, or . . . taking her to a carnival."

"Don't remind me," Daisy mumbled.

Vi glanced at Ramona. "Mom has trouble admitting that Jazzi is growing up. That *is* the point. She's still growing up. Ramona understands how I feel at my age and in my marriage. In fact, a lot of women in the mommy group do. That's why we enjoy it so much. I just wish—"

"Wish what?" Daisy asked.

"I wish so many women hadn't been affected by what happened at the clinic. It caused a lot of heartache, Mom."

Daisy studied both young women who were sharing

their hearts and their lives. "I know. Maybe once this murder is solved, it will help everyone move on. Maybe the clinic will try to do what's best for everyone."

However, Daisy saw Ramona and Vi exchange a look, and it wasn't an optimistic one.

The next morning Daisy sat in her tea garden office, catching up on bookwork, when her cell phone played its tuba sound. She took it from her pocket and checked the screen. Jazzi was working today so she knew it wasn't her. It could be Jonas, Vi, or Foster she supposed. She was surprised, though, when she saw Glorie Beck's name. Glorie didn't use her cell phone often. She usually only used it for emergencies.

Daisy hoped it wasn't an emergency this time. She kept her voice cheerful, not letting worry creep into it. "Hi, Glorie."

"Daisy, I need your help."

With that opening, Daisy *was* worried. "Did you fall again?" That had happened a few months ago and she suspected that it could happen again. It was one of the reasons Brielle was staying with her.

"No," Glorie said, almost whispering. That should have alerted Daisy as to what this call was about. She listened.

"Brielle isn't eating. She's upset about her parents."

"How can I help?" Daisy asked without hesitating.

"I want you to come out here. We can have tea together and talk about this. Don't you think that's the best thing to do?"

"I suppose it could be. When do you want me to come out?"

"I don't want to take you from your work."

"Brielle is important to me too," Daisy said. "I have to be at A Penny Saved for a volunteer shift around six. Why don't I come out to your place, maybe four-thirty?"

"That sounds fine."

"I'll see you at four-thirty."

At exactly four-thirty, Daisy drove down the gravel lane to the small farm. Glorie must have heard her because she came out to the small front porch and waited.

The white clapboard house looked as if it had just been painted. The porch with its little roof had gray floorboards and window trim with the same gray. Glorie had lived here for seventy years and Daisy knew she didn't want to move. This had been her home when she'd been a little girl. When she got married, she and her husband had lived here. The house had heat, electricity, and running water. Now it probably had a window air conditioner in Glorie's bedroom.

As Glorie stood on the porch, the sun hit the gray in her brown hair, which was curly with the summer humidity. She was wearing her usual uniform—jeans and an oversized pink T-shirt that made her look smaller than she actually was. Although her face was always lined, today those creases looked even deeper in the tan that might fade if Glorie stayed indoors more. Daisy knew Glorie's arthritis was getting worse. She was using a pink flowered cane today and Daisy suspected it was one Brielle had bought for her.

"I hope you like iced tea, Daisy. It's just too warm for hot tea, unless you have the air conditioning Nola wants me to put in."

"Iced tea will be fine." Daisy lowered her voice. "What did you tell Brielle?"

"I just told her you were coming for a visit. Really, that's what it's going to be, right? A visit with talking . . . lots of talking."

They'd be talking only if Brielle and Glorie could open up about what they wanted for the future.

Daisy followed Glorie inside and onto the beautiful varied-color rag rug on the floor . . . an eight-by-ten oval. It softened footsteps around the sofa, armchair, wood rocker, and coffee table. A breeze blew in the window, ruffling the curtains, but it was still hot inside.

"You like that rug, don't you?" Glorie asked as she spotted Daisy gazing at it.

"Every time I visit, I admire it. I know you made it before Brielle's mom went to college and your husband wanted you to put all kinds of colors in it. I love that you included old dresses that belonged to Brielle's mom, a couple of your husband's threadbare shirts, and an apron or two of your own. It's a wonderful memory rug, right?"

"It is," Glorie agreed with a nod.

On her first visit here, Glorie had told Daisy that she'd made the slipcovers that were green plaid along with the curtains hanging around the window in the same fabric.

Brielle was seated in the worn, burgundy armchair that Daisy had assessed as a Chippendale.

After studying her phone, Brielle finally looked up. "Hi, Daisy. Grammy told me you were coming. I made the peanut butter blondies you liked. Do you want to sit in the kitchen?"

The white metal cabinets in the kitchen had been popular in years gone by though they were pristine without any chips. The counter was gray-speckled Formica and that did have a few chips and stains. The refrigerator with its rounded top and the white gas stove could be vintage. Many times, Daisy had sat in one of the oak chairs at the square pedestal table with Glorie and talked about whatever came into their heads.

A flight of stairs led up to a loft, and that's where Brielle had been sleeping. Daisy could hear a fan going up there.

When Brielle noticed the focus of Daisy's gaze, she explained, "I've been sleeping on the floor in Grammy's room where the air conditioner is." She emphasized the last three words. "It's so much more comfortable than the heat, right Grammy?"

Glorie murmured, "If you say so. Why don't we sit in here and be comfortable. It's cooler than the kitchen. Daisy, you can put the glasses and the iced tea on the tray on the counter to bring in, and then Brielle can fetch the cookies."

"Will do," Brielle said, and Daisy seconded the motion.

Brielle carried the cookies in. She had placed them on a brown-and-off-white Pfaltzgraff pottery dish. They sat in a semicircle of sorts discussing their day and the weather and Vi and Sammy.

Brielle had hardly nibbled at a cookie and Glorie was watching her with worry in her eyes. Finally Glorie said, "Brielle, honey, I asked Daisy here so we could talk."

"Talk about what?" Brielle asked with wariness in her tone.

"I think your grandmother wants us to talk about you and her for starters," Daisy offered.

At first Brielle's face was closed. It was so impassive that Daisy thought it might crack if somebody touched it.

Then Brielle's eyes misted over. "I can't talk about it. Somebody will get upset."

"Getting upset isn't the end of the world, honey," Daisy said. "Maybe getting upset will help you tell us what you're feeling. If you do that, your grandmother can tell you what *she's* feeling. I have to say, your mom already told me what *she's* thinking."

At that Brielle frowned. "Why didn't she tell *me*?"

"I think she's afraid you won't listen to her, or that you'll be closed minded if you do."

Already Brielle was crossing her arms over her chest. That was a defense move if Daisy ever saw one.

"I don't know what to do," Brielle admitted.

"I want you to talk to me, honey," her grandmother told her. "I won't get upset. I'll think about what you have to say."

Brielle studied her grandmother and then her eyes turned to Daisy. Daisy nodded.

Brielle began with an uncharacteristic stammer. "I know . . . I know you want to stay here, Grammy. But I know what my mother wants too. She wants me to come to stay with her and you too. I don't know *what's* right."

Glorie looked crestfallen as if the reality of this situation was actually sinking in this time.

Sitting next to Glorie on the sofa, Daisy turned to her. "Tell me something," she suggested gently. "Do you really feel you can stay in your house much longer?"

Brielle was the one who answered. "Grammy can stay here if I stay with her." Her voice had gone higher, and Daisy knew that was a sign of distress.

Glorie must have heard it too. She reached over to the

armchair and took Brielle's hand. "If I'm taken care of . . . if I would go live with your mother, you would go to college, wouldn't you?"

"I might," Brielle answered hesitantly. "But I know you don't want to move into the big house with my mother."

"What if there's another option?" Daisy asked.

"How can there be another option?" Glorie wanted to know.

"Have you thought about the fact that Nola might not want to stay in that house since her divorce?"

After a few moments of thought-filled silence, Glorie said, "That would open up several possibilities."

"What kind of possibilities?" Brielle asked.

"Well, let's think about this. What if your mother sells her house?"

"She can't move in here," Brielle protested. "It's too small."

"It is that," Glorie agreed. "But what if I sold my property too, or maybe kept it and rented it?"

Brielle was getting the gist of this idea. "Then maybe we could find a house to suit all three of us," Brielle said. "It wouldn't be so big and you'd be living with Mom. The thing is, Grammy, can you live with Mom?"

Glorie gave a little smile. "I imagine that could be a challenge for both of us." She looked at Daisy. "Would you live with *your* mother?"

As Daisy thought about it, she answered truthfully. "If you had asked me that a year ago, I'd probably tell you I couldn't. But now things are different. Mom told me about situations in her past, and I understand her so much better now. I know if my parents needed help, I *could* live with them. If relationships don't grow, they just shrivel up. I don't think any of us want that to happen as we get older."

"I believe you're right," Glorie said. "I think Brielle and I will have to have a talk with Nola."

After her visit with Glorie and Brielle, Daisy put in her volunteer shift at A Penny Saved. Patrons had left and it was time for her to close up. She scanned the inside sales room of Willow Creek's thrift store. The shop always seemed filled to capacity with racks of skirts, blouses, dresses, and slacks. Shoes were lined up against the wall according to sizes—men's, women's, and children's.

Daisy took one last look around the sales floor after she closed down the computer. She was the one locking up tonight. She'd done it before.

She was turning her key in the lock, facing the door, when she suddenly felt fire flashing throughout her whole body. Her ears buzzed . . . her skin tingled . . . she felt as if she couldn't think through a gray cloud that pressed in on her. She couldn't even lift her hands to break her fall as she dropped to the ground like a heavy sack of flour. Through the pain in her body and the fog in her mind, someone hoarsely whispered in her ear, "Stop asking questions or the same thing that happened to Hiram will happen to you."

Gasping, Daisy fought to catch her breath. There was no air in her lungs. She saw spots in front of her eyes. Her limbs were frozen.

Even Daisy's stomach felt as if it had collapsed upon itself. Yet there was pain too—a burning pain in her legs and in her arms. She couldn't move them.

Time meant little as Daisy fought to catch her breath.

Finally she sucked in air and mostly felt relief. Her muscles began to respond when she attempted to move them. Fumbling in her pocket, she gripped her phone. After she tapped her Favorites icon, she tapped Jonas's name.

He answered.

She found her voice was crackly as without an intro she managed, "I think someone just used a stun gun on me."

"Where are you?" he asked tersely.

She told him.

"Stay put. I'm calling the police and an ambulance."

Feeling stronger, she offered, "Jonas, I can probably stand up . . ."

"Don't," he chided. "Stay put. Promise me, Daisy."

Her voice stronger now, her mind clearer, she answered, "I will."

It seemed as if Daisy closed her eyes and Jonas was there. His arm around her, she laid her head on his shoulder as he squeezed her tighter.

"How do you feel?" he asked.

"Safe with you."

"That's good. But I mean how do you feel physically?"

"Just very tired."

Jonas had rested his chin on the top of her head, and she could feel his jaw tense along with his arm as he held her.

It wasn't long before Detective Rappaport showed up along with the ambulance. Daisy didn't believe she needed an ambulance . . . that she could stand on her own two feet and walk where she needed to go. However, Jonas and the paramedics wouldn't let her.

Jonas climbed into the ambulance with her and held

her hand the whole way to the hospital in Lancaster, even as the paramedics put an oximeter on her finger, took her vitals every five minutes and added an oxygen cannula to her nose. She hated all this fuss, but she was also feeling weak and didn't have enough energy to protest too much. At least she didn't until they arrived at the hospital and she was feeling stronger.

She didn't let go of Jonas's hand very often. She wanted him to stay in the room even when the internist, a doctor in his mid-forties, with a name tag on his jacket that read DR. STILLWATER, spoke to her about HIPAA laws.

Feeling her ire rise, she said to him with more vigor than she'd felt since this happened, "I want Jonas here. You have my permission to tell him anything either of us need to know."

The doctor glanced outside the cubicle. "There's a detective out there who wants information too."

"Then he might as well come in," Daisy said. "Detective Rappaport?" she called.

Morris Rappaport looked a bit sheepish when he stepped inside. "I can wait," he said.

"Then we'll just have to go through this all over again," she decided. "Let's do this."

The detective looked at Jonas. "I think she's feeling better."

With a sigh the doctor said, "I believe you'll be fine, but we want to keep you here for a few hours just to make sure your electrical circuits weren't completely scrambled. We'll do another EKG in a little while. There are two burn marks on your neck. I've seen those before. You were attacked with a stun gun."

Daisy's mind raced and she murmured, "The same stun gun that was used on Hiram."

The detective said, "We don't know that, Daisy. You've riled up *someone,* just like you always do."

"I haven't done anything but listen," she insisted.

The doctor said brusquely, "I have other patients to see. I'll be back in an hour or so. Rest," he ordered Daisy and shot a warning look at Detective Rappaport and Jonas.

Detective Rappaport asked, "What did you do that you shouldn't have done? Who did you talk to that you shouldn't have?"

She supposed the best thing to do was to come clean. She had told Jonas she'd visited the clinic but not exactly how she'd done it.

Now she explained to them both, "I went undercover at the Hope Clinic. I pretended I was a woman who was looking to freeze my eggs. The director showed me around. I talked to one of the techs and the janitor. And then I didn't make a follow-up appointment."

Rappaport rolled his eyes as he often did with her. "Daisy—" he began.

She held up her hand and he stopped. She knew what he was going to say, and he knew she knew what he was going to say.

Jonas's mouth tightened into a grim line.

After Detective Rappaport left, Jonas sat by her bed and took her hand. "Do you trust me?"

There was no hesitation when she answered, "Yes, I trust you."

"Then the next time tell me *everything*."

She'd been alone for years now and taking care of her

daughters on her own. She'd handled the renovation of the barn into a house on her own. She'd bought the Victorian with her aunt but basically she'd made the decisions on her own. She was used to running a business and caring for her family, making financial decisions as well as personal ones all on her own. Now, however, as she gazed into Jonas's eyes, she knew she wasn't on her own.

She said simply, "I promise. From now on, I will tell you *everything*."

Three hours later, Daisy had become impatient. She'd sent Jonas to get himself a sandwich while she mulled over everything that had happened . . . everything since Hiram's murder.

When Dr. Stillwater returned for one final check, she said, "I have a question for you."

"About how you're feeling?" His dark brown almost black eyes told her he was in a hurry, but he would answer any questions she posed.

"Does someone have to know what they're doing to inject insulin?"

His face changed and he looked shocked by her question. "What does that have to do with *you*? Your records didn't show you as even a prediabetic."

"That's not why I'm asking. I was hit with a stun gun, doctor. I'm semi-involved in the investigation into Hiram Hershberger's murder."

The doctor's face paled, and he looked even more disconcerted. He hooked his shoe into the bottom of a rolling stool and brought it over beside the bed. He sank down on it. "Why would you be involved?"

"It's a long story, but asking questions is what put me in here today. So can you answer *my* question?"

After he thought about it for a moment and gave her another look that held disapproval, he responded, "Anyone who's been instructed by a doctor to give shots would know how to inject into fatty tissue."

"Fatty tissue like a stomach or thigh?"

"That's usually where patients inject their insulin, but . . ."

"But?" she prompted.

"Unfortunately anyone who researched insulin on the Internet could easily find out how to inject it, and not only inject it. They could probably learn that if they inject it into a muscle, the insulin would work faster."

Listening to the doctor and absorbing that information, Daisy realized Hiram Hershberger's murderer did not have to be a medical professional. The killer could be *anyone*.

CHAPTER FIFTEEN

Jonas kept looking over at Daisy as he drove her home after she was discharged. Daisy had stayed in the car while he'd stopped at Woods to pick up Felix. It had seemed safer to leave him there with Elijah than to bring him along when he'd rushed to Daisy at A Penny Saved.

Felix had climbed into the car all excited to see Jonas and Daisy. But when Jonas commanded, "Quiet, boy," the dog looked at Daisy and seemed to decide on his own that he *would* be quiet. Quiet, maybe, but still compassionate.

Leaning up between the seats he'd laid his head on Daisy's arm.

With another glance at Daisy, Jonas asked, "Can you tell me how you're feeling?"

She took a moment to think about it. "I still feel a little

odd . . . like my thoughts aren't in the order they're supposed to be in."

"That's to be expected," Jonas said. "Your whole body got an electric shock, including your brain. You're going to have to give it time to recover."

"How much time?"

"The doctor wasn't specific about that because everyone's different and stun guns have different voltages. It depends on the circumstances. I'm more worried about your emotional health than your physical health."

Daisy shifted in her seat toward him. "I don't know what you mean."

"Do you feel safe? Like you can walk anywhere . . . be anywhere . . . do anything and not look over your shoulder?"

"That's not a fair question," she murmured.

"It's fair enough," he gently insisted. "You were attacked. Is your mind saying that will never happen again? Or is it saying it might happen again and you'd better be careful?"

"I'd better be careful," Daisy whispered.

They were both quiet for the rest of the drive. When they drove up to the garage, Daisy sighed. "That's Mom and Dad's car."

"You can tell them you're still feeling shaky and go to your room," Jonas suggested.

When she shook her head, a headache pounded in her temples. "That doesn't work with them. They'd be in my room . . . sitting on my bed . . . holding my hand."

"You're going to have a lot of people around and I don't want to add to the noise."

Panicking a bit, she reached out and gripped his arm. "I *like* you being there."

Obviously reading her expression and her dismay, he smiled. "I'll go in with you and help you get settled. Your parents haven't met Felix yet so that should take some of the attention off of you. I'd like to leave him with you overnight. He's a good protector. Jazzi can let him go out into your yard or take him for a walk while you rest."

She would definitely like to ask Jonas to stay, but she didn't want him to get the wrong message . . . that she couldn't handle what had happened to her. And she didn't want him to feel as if she were using him as a bodyguard. Still, she'd accept his offer of letting Felix stay. She would feel protected when he was around, and Jazzi would be with her too. She had a security system. She wasn't going to be weak about this whole situation.

"I'd love to have Felix stay with me. I'll even let him share my bed. That way he doesn't need one of his own."

Jonas had stopped the SUV now and he turned to look at her. She wondered what he was thinking. His green eyes were bright and dark with many emotions sliding under the surface.

"I think that's a good idea unless Marjoram and Pepper decide to join you on the bed too. *You* might have to sleep on the floor."

He was trying to make her laugh, and she did manage a small smile.

As soon as Daisy walked into the house, she realized her parents had brought along her Aunt Iris. She could see they were all terribly concerned.

Her mother and her aunt rushed to her first. They studied her for a long minute as if they were afraid to touch her.

"I won't shock you back," she told them. "I'm going to be fine."

Her dad came to her and put his arms around her, giving her a big hug. "We're not going to stay. Your mom and Iris brought food. We just want to make sure you have everything you need."

Jonas and Felix walked in behind her. Felix came to her side and put his nose into her palm.

"Who's this?" her dad asked.

"This is Felix. Jonas adopted him. Jonas is going to leave him with me tonight to help me feel more secure."

"Are you afraid someone will break in?" Rose asked, often saying her thoughts before she filtered them.

"Rose, don't even suggest such a thing," Iris scolded. "No one can break in here. The security system is tied into the police department. And Daisy won't open the door until she sees who is outside either on her phone monitor or through the peephole. Right, Daisy?"

Daisy was still feeling a little shaky. As if Jonas could see that, he wrapped his arm around her waist and guided her over to the sofa. "Why don't you get comfy there?"

"I'll bring you iced tea, Mom," Jazzi offered. "Vi's going to come over in a little bit." She shifted her attention to Jonas. "Do you think that's okay? She'll leave Sammy with Foster."

Daisy raised her hand. "Of course, Vi can come. I just need to catch my breath and let everything go back to normal."

"We're going to go," her father said.

"But, Sean . . ." Rose protested.

"I think it's best for Daisy if fewer people are here."

Felix was at the arm of the sofa by Daisy's head. He

looked as if he'd stationed himself there and he wasn't budging.

Rose sat on the edge of the sofa. "I brought left over roast beef that you can use for sandwiches or a main course and mashed potatoes. There's fruit salad, too. Your aunt made some of that tapioca pudding you like so much."

"What did you two do, start cooking as soon as you got the call about me?" Daisy asked with a bit of amusement.

Her aunt and her mother exchanged glances.

"You did." Daisy actually laughed. "I promise I'll use the food and I won't starve."

"I can cook too," Jazzi said, bringing Daisy a glass of iced tea. "I put a little sugar in it," she said. "I thought that might help."

Daisy smiled again. They were all going to take care of her in their own ways.

Her mother moved her attention from Daisy to Felix. She reached out her hand to him and he sniffed it. After another sniff of her fingers and her wrist, he took a step away from Daisy toward Rose and lowered his head.

"Does that mean he wants me to pet him?" Rose asked, looking up at Jonas.

"You read him right," Jonas said. "It does. I hadn't even brought him home yet when I got a call from his previous owner. She had to go into assisted living and it was obvious she loved Felix a great deal. So had her husband. Her son trained him. I'm just learning what commands he knows. The best part is he's very intuitive and understands my tone of voice and gestures."

By now Rose was scratching behind the dog's ears and down his flank. "He really is beautiful. Such gold and cream fur." She looked up at Jonas. "I think the two of you are going to fit together well."

"But what about the cats when he's here?" Daisy's dad asked.

Jazzi answered, "They're going to get along. After everybody leaves, I'm sure Marjoram and Pepper will come down and sit on the back of the sofa with Mom. They met Felix the other night and after the initial she-nanigans were over, they got along. It must be the good vibes in this house," she joked.

"I think that's very true," Daisy said. "There are good vibes in this house. It's filled with care and love, and we all keep it that way."

Sean took Rose's elbow and helped her up. "Come on. Let's leave Daisy in peace so she can get some rest."

Aunt Iris came over to her, bent down and kissed her cheek. "You stay safe. Keep a low profile. Just bake and serve tea and spend time with Jonas, the girls, and Felix. The police will take care of this murder."

Daisy hoped that was so, but she wasn't sure about it. When Detective Rappaport had taken her statement at the hospital, she couldn't tell him much at all. Her back had been to her assailant. The assailant's voice had been grav-elly and low. It could have been a man whispering. It could have been a woman lowering her voice. There was no way to know. The thrift shop didn't have security cam-eras. The detective would be checking with the other businesses to see if they had cameras that could have caught something. But Daisy had a feeling that this per-son had been very careful.

Once everyone but Jonas, Jazzi, and Felix had left, Daisy propped pillows on the arm of the sofa and slid down, resting her head against them. Felix sat on the floor right beside her and she could put her hand down into his soft buff fur and feel his comfort. Jazzi bustled about making sure Daisy had iced tea, water, a cookie, and anything else she might want. The truth was, Daisy's stomach was queasy and she didn't want to think about eating.

She said to Jazzi, "Can you turn the air conditioning down. I think it's cold in here."

"You're having a reaction to the adrenaline crash after the event." Jonas stood, took the afghan from the back of the sofa, and spread it out over Daisy. As he folded it down under her neck, he said, "You just have to relax. Think of Jazzi and the college she wants to go to . . . think about Felix and playing ball with him out in the backyard. Remember how much fun it is to play with Sammy. Good thoughts, Daisy. Your body just needs time to recover from the shock. The best way for it to do that is for you to relax."

Sitting on the edge of the sofa, he took her hand. He stroked her palm and then the top of her hand.

"That feels good," she said, letting her eyes drift closed.

He continued to stroke her wrist and palm. "It would be better if you don't go into work tomorrow."

Her eyes opened and she almost sat up. But he pushed on her shoulders so she tilted back again.

"I'm not going to let whoever did this win," she protested. "I'll be fine in the morning and—"

Jonas cut her off. "Maybe you will be. Maybe you won't be."

"Jonas, I'm not someone who curls up into a ball after a scare."

"I know that better than anyone," he assured her.

Her eyes grew moist with determination. Then she let out a sigh. "I can take the day off tomorrow. But I'm not going to just sit around."

"Of course, you're not. But I'm going to check in often."

"You're a good man." All of the feelings she had for Jonas made her voice wobbly.

Jazzi had been making another pitcher of iced tea in the kitchen but now she came into the living room area and eyed the three of them. "I just got a text from Vi. She's on her way."

"That's fine," Daisy assured her.

Jazzi returned to the kitchen and in the few minutes it took until Vi arrived, Jonas leaned down and kissed Daisy. She knew when he straightened and gazed at her, her cheeks definitely had more color.

The doorbell rang and Jazzi went to open the door.

The next day Daisy rested as the doctor and Jonas suggested. However, late morning she called Vi and asked her to come over for lunch. Sammy would have a chance to play with Felix and they could get to know each other.

Vi arrived around noon.

After a kiss and a hug from Daisy, Sammy wanted to be put down. "How do you think we should do this?" Daisy asked Vi.

"Let's let Felix smell him first. That might get them used to each other."

"You sound like you know how to coax a dog and a kid into a friendly situation," Daisy said.

"I've heard talk about it in the mommy group. And the truth is, I looked it up on the Internet too. I read what vets suggested. Someday Foster and I might want to adopt a dog for Sammy. This will be good practice."

"Felix is pretty mellow. That's good when you have kids. I did some reading too. English cream golden retrievers are supposed to have sweet dispositions. He certainly does."

Vi, who was holding Sammy, set him on the sofa. Daisy knew she had to watch him continuously to make sure he didn't get up on his knees and hands and fall off wherever she put him. Right now, however, he was staring at Felix who had been lying on the other side of the coffee table. Daisy and Vi both watched as Sammy squealed and giggled.

As if taking that as a signal, Felix got to his feet, rounded the coffee table and sat at the sofa, his nose at Sammy's feet.

Sammy immediately tried to reach for the dog. He couldn't.

"He's going to cry," Vi warned. "He gets frustrated when he can't get to where he wants to go."

Instead of crying though, Sammy used the back of the sofa to squiggle around and end up on his knees and hands. Vi was ready to swoop in if he moved toward the edge.

Felix put his nose toward Sammy and positioned his head in such a way as to prevent Sammy from falling off.

"Does Felix know what he's doing?" Vi asked with surprise. "He looks as if he's protecting him."

"That's possible."

Vi went over to the sofa, lifted Sammy and put him on the floor between her legs. Felix nudged the little boy's arm and Sammy giggled. Moving fast, Sammy curled around on Vi's foot. In a second, he was on his hands and knees again.

Felix hunkered down so he was face to face with Sammy.

After Vi swooped Sammy up again, she sat him on her lap. Felix was tall enough that he could put his head beside Vi's legs. Taking Sammy's hand, Vi helped him touch one of the dog's ears.

Felix stood absolutely still.

As Sammy laughed, a big smile crossed his face.

"I think they're making friends," Vi said.

Relaxing, Daisy sank down on the armchair. "Ready for lunch? I'm going to make grilled cheese."

"Sammy will like that."

Daisy knew that Vi tore the sandwich into little pieces for Sammy to tuck into his mouth.

"I have homemade applesauce too."

"That sounds good. This was a nice idea. It will break up my day. Foster won't be home for supper."

"Does he have a class?"

"No, he's taking Ben out for a burger. They haven't had much time at all together lately. A couple of times, Ben called Foster to get together and Foster was either working at the tea garden, doing website business, or attending a class. I like Ben to come over to our place too, but I know they need some guy time. The older Ben gets, the less he's going to want to hang out with me and Sammy."

"I don't know about that," Daisy protested. "Ben seems comfortable around you."

"I'm comfortable around him. I always wished I had a brother. Now Ben feels like my little brother too. It's a nice feeling."

"I'm sure it is," Daisy said. "I always wanted a brother too. The truth is, when I met Cade Bankert in high school, he seemed like that brother." Cade was a real estate agent now. He had sold Daisy the barn property and the Victorian.

"How is Cade?" Vi asked.

"He's still selling real estate. I've heard he's doing well. I haven't seen him lately."

"Not since you and Jonas got serious?"

"I guess you could say that." He had asked Daisy on a couple of dates, but then her relationship with Jonas had deepened. "I think Cade and I never took off romantically because we always did seem like brother and sister. Even though he asked me to prom in high school, I never thought about him the way I think about Jonas." Daisy felt her cheeks redden as she admitted it.

"You shouldn't lose touch with him," Vi said.

"He doesn't agree when I get curious about a murder investigation, though he did give me some information on the last one that helped."

"See? Like a big brother. Maybe he and Jonas can be friends."

"I'll have to ask Jonas how he feels about that."

"I haven't really stayed friends with anybody from high school. My life changed so much so fast. But you"—Vi gave her a wistful smile—"you and Tessa are still best friends. So you shouldn't lose Cade's friendship."

"I'll give it some thought," Daisy said, watching Sammy as he cuddled in Vi's arms with Felix's nose on his leg.

"You know, we do talk a lot about brothers and sisters in the mommy group."

"How important they are?"

"Yes. It's good to learn how other moms juggle more than one child. They admit some brothers and sisters get along, and some kids constantly squabble. I haven't said so there, but I think that depends a lot on the parents, don't you think?"

"A certain amount of squabbling is natural," Daisy said. "You and Jazzi sure got into it now and then. But I let you work it out unless the argument got too loud or went on too long. How do moms in your group handle the discussion of it?"

"No one wants to call anyone a bad parent," Vi explained. "We're careful as to how we communicate there. You know, we always try to stay positive, and then add advice if somebody wants it."

"I get that."

"Ramona has said on the side that she wants a brother or sister for Petey, so he has somebody to depend upon other than his parents. I think that's what I'd want for Sammy too."

"A brother or sister who's a friend."

"For sure," Vi said with a nod, bringing her head down to Sammy's and giving him a kiss on his forehead. "I think Ramona wants it so badly for Petey because she has a stepbrother and she doesn't get along with him at all. That's such a shame."

"Camellia and I didn't squabble that much as kids, but there was always a tension between us."

"Why do you think that was, Mom?"

"Maybe because I gravitated toward Dad and Camellia gravitated toward your grandmother. As we grew older, we didn't stay close. We have very different ideas of what we want our lives to be."

"I hope that never happens to me and Jazzi."

"If the two of you make a point of talking to each other and sharing, not judging, then you can probably stay close."

"That's a tall order." Vi had teasing in her voice. "Maybe Jazzi and I'll have a talk about it before she goes to college. I don't want her to forget about me."

"I don't think she will."

Daisy hoped her two daughters could depend on each other for the rest of their lives.

CHAPTER SIXTEEN

Canoeing on the creek should have been just what Daisy needed.

Jonas had suggested going canoeing on Willow Creek that evening and she'd thought the outing would be a good idea. But ever since she'd gotten into the canoe at a docking ramp outside of town, she'd felt anxious. She'd felt as if someone was spying on her. Although the sky was still cerulean blue and the puffy white clouds were floating, forming pictures like she and Rachel imagined when they were young girls lying on their backs in the grass, Daisy felt exposed. The willows lazily dipped along the creek as she and Jonas floated along.

Still, who was standing behind those beautiful fronds? Anyone?

Why was she even thinking that?

She and Jonas were facing in the same direction and

paddling lazily in the center of the creek. He tapped her arm with the tip of his oar. "What are you thinking about?"

What *was* she thinking? She couldn't even begin to tell him her list of fears because they weren't real. Irrationally, she felt as if someone was chasing her when she was sitting in a canoe, floating on this serene creek.

Swinging her legs around on the seat and rocking the canoe, she faced Jonas. Distracting herself, she studied him. He looked as if he belonged in the canoe. His jeans were worn and hugged his thighs. His green T-shirt looked as if it had seen many washings and fit him superbly. His feet were braced in the bottom of the canoe in his deck shoes. They seemed loose enough to fall off but he didn't seem concerned about that. After his hair blew in the breeze, it slipped down over his brow.

"Do you do this often?" She stalled from answering his question. "I just wondered. You look as if you could row the whole creek up and down twice and not be winded or tired."

He narrowed his eyes at her. "You're changing the subject." Nevertheless, he gave in to responding to her question and motioned to the shores. "Sometimes I think I belong in the middle of oaks and evergreens and willows." Pointing his oar over the water, he said, "Just look at those sparkles. They make me think that everything is crystal clear and clean. Isn't that why we came out here?"

She kept her eyes on the water, sparkling like white diamonds catching the rays of the sun. To the right of them near the shore she caught sight of a momma duck and four ducklings. They took turns dipping their heads into the water. When they raised their little heads again, they shook away excess droplets from their feathers.

She murmured, "I bet Felix wishes he was out here with us."

As if he was perplexed by the change in subject, Jonas cocked his head and studied her. "I imagine he's having plenty of fun with Jazzi. Hopefully she'll tire him out fetching a ball and, when we go home, he'll be ready to sleep. Sometimes he paces back and forth like a guard dog at my townhouse. I'm not sure what that's about. I'll have to ask Mrs. Gunnarsen when we visit her."

"Maybe he guarded her when she wasn't feeling well."

"That's possible."

"Did you get all the furniture delivered from the sale?"

He let her continue guiding their conversation. "Only a few pieces left. They go to people who wanted to make a place for them. That required cleaning and rearranging. All in all, we did well. I'm thinking we can do it again next year, maybe earlier in the spring."

Daisy glanced over her shoulder and checked both shorelines. "Do you think we've rowed far enough? Maybe we should turn around and head back."

His brows furrowed. "Are you in a hurry? The sunset will be beautiful out here."

"I guess it will be. I wasn't thinking about that."

He laid his oar inside the canoe. "I should have brought a rowboat so we could both sit on the same seat. Or maybe a drifter."

"A drifter?"

"They're called drift boats or drifters. It's a type of fishing boat."

"Is there a reason they're called that?"

"They're designed to catch fish with long drift nets. You can fish fresh water streams, rivers, and lakes with them as well as bays. One person can handle a small one.

They're not cheap. I saw a fourteen-foot one that I liked at a boat show. There are YouTube videos on how fishermen use drift boats."

"There are YouTube videos about anything," she said distractedly.

They floated for a while longer, watching the horizon change with the sun slipping lower. In the silent dusk, willow fronds floated in the creek and shadows steadily lengthened. Daisy's anxiety increased.

Suddenly, a shot rang out. At least that's what it sounded like to Daisy. Instinctively she folded her arms over her head, ducked down between her legs, and slid to the floor of the canoe.

"Daisy!" Jonas called. "Daisy! Are you hurt?"

The canoe rocked as he lowered himself to the bottom of the boat with her. As best he could, he folded her into his arms. "Daisy, what's wrong? I think that was fireworks going off. Somebody's practicing for the Fourth of July."

Trembling, she felt Jonas's arms around her and heard his voice. His words didn't sink in. Her heart was racing so fast she thought it would beat out of her chest. Her breaths came hard and heavy as tears filled her eyes.

Holding onto Jonas, trying to be rational, she responded breathily, "I didn't know what was happening."

"Easy," Jonas said again, putting his cheek next to hers. "Come on, sweetheart. I think you're fine. Did the noise scare you?"

Noise, she repeated to herself. *Not a gunshot.*

"Daisy, it was fireworks. I'm pretty sure of that."

Fireworks. She measured the word in her mind. *Fireworks.*

Slowly she lifted her head and gazed into Jonas's

green eyes. They were steady, calm and comforting. She sucked in a couple of deep breaths.

"Daisy, tell me what's happening. What are you feeling?"

She was the one who had taught him how to express *his* feelings, wasn't she?

She straightened and he helped her up onto the seat though he still stayed on the bottom of the canoe. Realizing tears were running down her cheeks, she swiped them away with her hand.

Since she wasn't communicating with him, he prompted her. "Did you think that was a gunshot?"

She nodded.

"I thought bringing you out here would help but it obviously hasn't."

She knew he'd tried hard to help her to relax, but she just couldn't.

"The other night scared you witless," he determined.

She nodded again. Her mouth was so dry and she licked dry lips. Finally she found her voice. "This should be a happy place . . . an easy place. The water, the sky, the trees, the ducks." Now that she was talking, she kept on going. "But it isn't. I feel like somebody's watching me."

"Did you see actual evidence of that?" he asked practically.

She shook her head. "No. It's just a feeling. I don't know. I felt anxious, almost panicked, ever since we came here into the open." They weren't really in the open now because trees rose on both sides of the creek.

"Did you feel safe at home?"

She thought about it. "Yes, I did. I had a good lunch with Vi and Sammy. When Jazzi came home, I made her beef barbecue so she'd have something when she got hungry. Having Felix there with us gave me a sense of security."

Jonas didn't speak for a few moments as if he were thinking something over. "I'm going to make a suggestion and I want you to feel free to say no."

She kept her eyes on his.

"I know your couch opens out. Why don't I sleep over at your place tonight? You'll have Felix *and* me guarding you."

She didn't want to seem weak. She didn't want to feel weak. But she also wasn't going to put her pride over her emotional health.

She said simply, "I'd like that very much."

The next morning, Daisy awoke to the smell of coffee brewing. Jonas.

Felix who had been sleeping beside her on the bed stood up, lifted his nose as if he smelled it too. "Let's go," she said. "I'm sure you want to go out."

After Felix jumped from the bed, she opened the bedroom door and he dashed out to the kitchen. She, on the other hand, went to her bathroom to freshen up. Afterward, she quickly dressed in yellow knit pants and a yellow T-shirt. She felt fine this morning but she'd agreed to stay home again today. Still, she didn't know if she was going to stay in the house *all* day.

When she went out to the kitchen, Jonas was already making an omelet.

Jazzi was sitting at the bar, drinking a cup of coffee.

Jonas crossed to Daisy, gave her a hug and a light kiss . . . probably because Jazzi was sitting nearby. Then he went back to the stove. "What would you like with your omelet? Toast? Bagels? There are some of those in the fridge."

"Toast is fine. I want to call Zeke before he goes to work."

"I already called Zeke for an update. He didn't have much to tell me."

"I have a couple of ideas I'd like to share with him."

"Your ideas make me nervous," Jonas said.

Jazzi laughed.

"It's true. How did you sleep last night?" he asked.

"I slept well. Why not with Felix as a bed partner, and you in the living room?"

Jazzi perked up. "Maybe you two should consider making that a more permanent arrangement."

Daisy blushed, ducked her head, and crossed to the coffee maker. She didn't make a comment and neither did Jonas.

The omelet was delicious, the coffee was strong, and the conversation between the three of them was kept casual.

"What are you going to do today?" Jonas asked as he picked up the plates off the bar and took them to the sink.

"This or that." It all depended on whether Trevor had the information she needed.

Jonas looked at Jazzi. "How about you?"

"I'm working at the tea garden today to relieve Mom. I'd better get going. I'm going to help Aunt Iris make a recipe for bread pudding.

"Will you be here tonight?" Jazzi asked Jonas.

"If your mom wants me to be, I will. She'll have to tell me at the end of the day. Felix can always stay even if I don't."

"Where are Marjoram and Pepper?" Daisy asked.

"They saw Felix in the kitchen so they ate their breakfast begrudgingly while he went outside and then they left for upstairs."

"They're working it out," Daisy said optimistically.

After breakfast, Jonas asked her, "Do you want me to leave Felix here with you today?"

"That would be great. I might run a few errands. I'd like to have him along. Do you think he'll take commands from me?"

"He has up until now. I don't see why not. I'd feel better if he's with you if I can't be."

"I think Felix and I will have a good day together. Are you coming over for supper tonight?"

"I can. What time?"

"How about six? I'll make shepherd's pie. I have the ingredients for it."

"You've never made that for me before."

"I didn't want you to compare it to Sarah Jane's."

"You know I'll like whatever you make. Six o'clock it is." This time, before he left, his kiss rocked her back on her heels. She was still smiling after he'd exited the house and closed the front door.

Alone, Daisy made sure the kitchen was cleaned up and Felix was happy. Then she picked up her phone, found her contacts, and tapped on Trevor's name.

"Are you at the tea garden?" he asked when he answered.

"No, I'm not. I need a favor."

"What kind of favor?"

"Do you know the name of the witness who saw someone running from Hiram's office the night he was killed?"

Trevor went silent. Finally he said, "Daisy, I don't know if I should give you that information."

"You know what happened to me. I still have the stun gun marks. I need to do some investigating on my own. Please, Trevor."

"If I don't give it to you," he said, "I'll never hear the end of it, will I? I probably won't hear the end of it from Tessa, either. If I give you the name, what do you intend to do with it?"

"I want to visit the witness."

Again there was silence. "You shouldn't go alone, but I'm tied up today. I have three interviews."

"You don't have to come with me. I'm fine. Besides, I'll have Felix with me. That should help, shouldn't it?"

After a grudging okay from Trevor, he gave her the name. "His name is Keith Farber. He works in a paint store in the four hundred block of Market. You can look up the exact address. It's a Sherwin-Williams store so you can't miss it."

"Thank you, Trevor. I really appreciate this, and I'll be all right. Felix will be with me and we'll go into the paint store and just ask a few questions. That's it."

"Text me when you get there and text me when you're finished. Tessa will have my head if I don't have you do that."

"I thought you said you'd be doing interviews."

He gave a sigh. "I can check a text."

"Got it," she agreed, and they both ended the call.

A half hour later, Daisy found herself in front of the paint store. She'd been here before to buy paint for the Victorian after they'd bought it and for her own home. When she walked in, she saw an open utilitarian aisle up to the desk in the rear of the store. To the side were shelves of wallpaper and a long table with high chairs where customers could sit to decide what kind of pattern they wanted. There were also two walls of brackets with paint samples from every color, exterior and interior paints. Today she wasn't interested in paint.

Felix walked with her to the desk and she asked the man there, "Is it okay to have Felix here with me?"

The man looked down at him. "Is he trained well?"

Daisy said, "Sure is. I wouldn't go anywhere without him."

The man smiled at her. "He's welcome then. How can I help you?"

Daisy studied the clerk who looked to be in his fifties. His brown hair was thinning and graying like his trimmed beard. "I'm looking for Keith. Is he here?"

"I'm Keith." His expression became more serious. "What can I do for you?"

"I need help with something." Daisy extended her hand. "My name is Daisy Swanson. I own Daisy's Tea Garden down the street."

"I know it," he acknowledged with a nod. "My wife goes in there at least once a week."

With a smile and the ease she experienced because she'd made a connection with him, she offered, "The next time she comes in, have her introduce herself to me. I'll give her her order on the house."

Keith eyed Daisy suspiciously. "Uh oh. If you're giving freebies away, then you *do* want something. I can't give you free paint."

"No, I don't want free paint. I'd like information. I've kept it quiet, but I was assaulted outside A Penny Saved the other night."

His expression manifested surprise and a new alertness. "I heard the ambulance. I wondered where it was going."

"That was me. Somebody assaulted me with a stun gun."

Keith's eyes widened more. "A stun gun? You mean like the one that was used on Hiram Hershberger?"

The news about Hiram had been leaked and publicized.

"Possibly. That's why I'm here. You were a witness to someone running away from Hiram's office. Correct?"

"Yes. That's right," he answered warily.

"I have an important question, and I want you to think about it before you answer me. Or better yet just give me your gut feeling, okay?"

Keith leaned down on the counter with his elbows in front of him. "All right. What's your question?"

"Could you tell if the person running away was a man or a woman? The police keep categorizing the assailant as a man, but I'd like to know what *you* think."

"All I can do is tell you what I saw."

"We'll start with that. What did you see?"

"The assailant was tall, probably not above six feet. The hoodie he or she was wearing was oversized."

"Was the person fat?"

"No, the person was slim. The hoodie slouched on the sides."

"Okay. This is the important question. You saw the person running, right?"

"Yes, I did."

"I want you to try to picture the person running. Picture the person's hips when running."

"Okay," he agreed.

"Did the person's hips rock, not remain . . . rigid?"

He thought about her question for a few moments, his eyes shut. "Yeah, I think they did."

"So that means the assailant could have been a woman."

He opened his eyes. "Yeah, it could have been," Keith said. "But remember, it was dark, and the person looked ordinary—black hoodie, black pants, black sneakers."

"I know. But when you instinctively watch someone run, I think you can tell if they're male or female. I think the person who assaulted me was a woman."

That afternoon Daisy phoned Jonas and told him about what she'd learned. She wasn't going to keep secrets from him. He said he'd pick her up and they could go talk to Zeke if that would ease her mind. She said that would be a good idea.

When they arrived at the police station, a patrol officer was at Zeke's cubicle. Unlike Detective Rappaport, Zeke didn't have his own office. At least not yet. They sat in the reception area until the receptionist came to get them and told them Zeke was free now. Daisy sat by Zeke's desk while Jonas stood against the wall. He was just there to listen.

Zeke said to her right off, "Don't tell me you've been investigating."

"I won't tell you that," Daisy agreed. "But are you going to listen to what I have to say?"

He leaned back in his chair and nodded his head one way and then the other as if he needed to stretch his neck. Apparently he'd had a long day. Apparently he'd had several of them.

"Do you think what you have to tell me is of import?"

"I think it could be. It all depends on what you do with it."

Zeke looked over at Jonas. "What do you think?"

"I think you should listen to her. If nothing else, it will give you a few minutes break from staring at that computer as if it holds the secrets to the universe."

Zeke scowled at Jonas. "And just how do you know I've been doing that? I was talking to another officer when you came in."

"I know how these cases work, Zeke. You not only add to a murder book, but you have a list of all the clues. You have a list of all the subjects and suspects, as well as notes on every one of them. You're going through it with a fine-tooth comb. Just listen to Daisy for a few minutes, then we'll leave."

Zeke crossed his arms on the desk and leaned forward. "Talk," he ordered.

"Talk? Should I take that as a voice command, Detective?"

"Are you going to fight me on everything I say?" He looked at Jonas. "Does she do this with you?"

Jonas smiled. "Nope. Not with me."

Zeke sighed. "Okay, I'm listening."

If the subject they were talking about weren't so serious, Daisy would have smiled. But it *was* serious. Her attack had been serious. She'd been scared to death. "Is it all right if I tell you what happened to me the other day first?"

"You mean the attack with the stun gun? I have notes on that."

"No. Yesterday. Jonas took me out for a canoe ride."

It was obvious from Zeke's expression that he didn't think this had anything to do with his case, but with a wave of his hand, he motioned her to go on.

"We were canoeing because Jonas thought it would help me relax. But we heard what I thought was a shot.

Jonas thought it was fireworks. I fell apart. I felt like someone's eyes were on me the whole time we were out on the canoe."

Again Zeke glanced at Jonas, but Jonas gave a shrug. "She does have a sixth sense sometimes."

"That's not what's important," Daisy pointed out. "What's important is that that stun gun attack really had me spooked. Jonas stayed overnight last night. He left Felix with me. I'm better today. I feel like myself again. But I don't want to be scared like that ever again."

"And now you're going to tell me something I don't want to hear, right?" Zeke asked.

"I don't care if you want to hear it or not. I visited the man at the paint store, the witness who had seen the suspect running away from Hiram's office the night of the murder."

Now the lines across Zeke's forehead deepened as well as the lines around his mouth. In fact, he had more than a scowl on his face. She could almost hear the growl that was coming.

She held up her hand. "I know you questioned him. I know you have notes on him. I know you probably even have a recording. But I want you to listen." She had never let Zeke bully her, or Detective Rappaport, and she wasn't going to start now, not even with the deepest scowl she'd ever seen on his face.

Zeke turned to his computer and tapped a few keys. He said, "Keith Farber was the man who saw someone running from Hiram's office. I ran a background check on him. He just has a couple of unpaid parking tickets. Other than that, he seems to be hard working. He has a family."

"I didn't care about all that," Daisy said.

Zeke pointed to his computer screen. "He couldn't tell

me anything about the person who ran away—no description except tall, slim, all in black. Tell me you got more than that."

"Not exactly," Daisy admitted. "I got that but maybe I got something more."

Zeke turned back to her, his eyes narrowed. "What did you find out?"

"I didn't see who used the stun gun on me, but as Jonas said, sometimes you simply sense something. Although the voice was deep, I think that could have been a fake voice."

"What do you mean *a fake voice*?"

"Like an actor uses. Or a ventriloquist uses. A voice to throw you off the scent. Anyway, I had the sense that it was a woman who did it."

"A woman. Someone in particular? And how could you tell? And what does this have to do with the paint store clerk?"

"Maybe you don't discover as much as I do because you don't give the witnesses you interrogate a chance to get a word in edgewise," she returned.

"Okay," he said with a long sigh. "Tell me."

"I asked the man in the paint store if he saw the person run, and he said he did. And I asked if he watched the hips."

"The hips," Zeke said deadpan.

"There's a different way a woman runs than a man runs. I asked him if the hips rocked."

Zeke looked nonplussed. "And?"

"Rocking hips could mean he saw a woman—oversized hoodie, loose trousers, sneakers. The way a person runs is unique. I think we're looking for a woman."

Zeke was already shaking his head. "Daisy."

"This is a clue. When you look over the suspects, look at the women . . . their alibis or lack thereof."

Jonas was no longer leaning against the wall. He straightened and came to stand beside Daisy. "She's not telling you she has the answers, Zeke. But she is telling you that a woman's intuition might mean something."

Daisy and Zeke had had their share of go-arounds, so had Jonas and Zeke for that matter. But this was different. This was a case that needed to be solved.

Zeke studied them both. "You've been right before. I don't see that it works in this case, especially with the motive, opportunity, and substance that I've learned along with the autopsy report. But I'll take what you said into consideration. I will, Daisy. I promise."

The reason Zeke had betrayed Jonas in the past had been for love. He and Jonas had both fallen in love with the same woman. Zeke had put his own needs over his friendship with Jonas. But Daisy knew deep down that Zeke was an honest man. She knew he meant what he said. That was the reason she'd come. That was all that she needed to know.

CHAPTER SEVENTEEN

The next day, Daisy was clearing the register at five fifteen when Jonas texted her. **"Can you stop at Woods before you go home? Just stop in the back."**

She quickly texted him that *of course* she could. Fifteen minutes later, the tearoom locked up, she walked along the macadam parking lot. The work van and Tessa's car were parked back there. She passed the hitching post and walked straight across the asphalt behind the other businesses. She easily walked on gravel, through grass, and even crossing stepping-stones.

At the rear entrance of Woods, she knocked on the door.

Jonas answered immediately. "Come on in," he said. "I have a surprise."

Her heart started beating faster, and she felt like a little kid on Christmas morning.

In Jonas's workshop near a highboy stood two bicycles. One was a man's bike and appeared to be about twenty-six inches. It was silver. The handlebars had wires that looked complicated and she imagined the bike had fifteen or twenty speeds. The one next to it looked a little smaller, less complicated, and was rose gold.

"What are these?"

"They're used bikes, though you can hardly tell it from their condition. I hope you don't mind that they're used. Until we find out if we like biking, I thought they'd be a modest investment. What do you think?"

First Daisy went to Jonas, wrapped her arms round his neck and gave him a long kiss. Then she backed up. "I think they're a marvelous idea. I want to pay for mine."

"Daisy . . ."

"I'm an independent woman, Jonas, you know that."

"You won't accept it as a Fourth of July gift?" he teased.

The Fourth was in two days. She gave him a you-should-know-better look and went over to the bicycle. She sat on it as well as she could while it was standing in the workshop.

"I'm hoping biking will be a great pastime for us," Jonas said.

"What about Jazzi?" Daisy asked.

"I actually found these at a yard sale when I was delivering furniture. The man I bought them from said they'd belonged to their son and daughter. They're in college and don't use them anymore. I took them to my mechanic who can do anything mechanical. He checked them over, and I touched them up and polished them. For Jazzi—I thought maybe we could buy her a new bike, maybe from Piper's shop."

Daisy thought about his idea. "I'd like to do that for Jazzi. She so often got hand-me-downs from Vi and never complained. She could take it to college with her if she goes somewhere within driving distance."

"She could," Jonas agreed. "Why don't we wait until she gets home from babysitting and go into Piper's shop and then out to eat?"

"That sounds like a good plan."

Not long afterward, Jazzi seemed to like the idea of getting a bicycle and the three of them going riding. They had plenty of roads they could ride them on that didn't have too much traffic, where there were more horses and buggies than cars.

She said to Daisy, "Are you sure you don't want me to look through ads to find a used bike?"

"No. I think you deserve a new one. Your grades were exceptional this year. You're working hard to save money for a car."

"Are you doing this because you bought things for Vi and the baby? Because you don't have to buy me things too."

"This has nothing to do with Vi and the baby. This is just something I want to do for you because you're a good kid. And we'd like you to take bike rides with us."

Jazzi smiled. "All right. Let's go buy a bike."

Jonas had carried the bikes on the multi-bike rack he'd had attached to the back of his SUV. They parked almost in front of Wheels and went inside. Jazzi looked all around and then headed toward one particular display of Schwinn bikes.

Piper saw them and came over immediately. No one else was in the store.

"You caught me right before closing," she said. "It looks as if Jazzi might have her eye on a bike."

Jazzi was pointing to a blue and purple one that looked to be about the right size for her.

"Jazzi wants to pick out a bike, something practical for riding around here on rural roads."

"The one she's looking at would be great for that. Let me pull it out for her."

Piper went over to the row of bikes on the rack. She easily lifted the one Jazzi wanted to look at up and over two others. Daisy found it suddenly hard to breathe. Piper had done that so easily. Just how strong was she?

As Piper explained the many features of the bike to Jazzi, Daisy stepped away for a minute toward the window. To her dismay she felt as if she were back outside of A Penny Saved, locking the door, ready to leave. Then someone had stepped behind her . . . someone who seemed tall. Someone who had seemed strong. *If . . .* she thought. *If her assailant had been a woman—*

Jonas came over to Daisy and settled his arm around her waist. "What's up?" he asked quietly.

"Piper's taller than I am."

"Yes, she is," Jonas said.

"She lifted that bike as if it had no weight at all."

"Yes, she did. What are you getting at?"

"I've got to be wrong. I'm probably totally wrong. But when I think about that night when someone used a stun gun on me, I wonder if it could have been Piper."

Jonas's expression hardened and his jaw became tense. His detective voice asked, "Any particular reason you think that?"

Daisy took a deep breath. "No particular reason. But I

think it's a possibility. After all, she has as much motive as anybody else . . . at least as much motive as Emory."

Jazzi called to them. "What do you think, Mom? Is this one okay?"

Piper was looking that way with a questioning expression. Was that a calculating look she gave Daisy? Or was Daisy just being paranoid?

Keeping her tone light, Daisy answered breezily, "Just imagining how you'd look on it while we're riding along the trees and through the covered bridge." She said to Piper, "Jonas and I were just discussing whether it's the right size for her. What do you think?"

Piper looked relieved that that's what they'd been talking about. "I think it's perfect for her height. Shall I ring it up?"

After Daisy paid for the bike, Jonas wheeled it outside toward his SUV. While Jazzi climbed into the back seat, he loaded it onto the bike rack. Three bikes hung in a row.

He said to Daisy, "You know, I feel as if I'm part of a family. It's a good feeling."

Daisy, who through the process of buying the bike had convinced herself she had to be wrong about Piper, now focused entirely on Jonas. She stood close to him and interlaced her fingers with his. "You *are* part of a family."

After bike shopping, Jonas drove to Sarah Jane's Diner for supper. Seated in a booth, they decided what to order from the large menu. The special of the day was pot roast, one of Jonas's favorite meals and he could have it served with mashed potatoes topped with sauerkraut. It wasn't Daisy's favorite, but then he was a meat and potatoes kind of guy. After all, her suppers now saved him from fast food burgers and fries.

Other specials for tonight were Sarah Jane's fried chicken, roasted turkey and stuffing, country-fried steaks smothered in gravy, liver and onions, and smoked ham. The sides were almost as good as the main dishes including Amish potato cakes, Amish noodles, mac and cheese, fried okra, chow-chow, homemade applesauce, or baked hot apples. Daisy and Jazzi decided to split a strawberry field salad that included fresh spring lettuce, strawberries, almonds, dried cranberries, and chunks of cheddar cheese. It was served with raspberry vinaigrette and homemade apple bread. In addition, Jazzi ordered a bowl of chili con carne while Daisy ordered a chicken orzo soup.

Sarah Jane's Diner was usually packed at supper time. Everyone had a favorite special and they came the night she served it. Her prices were reasonable and the food was delicious. Along with her personality, Sarah Jane managed a tight ship, stuck to her budget, took advantage of sales, and always produced dinners a family could enjoy. Not only were all of those conditions met for running a successful business, but Sarah Jane knew how to pick the waitstaff and her kitchen staff. They were loyal to her and only wanted to do their best.

An older woman in her fifties came to take their order. Eunice Jones had been with Sarah Jane almost since Sarah Jane had opened the restaurant. Before waitressing here, Eunice had worked at a chain restaurant in one of the Lancaster malls. She'd told Daisy more than once that working for Sarah Jane here was like being in heaven. She knew her exact hours from week to week, mostly what her tips would be, and on top of all that, she liked everyone she worked with.

As Eunice stood at their table, Jonas ordered coffee as

did Daisy. Jazzi opted for unsweetened iced tea. Eunice took their orders efficiently and then winked at Daisy. "Sarah Jane told me she has something she wants to speak with you about, but she's too busy right now. She just wants to make sure you don't leave without talking with her."

"No problem," Daisy assured her. "If she has a break, let me know and I'll come back there to her office to talk with her."

"She wouldn't want you to interrupt your dinner. You know she thinks that would give you indigestion," Eunice explained with a wink as she left the table with their menus.

"What do you think that's about?" Jonas asked.

Jazzi unwrapped her silverware and laid the napkin on her lap. "I bet any money she has something to tell you about the investigation."

"Jazzi, not everything revolves around that," Daisy reminded her.

"Sarah Jane doesn't interfere with her supper service for just anyone," Jazzi concluded.

The laugh lines around Jonas's eyes crinkled. The scar along his cheek wasn't evident tonight which meant he was relaxed. When he smiled, she didn't notice the scar at all. "Your daughter knows you and Sarah Jane pretty well, I'd say."

Daisy scrunched up her nose in disagreement. "I'm more interested in discussing where we're going to ride those bicycles. You and Jazzi might want to take yours out before I can get to mine. Aunt Iris, Tessa, and I will be preparing for the garden event this weekend."

"Ned told me that he's going to be playing his guitar," Jazzi said as if she was looking forward to that. "I've never heard him play while I'm waiting tables. It will make the time go faster."

"I'm hoping we'll be so busy time will fly by," Daisy said. "We've sold enough tickets for a full house."

"Since Brielle will be serving with me," Jazzi said, "she told me her mom's going to bring Glorie. It will give her a nice day out. I didn't see a flyer for your garden party in Piper's store, but the flyers are in most of the other windows."

Most of the shops had a pact that if they had a special event going on, each business in the chamber of commerce would help promote it. Daisy had several flyers in her windows because many businesses were having events on Fourth of July weekend.

Eunice brought their drinks and they all took a few minutes to relax and sip.

Jonas asked Daisy, "Do you still need me to help set up the tables tomorrow evening?"

"I'd love to have your help. Foster will be there and I think Ben's coming too. I told Foster I'd tip Ben if he helped."

"It shouldn't take us too long," Jonas said. "And then you have a day off on Monday, right? Maybe we could take the bikes out on Monday, all three of us. I also thought we might visit Adele Gunnarsen, Felix's mom."

"Sounds like a plan," Daisy said.

They were just finishing up their dinners when Eunice beckoned to Daisy.

Daisy said, "Don't leave without me. This shouldn't take too long." She slipped out of the booth and headed toward the back and Sarah Jane's office.

Most of Sarah Jane's staff knew Daisy, and they smiled

or waved or said hello as she made her way to the back with Eunice showing her the way.

Sarah Jane emerged from the kitchen and met Daisy at the office door. "Come on in," she said. "I've something to tell you and I think it's important."

Sarah Jane's office was about as big as Jonas's in the back of his workshop . . . very small. Piles of papers were stacked on the desk while magazines and cookbooks lined the short bookshelves. Two wooden straight-back chairs weren't comfortable but rather utilitarian.

As Sarah Jane sat behind the desk, Daisy took the other chair in front of the desk.

"What's this about?" Daisy asked.

"I overhear lots of conversations in a day and evening," Sarah Jane said. "Many of them I'm not supposed to hear, but while I'm circulating, people don't notice me and they just keep talking."

"Who did you hear?"

"I overheard two of the nurses from the Hope Clinic talking. It's possible they were techs, I'm not sure. They had those scrub outfits on."

"Blue ones," Daisy said, remembering.

Sarah Jane nodded. "Yes, that's right. How did you know?"

"I just happened to visit the clinic not so long ago."

Sarah Jane stared at Daisy. "I suppose that had something to do with Hiram's murder?"

"I'm not saying one way or another." She still wasn't sure she wanted her visit to the Hope Clinic to be public knowledge.

After a pause, Sarah Jane went on. "I got the sense that the two of them didn't really know where Thelma Bartik is. But they did say she wasn't the one who caused the malfunction. One of them said that Thelma knows who did it."

"Wow, that's news. I wonder if Zeke Willet knows."

"I didn't want to call him because, after all, this is gossip, I guess. But if you believe I should, I will."

"Did they say anything else?"

"They think they know why Thelma ran." Sarah Jane held up one finger. "They're supposing that she's afraid that the person who caused the malfunction might want to quiet her because she knows who it is and might spill it!"

CHAPTER EIGHTEEN

Daisy stood outside the side door of the tea garden the day of the Fourth of July garden party. The herbs in the ceramic pots along the patio gave off fragrant aromas as the sun hit them. Especially the lavender perfumed the area. The ornamental oregano was taking off now and wound around a large royal blue pot and the bronze cat statue. Since daylight still prevailed, the tall lantern on a hook near the side door wasn't glowing with the flameless candle that came on at dusk. Nevertheless, the lantern with its copper exterior and red, white, and blue ribbon, stood out and presented the ambience Daisy and Iris wanted outside.

Still, Daisy's mind wasn't completely on the event. Even as the breeze caught the side of a yellow-and-white umbrella and the red, white, and blue streamers beneath it, Daisy was thinking about dinner the other night and her talk with Sarah Jane. Sarah Jane had called Zeke right after their conversation. He was going to track down the women who had eaten at the diner.

Cora Sue came up to Daisy, startling her out of her thoughts. "I didn't expect this many people, did you? Customers are lined up at all the tents."

Colorful canopies stretched along the grass down to the creek. Pirated Treasures sold tea ware, antique and new. Otis Murdock was manning the stand and Vi was helping him. She worked part-time for Otis and enjoyed it. Quilts and Notions also had a spot under a blue canopy. Today a part-time helper from Rachel's shop was selling tea cozies and pot holders. She also had a few quilts that might draw anyone who liked them into Quilts and Notions later in the week to buy others. The thing was, Rachel wasn't selling her own wares because it was Sunday. Her *Englischer* clerk was manning the booth. Under the red canopy, Betty Furhman from Wisps and Wicks sold tealights and homemade candles. There were drip pillar candles, tapers, tealights, scented beeswax and soy candles.

In buckskin breeches with a loose cream shirt, Ned Pachenko was already playing his guitar. It added ambience to the day that was calm, pleasurable, and friendly.

Lawrence Bishop who was sitting at a table with Piper and Emory waved at Daisy and motioned to her. She approached their table.

"Are you enjoying the tea service?" she asked them, dismissing her previous fearful thoughts about Piper.

Piper assured her quickly, "We are. Emory especially likes the whoopie pies, and I think Dad's ready to buy a couple dozen snickerdoodles."

After studying Emory, Daisy wasn't sure he even

wanted to be there. His expression wasn't one of pleasure but of resigned resistance.

"The whoopie pies come in several different flavors," she told him.

"Chocolate's fine," he said, an odd inflection in his voice.

Piper gave him a look. "Emory, we're supposed to be enjoying today, relaxing, getting away from everything that's making us so tense. Why can't you just enjoy the weather, music, and company?"

He looked at Piper as if she should understand exactly the expression that was on his face. Then he stood and laid his patriotic napkin on the table. "I think I've had enough enjoyment for one day. I'm going home. You can get a ride home with your father."

Piper stood too. "Emory, wait."

But Emory was already walking out toward the front of the tea garden and Market Street.

Lawrence put his hand on Piper's shoulder. "Come on, honey. *You* try to relax."

"It's hard to do when I know I have to deal with Emory later."

Daisy wasn't exactly sure what to do next when she eyed Zeke standing at the back door of the tea garden. He was studying everyone with a detective's eye. Had he just seen the argument between Emory and Piper? Did it matter if he had?

"Excuse me," she said. "I need to talk to someone."

"I see Willet over there," Lawrence said. "Is that who you're going to talk to? Maybe you can find out where this investigation is headed."

"Lawrence, Zeke won't tell me what he's planning. That's the way detectives are. I do want to find out why he's here, though. So if you'll excuse me . . . Please try to enjoy your tea."

After heading Zeke's way, she stood beside him and asked, "Can I convince you to have a tea service?"

"I thought I'd look at candles," he joked.

Becoming serious, she faced him. "Why are you here?"

"I like to see suspects in their everyday lives. It helps me get a better picture of them . . . like the picture I just noticed of Emory and Piper."

"They're under a lot of tension right now."

"I guess they are, but I think Emory has a short fuse. That's what I noticed most."

"Who else are you interested in?" Daisy asked, hoping to catch him off guard.

With an impassive expression, he gave her one of those detective looks. "I'm not telling *you*. I'm just going to mosey around and overhear lots of people's conversations. Isn't that how you find clues?"

"Sometimes," she admitted.

"Is Jonas around?" Zeke asked

"Not right now. He's down at his shop. He's going to come back at the end of this and help tear down and clean up."

"You have a real event going on here. The tea garden's packed inside too."

"That's how I keep the place running, Zeke. These special events help."

"I've got to give you credit, Daisy. When I first met you, I just thought you were a pretty blond with deep blue eyes, and that Jonas had made a good choice."

"We weren't seriously together then," she reminded him.

"Oh, you were together. The two of you just didn't know it yet. Anyway, I've realized since then that you have good business sense. Not only that, but you have good deductive skills."

"Why, Detective, you flatter me."

"That's not flattery if it's true. There's somebody waving to you. You'd better go see what she wants."

"Tell me one thing before you leave. Did Sarah Jane help you?"

"She helped some. Every little clue helps. But we still don't know where Thelma Bartik is."

Ramona was the one waving at Daisy. She was sitting at a table for two with her little boy Petey. From the way he was jittering around on his seat, Daisy didn't think they'd be there very long.

After an "excuse me" to Zeke, she went to the table where Ramona was seated. Instead of asking Ramona what she thought of the day, she looked at Petey. "Hey, little guy, do you like all this?" She motioned to Ned who was playing the guitar.

Petey wrinkled his nose. "I don't know his songs."

Daisy easily saw that Petey's plate was empty. "What about the goodies? Did you like any of them?"

Now his head bobbed up and down enthusiastically. "I liked them *all*."

Ramona laughed. "Yes, he did. When we get home, I have a feeling he's going to be wound up. It's worth it to sit out here on this beautiful day, hear the birds chirp, and just enjoy everybody's company."

Daisy agreed. "Sometimes we just have to slow down."

Ramona brushed crumbs from above Petey's upper lip. "I imagine this was a lot of work to plan."

"It was, but I have help."

"I suppose you do need a team to get anything done," Ramona said.

Suddenly her pleasant, relaxed expression changed. Lines formed around her lips as she frowned and glanced toward a table closer to the side door.

"Is something wrong?" Daisy asked. Maybe Ramona had just gotten a bad swig of tea and didn't like it.

The young adult brought her attention back to Daisy. "No, nothing's wrong. I'm not going to let my stepbrother spoil my afternoon out."

"The two of you don't get along?"

"Let's just say we have different values and ideas about family. Fred was totally against Jim and me trying *in vitro*. He said it was unnatural. He and I never agreed on much, but that really separated us. I haven't talked to him since *that* discussion."

So many questions filed through Daisy's head about Ramona's relationship with her stepbrother. On the other hand, none of it was her business. Families were what they were, and sometimes they just didn't get along.

Brielle and Glorie Beck were sitting under one of the maple trees.

Daisy said to Ramona, "You enjoy the rest of your afternoon. I've got to circulate a little more."

Ramona said, "I understand, and Petey's getting restless. We'll probably leave soon."

As Daisy walked toward Brielle and Glorie, she had to sidestep Ramona's stepbrother and the man he was talking to. They looked as if they were having an animated discussion. Passing them, she heard Ramona's stepbrother say, "Hiram was a good lawyer. He could win a case with one arm tied behind his back."

Daisy knew what Ramona thought about lawyers. She wondered if Ramona's stepbrother had been a client of Hiram's.

Monday was Daisy's day off, and she needed it after yesterday. The event had been a success. This morning she'd gone with Jonas and Jazzi on a five-mile biking trek. Now she and Jonas were driving to visit Adele Gunnarsen at Whispering Willows Assisted Living Facility which was about two miles outside of Willow Creek. Daisy realized why it was named that as they drove up to it. There were willow trees all over the property. Daisy guessed the back of the property stretched to Willow Creek. Willow tree roots searched for water and they did well along the shoreline of the deep creek.

On the drive here, Jonas and Daisy had discussed Ramona's stepbrother and his comments about Hiram. She'd said, "Hiram was involved with so many people. In a practice, when somebody loses and somebody wins, you can bet Hiram made enemies."

Jonas had agreed with a nod. "I don't think we realized how many. I hope Zeke does, though."

Suddenly Felix, who was accompanying them to see his former mistress, nudged his head up between their seats.

Daisy reached up and rubbed his neck. "I know you're going to like where we're going," she told him. "I'm sure Mrs. Gunnarsen is going to be pleased to see you." Daisy had called the facility that morning to make sure Felix would be welcome and to ask about visiting hours. The person she'd talked to said their visiting hours were very flexible and, of course, Felix was welcome too if he made one of their residents happy. Afterward she'd spoken to Adele to ask if she ate sweets. She assured Daisy that she did.

Daisy retrieved the basket of baked goods she'd assembled for Adele from the back of the SUV. After they walked inside the pleasant lobby decorated in mostly green and yellow with a few roses in a wallpaper border around the ceiling, they signed in. The receptionist told them that they kept a log of everyone who visited their residents. She informed them that Adele had a suite with one bedroom and a kitchen.

Afterward, the receptionist pointed to a board that listed the activities for the day. She told Daisy and Jonas, "If Adele feels like it, you can all join the bingo game. We have gift cards today for their favorite online stores as prizes. A girl scout troop is coming in later to sing some of their favorite Broadway songs."

As Daisy, Jonas, and Felix started down the hall toward Adele's room, Daisy said, "They even have chair yoga listed with the activities. I'm glad to see that. The more active the residents are, the happier they are. Wouldn't you think?"

"The activities keep them motivated, I suppose," Jonas agreed. "We'll have to ask Adele if we're keeping her from anything."

At the door to room twenty-three, a welcome wreath with sunflowers hanging on it, Daisy knocked lightly. The door was propped open and Felix decided he didn't need to wait. He ran right in.

By the time Jonas and Daisy walked inside, Felix was sitting at Adele's feet, being loved on all over. Adele's book lay open on the sofa beside her and she had obviously been reading.

She looked up at Jonas and Daisy with a wide smile but tears in her eyes. "I'm happy to see him," she said.

Jonas's voice was husky when he responded, "This is only the first of many visits."

Daisy put the basket of goodies on the small coffee table. "Mrs. Gunnarsen, we just want to tell you how happy we are that Felix has come to live with Jonas. He's a wonderful dog."

"Please call me Adele. Have a seat so we can have a real visit."

To Daisy, Adele Gunnarsen looked a little like Betty White with snowy white hair and curly bangs brushed to the right. A bobby pin held her hair back over the left ear. Wire-rimmed glasses hung from a turquoise beaded chain around her neck. When she smiled, huge dimples appeared on either side of her mouth. She was wearing a mauve flowered blouse with buttons down the front. It hung out over mauve knit slacks.

Felix now rested across her white tennis shoes, his tail swishing back and forth.

A gray-and-black tweed throw rug lay across the vinyl tile floor. As Daisy glanced around the small suite, she saw that the cabinets were finished in pale green. The counter was a dark sage laminate. White appliances matched a small round white table with two chairs.

Adele peered under the cloth napkin covering the treats Daisy had brought. She watched Daisy glance around and she asked, "What do you think of my home?"

"I think the question is," Jonas said, "how do *you* like it?"

She motioned Jonas to a chair. "Don't hover. My son does that."

He sank down into a small side chair. The fabric on the

sofa where Adele was sitting was a sunflower print. The easy chair Daisy had chosen was covered in a pale green fabric.

Felix raised up again and laid his head across Adele's legs. He looked up at her with adoring brown eyes.

"I miss my home," Adele said. "I miss it a whole lot. It was a craftsman with two floors and a backyard. My rose bushes were my pride and joy along with Felix here. But the truth is, I couldn't take care of most of it any more. The hardest part was giving up Felix. I told my son I wanted a background check on anybody who adopted him."

She made eye contact with Jonas. "We went over your adoption application with a fine-tooth comb. We saw that you had been a police detective but now you made hand-crafted wood items. We were intrigued. He stopped into your shop without you knowing it, I'm afraid. I'm sorry for that little bit of spy work."

"If I was giving up a pet, I might have done the same thing," Jonas said. "You know, that means your son cares about you a lot. He wanted you and Felix to be happy."

"Yes, he did. He said he liked what he saw when he met you. Your furniture is worth the money and he didn't feel as if you tried to take advantage of anyone. He heard you talking with other customers and you didn't high pressure them, you just stood by your work."

"I'm glad I passed muster." Jonas gave her a crooked smile. "Felix goes to work with me every day. Customers will soon find out he's part of the shop. We're still getting to know each other, but I think we're becoming good friends."

Adele looked down at Felix and asked the dog, "Are you obeying his commands?"

Felix gave a little ruff as if he understood exactly what she was saying. Smiling, she petted him more.

Adele looked at Daisy. "You told me a little about yourself when we talked. You have that nice tea garden restaurant downtown."

"I do. My aunt and I run it."

"Since I'm too old to mince words . . ." Adele paused and pointed her finger first at Jonas and then at Daisy, then back to Jonas. "Are you two involved?"

Jonas's gaze connected to Daisy's. He answered, "We're dating and finding out how much we mean to each other more every day."

"That's a nice way of putting it," Adele agreed approvingly.

Their conversational ball never dropped as Adele wanted to know about their lives and she revealed much of hers. She explained how she and her husband Horace had been inseparable. Her husband had been a plumber. After he retired, they played cards with friends, went on daylong road trips, and ran a book fair at the elementary school twice a year.

"When Horace passed, I was lonelier than I ever thought I could be. I had Felix, though, and that helped, and my son stopped in whenever he could. Then I moved here for lots of reasons, mostly because I wanted to make new friendships and those are nice to have at my age."

Felix had settled on the floor, his back against Adele's foot.

Adele went on, "I have a subscription for the *Willow Creek Messenger* so I keep up-to-date on most of what's going on. My son got me one of those electronic tablets. I use it for games. I have a cell phone too. It's nothing fancy. My son made sure I'm on what he calls a neighborhood app. People post on there what they're concerned about and there's all kinds of replies. There was a big back and forth about that protest at the social for the homeless shelter."

"I served tea and baked goods that day," Daisy said.

"I'm curious," Jonas asked. "What did most of the people say on there about the protest?"

Adele glanced at her phone on the coffee table. "Neighbors mentioned how scary it was to have those men coming toward them with masks on and yelling what they did. One or two said they understood why those men were protesting. I'm not sure. Shouldn't kindness rule our lives? Shouldn't we want to help people in need?"

"I think so," Daisy said. "We knew a man who was homeless and with help he got back on his feet for himself and his daughter."

Adele nodded. "That app's also talking about the murder of that lawyer, Hiram Hershberger."

"There's a lot of talk about that around town," Jonas said.

"I knew Mr. Hershberger," Adele said.

"How did you know him?" Jonas asked before Daisy could.

"I went to him to have my will, living will, and power of attorney drawn up. I imagine many residents of Willow Creek did. He had a good reputation for that. He was a gentleman with me and didn't overcharge from what I could tell. But not everyone was happy with him."

Jonas leaned forward. "How so?"

"I knew one elderly man whose children wanted to declare him incompetent so they could take over his estate. Mr. Hershberger made that happen. The thing was, it wasn't *all* the children who wanted that to happen. Two brothers against another brother. That brother looked so cross. I saw him one day I was in town. I could tell the whole thing was still eating at him. I talked with him and he believed his brothers were wrong. He believed Mr. Hershberger had done the wrong thing by taking on their case. He was finding another lawyer to try to have it reversed. I had to ask myself, what would have happened if Mr. Hershberger would have sat down with all of them and they would have talked it out. But I guess that isn't the way of things these days."

"Hiram seemed to have a lot of enemies," Daisy suggested.

"I suppose so," Adele agreed. "Just imagine him defending that clinic against all those couples who were planning on having babies and were disappointed. That had to be a mark against him."

"I think the police are looking at that angle most of all," Jonas confided.

With a sad expression, Adele shook her head. "So many unhappy people. It was fortunate that Horace and I could save money over the years. I'm grateful that my son helped me make the choice to move in here. And I'm so very happy that Felix found a wonderful home."

Jonas said, "My yard isn't huge, but I see Daisy almost every night and Felix loves to play fetch in her huge backyard. She renovated a barn into her home and has lots of running room for him. She introduced him to her grandson."

Adele studied Daisy. "You don't look old enough to have a grandchild."

"But I do. I love Sammy to the moon and back."

"Why don't I make us all a cup of tea and we can dig into some of those goodies you brought. Do you have time for that?"

"Are you sure you don't want to go to bingo?" Daisy asked.

"I can go to bingo any day. Right now, I'd rather just visit with you and spend time with Felix."

Daisy truly liked Adele. She even thought that Glorie Beck and Adele might become good friends if they could meet and have tea. She'd have to talk to Glorie about that. But right now, they were taking a break to give Adele the company she needed . . . the friendship she needed. Most of all the time to love Felix as she once did.

Daisy was sure they'd be coming back often. Maybe she could convince Jazzi to visit with her, and maybe Vi and Sammy too. Maybe, just maybe, they'd all make a new friend. Maybe, just maybe, Daisy had learned more about Hiram Hershberger too.

CHAPTER NINETEEN

On Tuesday evening, Daisy felt Felix's nose on her arm. He'd nudged up between the seats in Jonas's SUV and she knew why. Jonas's expression was sober. She was worried. Felix could feel the tension in the vehicle.

An hour ago, Daisy had received a call from the janitor at the Hope Clinic. "Mrs. Swanson?" he'd asked tentatively when she'd answered her phone.

She hadn't recognized the number and for a few moments was fearful that it might be her attacker. Still she'd said, "Yes, this is Daisy Swanson."

"You wanted me to call you if I knew anything about Thelma."

Then she'd placed the voice . . . Cletus Simpson. Her heart increased its beats until her pulse was *rat-a-tat* at her temples. "Go ahead," she'd told Cletus.

"I might know where Thelma is."

"Might?"

"I don't know for sure. I suppose the police have looked at all of the usual places."

"Yes, I guess they have. I'm sure they've checked her house and friends and any relatives."

"Yeah, well, there's something they might not know about."

"And what's that?" She couldn't imagine that Zeke and Detective Rappaport wouldn't have followed up on every lead they possibly could. Thelma was a lead, an important one.

"Thelma was divorced about six years ago."

"Okay," Daisy had prompted.

"Her ex-husband had a house, more like a cabin, along the Susquehanna River."

Daisy's heart had tripped so fast she'd had to sit down. "Was the divorce friendly?"

"Not exactly. He don't use it that much. He's got hip issues now. It was part of the settlement that Thelma could go up there whenever she wanted . . . as long as he still owned it."

"Does he still own it?"

"I don't know for sure, and I don't know that's where she went."

"Do you know the exact location?"

"Nope. Don't know that either."

Daisy's hopes had dimmed a bit. "But you do know her ex's name?"

"Sure do. His name is Wilson Bartik. Like I said, she don't have to tell him when she's up there, so he probably don't know anything either."

"Cletus, thank you. I'll check this out and I'll let the police know if she's there."

"You didn't get no information from me."

"I'll remember that," Daisy had assured him.

Daisy had called Jonas. Using skills he'd honed as a detective, he'd immediately searched property records and found the location of the property.

On the road now, they took Route 462 to Wrightsville, a borough in York County with about 2500 residents. From a distance, it looked like and was a village with a long street that led down a steep hill to the riverfront. It had been settled in the early 1700s. A quiet river town, it had gained historic notice during the Civil War.

Jonas turned onto South Front Street which turned into a five-mile stretch along the river called Long Level.

When Daisy realized her hands were clenched, she opened them and told herself to relax. "Do you think we should have called Zeke or Rappaport?"

"What good would that have done? We don't even know if Thelma's at her ex's house."

"I know, but I told Zeke if I learned anything, I'd let him know."

"We *will* let him know. We'll just scout out the place and see if Thelma's there. If she is, I'll call him, or you can. If she's there, we've saved him foot- and roadwork. If she's not, it was a lead that went south. He didn't have to waste his time."

The way Jonas put it, that all made sense. But she wasn't sure.

Driving along the road, they passed a mobile home park and a quarry on the right. The river rolled along the left, at times not far from the road. It was easy to see how this stretch would flood with unusually heavy rains. Felix nudged his head up between the seats as if he was considering a run in the woods that flanked both sides of the road. Not long after, they reached Susquehanna Heritage Park on the right. It was one of the landmarks Jonas had told her they could watch for.

Felix gave a short bark as if he thought they'd reached their destination.

"Not today, boy," Jonas said. "Maybe we can return another time and let you explore the park."

Daisy rubbed Felix's ear the way he liked and he seemed satisfied.

Soon they approached the marina on the left. It was small as marinas went with dock ramps and boats moored close by.

"The house should be coming up on the right," Jonas advised her. "From what I could see on the aerial map, it sits on a hill and has concrete block pillars for support under a screened-in porch."

"And the rest is wood-shingled?" She'd taken in all the information quickly and wanted to make sure she had a clear picture in her mind of the house they were searching for.

"You'll see the house up on the hill before I find the lane that leads up to it. There are binoculars in the glove compartment that we might need."

Reaching forward, Daisy pulled open the glove compartment. There were binoculars in there all right, but there was also something else. "Jonas . . ."

"It's just a precaution, Daisy."

The gun in Jonas's glove compartment was usually kept in the locked safe at Woods. She shivered at the thought that he'd ever have to use it.

Suddenly Jonas made a sharp right turn onto a gravel lane. "This could easily wash out," he said as he navigated over potholes. The narrow road headed up a steep incline.

Finally, at the head of the lane sat a small house. The cedar-stained siding was old and weathered. The shingled roof was covered with green algae.

"It's twelve-hundred square feet," Jonas said, "with two bedrooms. I saw the plans online."

Daisy used the binoculars for a close-up view. The wood surrounding the screens had darkened and was cracked. One of the screen panels had a hole in it.

"It doesn't look as if much upkeep goes on here."

"You know what Cletus said. I don't think the house gets much use."

Jonas nodded toward the detached shed about twenty yards from the house. Tracks to it in the dirt had come from a vehicle or vehicles.

"It doesn't look as if anybody's around," Daisy observed, almost hopeful of the prospect.

"I'm going to go check around." Jonas unfastened his seatbelt.

"Without the gun?"

"Yes, without the gun. I'll take Felix. You stay here."

"No way. I'm going with you."

After a quiet perusing look, Jonas didn't try to argue with her. She was glad for that. He respected her determination.

After he let Felix out of the SUV, the dog walked with him ahead of Daisy up the path to the screened-in porch. When she reached the porch, she peered inside through the screen door and could see an old-fashioned clothes tree in a corner. A red flannel jacket hung on it. A pair of old sneakers covered in mud sprawled underneath it.

"I think she's here," Jonas said quietly. "Let's go into the porch and rap on the—" He cut off his sentence when Felix suddenly turned and pointed toward the side of the house. Felix's nose was high and his tail was too.

"What is it, boy?" Jonas asked.

Felix barked.

"I don't know what he sees but I'm going to let him find it. Go Felix."

Jonas took off at a sprint after the dog and kept up with him around the back of the house.

Daisy ran after them.

Holly bushes out back against the house were matted with undergrowth that had grown too long and too tangled in between their branches. Daisy caught a whiff of mock orange as she tried to keep up with Jonas's hurried stride in the long, tall grass. If there had been a path at the back of the house, it was now overgrown.

"Thelma!" Jonas called.

Daisy stopped to catch her breath and saw a woman in a tan T-shirt and jeans. Daisy had no idea what Thelma might be running toward. At the back of the property stood poplars and Alaskan cedars so thick you could hardly see daylight through them.

If the woman they were chasing was Thelma Bartik, she didn't stop when Jonas called. However, Felix took off even faster and reached her before Jonas could. When the woman saw the dog, she stopped, wrapped her arms around herself, and sunk down onto the ground.

Jonas and Daisy reached her to see Thelma was holding onto Felix, her head in his fur as if the dog were a lifeline.

"Please don't hurt me," she was mumbling into Felix's fur.

Thelma Bartik looked to be around fifty. She had scraggly dark brown hair unevenly cut that hit the collar of her shirt in the back. Dainty silver hummingbird earrings hung from her earlobes. There were blue-black circles under her eyes. The lines from her nose to around her mouth pulled taut as she grimaced and looked up at them.

"What do you want?" she asked in a soft voice.

"We're trying to find out who killed Hiram Hershberger," Jonas said.

"How did you find me?"

Daisy shook her head. "Does it matter? Someone knew your ex-husband had kept this property, so we just made a lucky guess that you might be here. Running away has confounded the police. They think you're a suspect."

"Me? That's not why I'm here. I came because . . ." She stopped, and ducked her head into Felix again. When she looked back up, there were tears in her eyes. "I came here because I'm trying to protect someone and myself too. Look what happened to Hiram."

"You've got to tell the police your story, Thelma," Daisy suggested. "The only way everybody's going to be safe is if they catch the murderer." Watching Thelma as she'd run, also noting the woman had done nothing for self-defense, Daisy was sure Thelma hadn't killed Hiram. But she might know who did.

Thelma looked from Daisy to Jonas again. "So you're not cops?"

Daisy gave a humorless laugh. "No. I run Daisy's Tea Garden downtown, and Jonas has a store that sells furniture. It's called Woods. But I help the police sometimes and Jonas is a former detective."

Thelma sat up a little straighter, crossed her legs in front of her, and patted Felix's back. "And who's this guy?"

"That's Felix," Jonas said. "I adopted him recently. He heard you or caught your scent before I did. I think maybe he could tell you didn't want to be running. He's big on protection."

Thelma ran her hand through Felix's fur. "Do you really think the only way I'm going to be safe is if I talk to you or the police?"

"We do," Daisy advised her. "I can call Detective Willet and have him come here . . . or we can take you to him."

Thelma's eyes were wild with fear. "I don't want him to come here. My ex-husband would divorce me all over again. Can I tell you what happened first? I don't want to get mixed up when I get to the police station. When I get nervous, my words don't come out right."

"We're here. We've no place to go. You can tell us anything you want," Jonas assured her.

They were sitting in a circle of sorts, the three humans and Felix. Thelma kept her hand on Felix as if by merely touching him, she was filled with courage. Daisy knew that was very possible.

"You know who I am. Do you know what I do?" Thelma asked.

"You're a tech at the Hope Clinic," Daisy said.

"Yeah, but I'm not the one who messed up."

"You're going to have to tell the police who did," Daisy warned her, "or they'll think you're hiding something."

"Oh, I've been hiding something all right. I saw Hiram . . . but he was dead."

Daisy couldn't help a little gasp. She'd never expected that.

"Why did you go to see him?" Jonas asked.

"I went there to make sure he was going to protect Joyce Getz. She's the one who miscalculated the numbers on the storage unit. She was in a hurry. I spotted her at the unit and I knew she'd been the last one to touch it. No one knew I knew, but the talk around the clinic was that there was going to be a deal. The CEO might give up the person who caused the malfunction if he could get the clinic out of hot water. Everybody could sue her. That wasn't right. My husband and I knew Hiram. He had done the settlement for our divorce. I liked him right enough. Things came out as best they could. I thought Hiram would be reasonable about Joyce if I could talk to him. I went to him to make sure he was going to protect her from the nonsense Mr. Richter wanted to pursue. I heard scuttlebutt that Joyce going bankrupt would be a small price to pay rather than the clinic going bankrupt. Can you imagine?"

"As CEO, mostly what Richter cares about is making money," Jonas said.

"I don't know what Hiram was going to do, but when I got there, he was already dead. I'm an LPN and I know how to tell. I ran out of there faster than lightning and went the back way down the alleys so nobody would see me. And nobody did as far as I know."

Thelma wasn't the person whom the witness, Keith Farber, had seen running away. According to Trevor, Keith had been standing on Spruce Street, not looking down an alley.

"Do you think this *Joyce* killed Hiram?" Jonas asked.

"I just don't know. I don't think she has it in her."

Jonas looked Thelma straight in the eye. "You need to go to the police and tell them everything. If they won't protect you, or if they can't spare anyone, I'll do it myself."

Daisy could see Thelma was fearful and she didn't know who to trust. Daisy said, "Jonas always keeps his word."

Thelma seemed to make up her mind after petting Felix again and studying Jonas for a good long while. Then she said, "All right. Let's go. I'll talk to the detective."

Daisy breathed a sigh of relief, hoping Zeke Willet would understand why they'd come here without him.

On her break, Daisy hurried across the street to Quilts and Notions, still thinking about yesterday and Thelma. It had been an eye-opening excursion in many ways—from the drive and finding Thelma to their visit to the police station. Somehow she had to put all of the questions that had stirred up out of her mind.

Rachel had phoned her, which was unusual in itself. Since she was New Order Amish, the district's bishop allowed Rachel to have a cell phone to use for business or emergency use or important calls. She rarely used it, but she'd used her phone to call Daisy. She'd said, "Eli is here and he'd like to talk to you."

"He can't just come over to the tea garden?" Daisy had asked.

"He doesn't want to do that, Daisy. There are more

people there and he's in my back room. He says he was at the police station and now he wants to talk to *you*."

Daisy's mind had swept around and around thinking of all the reasons Eli might want to speak with her. Had he been cleared?

Daisy had said, "I'll be there in about ten minutes when I'm on my break. If he can't wait, then he'll just have to come over here."

She hadn't heard from Rachel again so she'd assumed ten minutes had been okay.

A long-striding bay gelding clomped down the street, pulling a wagon with two teenage boys. One of them tipped his hat to her. She recognized him as the son of her neighbor. She smiled and waved and continued across the street.

When Daisy entered Rachel's shop, she noticed tourists looking around at the materials and trims. Three were standing at the checkout desk holding items they wanted to purchase. Rachel was there and pointed Daisy to the back room. Daisy knew her way because she'd had discussions with Rachel there before. It was a storage room that often held the quilting supplies that Rachel's quilting circle needed. Daisy had joined the circle at times when she could. The small baby quilt topper she'd started wasn't nearly finished. Her stitches compared to the other women's in the group were irregular, too big, and definitely of poorer quality. She always thought she could make time to work on it, but she never did.

Making her way around the tourists, she passed the powder room and saw the door to the storage room was open. Eli was standing there, his hat in his hand, looking nervous.

She stepped inside and he motioned for her to close the door. She looked him straight in the eyes and decided she trusted him enough to do that.

"Miriam talked to me and convinced me to go to the police station," he started, running his fingers around the brim of his straw hat.

"Rachel told me you went, but she didn't tell me why you were there."

"First off, I had nothing to do with the murder of Hiram. I told Detective Willet that, and I think he believes me now."

When Zeke kept a poker face, it was hard to know what he believed, but she didn't burst Eli's bubble.

"I told him other things, though, other things that I hope *made* him believe me."

"Other things that had to do with the protest?" she guessed.

He nodded, looking forlorn. "I was paid to protest against the homeless shelter."

"Paid by the other protestor I saw you with?" she asked.

"I didn't tell the police who paid me. I believe in trust."

Almost exasperated with him, she leaned against the shelving, trying to decide what was the best thing to say. "I understand that you believe in trust, Eli, but what happens when you trust the wrong person? What happens when you trust someone who gets you into trouble, especially trouble with the police?"

The look he gave her was one that she'd seen on her own daughters' faces when she'd scolded them. He looked unhappy and he shifted from one work boot to the other.

She softened her tone. "I saw who you were paid by. I just don't know his name. But I'm sure I could pick him out on the TV footage."

"Please, Mrs. Swanson, don't do that. He handed me the money but he is not the one who paid us."

"Who is?"

"I can't tell you! She thought—" He cut off his words and his lips thinned as he scowled at what he'd given her.

"She what?" Daisy asked, pressing hard.

"She thought she was doing the right thing. She thought she was doing good. She thought the newspaper would do a story." He stopped again. "She thought bad publicity could be good publicity."

Something Arden Botterill had said nudged at Daisy's memory. The day when Daisy had picked out the spices, Arden had said to her that negative PR had paid off.

"You don't have to tell me who paid you. I think I know. I'll find out on my own."

"Mrs. Swanson, I don't want to cause new trouble for anyone. I just want to go back to my family and my district and start a good life with Miriam. I need money to start a business, and for us to get married. I thought taking that money for protesting was an easy way to do it."

"You told the police all this?"

"I did."

She considered something else. "Now you'll have an inheritance from Hiram to get you started."

"I will, but . . . I spoke with the bishop. I'm only going to take what I need to build a house for me and Miriam and to buy the bare essentials to start my business. The rest will go into a community fund in my district. There's always someone who needs something."

Daisy could see the sincerity in Eli's eyes. She knew what he was telling her was the truth.

"I wish you well, Eli. Thank you for telling me all this. I hope you're right that the police no longer suspect you. Jonas and I found someone who might be able to give the detectives a good lead to take them to exactly who killed Hiram."

Last evening Zeke had called after she, Jonas, and Felix had taken Thelma to the station. He'd said they'd put a patrol officer outside of Thelma's house for a couple of days and definitely talk to Joyce. Beyond that, Thelma would be on her own. Jonas had told her he'd help her put in a security system. She'd accepted his offer.

The rest was up to Zeke and Detective Rappaport.

Except for Arden. Daisy was going to confront the shopkeeper now!

CHAPTER TWENTY

"I did nothing illegal," Arden Botterill claimed.

With fifteen minutes still left from her hour break, Daisy had gone straight to Vinegar and Spice. The store was empty but for Arden. Daisy had walked straight up to the counter. "Eli told me he was paid by someone who paid all the protestors."

"And he named me?" Arden asked looking surprised.

"No, he didn't name you. But he didn't have to. He said *bad publicity could be good publicity*. And where could he have gotten that? You said the same to me."

"Lots of people use those terms."

"You thought by using that kind of coverage you would get us on TV and more exposure for the homeless shelter."

"I didn't do anything wrong."

"You didn't do anything wrong? The police were called

to the scene. That costs the town money. They could charge you. Maybe you had good intentions, but what do you think might have happened if those protestors with hot tempers had met people on the other side with hot tempers?"

Arden brushed Daisy's concern away with her hands. "Sometimes I think you pay too much attention to Amish values. Everything isn't black and white. There are shades of gray too, and sometimes you have to do what's good for the greater good. The greater good is getting that homeless shelter built. Fundraising isn't easy, Daisy. You're naïve when it comes to that. You think the good citizens of Willow Creek are just going to empty their accounts and safes and give thousands of dollars to this fine, fine benefit? Guess again. Somebody has to give them a reason to empty those pockets. Somehow the word has to get out about what we're even doing. Image is everything. What better image to show than to have nasty people protest against good people? There were a lot of Amish in that crowd on tape, and that was good for us too."

"Arden, I think you should rethink your publicity campaign and, if you can't, maybe you should resign from doing it."

"And just who else will volunteer unpaid?"

Daisy studied Arden as if she hadn't seen her before, as if all their previous encounters hadn't been friendly, as if Arden had never understood what this community meant and what it was about.

The Amish and English had worked hard to live together in and around Willow Creek, respecting each other. There was no room for division. Any division that came up had to be settled, had to be mediated, had to be ended, not provoked. Before she said something to Arden that she shouldn't, before her indignation took over, she knew the best thing for her to do was leave. That's what she did.

Without another word to Arden, she turned and left the shop.

That evening Daisy and Jonas were admiring the tomato and pepper plants in her garden. She explained what had happened with Eli and Arden.

"It's probably good you walked away." After he examined a tomato on a plant, he said, "I talked to Zeke today."

"About the murder?"

"He told me this is the last day of protection for Thelma. I volunteered to sit in my car in front of her place tonight. He doesn't want her to run away again and wants to question her more. He feels she might know something that she doesn't think she knows."

"About the clinic or about Hiram?"

"He's just trying to follow up every lead. There *is* something else he told me. He's connecting clients of Hiram's who also had contact with the clinic. That could come up with unique matches for suspects. But it's going to take time."

"In other words, he's thinking out of the box."

"Or, he's doing what some algorithms on computers do—find matches when you don't think there are any."

"I was thinking of going out of the box a little myself."

"How?" he asked warily.

"Maybe Zeke or Rappaport don't know enough about any of the suspects to put clues together. They know what questions they want to ask, and that's what they ask.

Sometimes they get the same answers over and over again. Maybe a round-about way that they don't have time for might be better."

Jonas carefully put his hand underneath another to-mato, studied it, and looked back at Daisy. "If you're telling me all this, then you're thinking about doing *something*."

"Nothing dangerous . . . at least no more dangerous than going into Piper's shop to buy a bike. I'd like to dig into Piper's background a little and there's a way to do that. I know Lawrence's wife Jeanette at least in passing. I could stop in and ask her how Piper's doing, mother to mother."

Felix, who had been snuffling around the ground in the garden for anything unusual or maybe even edible, came back to Daisy and dropped down at her feet. She lowered herself to her knees to pet him. This wasn't just a quick pet but a long petting session. He lifted his head so she could rub under his chin, then he rolled over on his side so she could rub his belly. At one point, he even had two paws up in the air and seemed to sigh with pleasure.

"You're spoiling him," Jonas warned.

"I'm not. I'm just giving him a little love. Men pet differently than women."

Jonas chuckled. "I guess they do. Felix has never seemed in doggy heaven when I pet him, or brush him, or groom him."

"I'll have to give you lessons," she joked.

"It's that mother's touch you have," Jonas said, serious now. "If you and Piper's mom relate, I don't know what you'll find out."

"Neither do I. But if we suspect Piper at all and we still

think it was a woman who used the stun gun on me, then this visit won't be wasted."

"Do you want to take Felix with you?"

"I don't think I'll need Felix. Not with Jeanette."

However, when Daisy found herself sitting in Jeanette's living room the following afternoon on her break, she was suddenly nervous. Maybe she should have brought along Felix. After all, he was a buffer.

Jeanette was a tall woman like Piper, but she was rail thin. Her flowered blouse with buttons down the front seemed to hang off her shoulders. Her white slacks looked as if they had a designer cut but they were roomy, not tight like the style now. Daisy had called ahead because she knew some people didn't like surprise visits. Jeanette had been pleasant, even eager to talk about Piper. She'd told Daisy she had bought a raspberry pie from the farmers' market and they could have that with tea.

The Bishops' living room, like their Cape Cod house, was old school. Set off the foyer, it had double windows on two sides of the room. Bookshelves stood between both sets of windows. And to Daisy's surprise, two gray tabby cats were asleep on the bookshelves between the books. She smiled as she studied the milk glass lamps on mahogany side tables with marble tops. As Daisy sank in to a paisley armchair, she admired the table next to her.

"I see you admire the tables," Jeannette said.

"They're beautiful."

"I inherited those from my mother. I think bringing the past into a house is a good way to keep memories alive."

"I suppose that's true," Daisy agreed.

"I wish things weren't so complicated for young people now. We didn't have very much when Lawrence and I started out, but we could make do. We were able to save a little from each paycheck so we could buy our first house. Now I think the problem is that young people want everything all at once rather than in stages."

It was time Daisy asked the questions that she wanted answers to. "Do you think Piper's like that, wanting everything at once?"

"I think Piper's view of life has been somewhat limited. All she ever wanted was a husband and a family. Lawrence and I have a good marriage. She saw that and she wanted something like it. But every marriage is different . . . every couple is different."

"Do you think Piper is disappointed in her marriage?"

"I don't know. I do know it's Emory's fault that they can't get pregnant, but that's part of *for better* or *for worse*. Piper was my miracle after two miscarriages. We have tried to give her everything, but we can't fix this. And I don't think a lawyer filing a class action suit will fix it either. Hiram Hershberger just made things worse."

"Did you know Hiram?"

"Just as a lawyer, nothing deeper than that. Lawrence and I used him for our wills. Emory's father had more dealings with him. He used Hiram in a lawsuit against a neighbor. Unfortunately, the neighbor won. The cases Hiram won were all publicized well. The cases he lost weren't. That's the way he spun his career. Really good lawyers don't have a spin. They just do the work."

Daisy supposed that was mostly true. Jeanette had just given her something to look into—a lawsuit between Emory's father and a neighbor.

* * *

That evening after the tea garden closed, Daisy sat in the office there, her computer screen glowing in front of her. Jazzi had left the tea garden with Brielle after their shift. They were going to spend the evening at Glorie's, pulling weeds in her garden. As far as Daisy knew, Glorie, Brielle, and Nola hadn't made a decisive decision yet on what they were going to do for the future. They were all thinking about it.

Eerie quiet surrounded Daisy with no activity in the tearoom or kitchen. She experienced an unexpected shiver up her neck, but that wasn't because she was afraid to be there alone. The shiver was warning her that what she was about to do might have consequences.

Daisy had learned a thing or two about exploring public records. Some of those strategies she'd learned on her own by simply searching, delving into public state websites, following links. Other means of searching Jonas had taught her. After all, as a detective he'd had to be facile at it.

Daisy found the page for recorded lawsuits in Pennsylvania. Since she didn't know what year Emory's father had filed a lawsuit against a neighbor, she searched for his name. The search engine found the name in short order and Daisy read over the narrative quickly.

Hiram had indeed lost the suit. The case seemed to be fairly cut and dried. The neighbor had had the right to erect his fence. Emory Wagner, Senior didn't have the right to tell him to take it down. Daisy wondered why Hiram had even taken the case. The lawsuit didn't seem to have much to do with the rage it took to commit murder. Then again, it was the only lawsuit she knew anything about with reference to Hiram, other than the Hope Clinic's.

Feeling as if she was tilting at windmills, she decided to keep tilting. The next name she searched was Hiram Hershberger, lawyer of record. This could take a while but she was determined to find at least part of the puzzle necessary to take her to the next clue or to lead the police to the next clue.

Did she know more than the detectives did? No, of course not. But she might have talked to more people than they had who weren't direct suspects. She might have discovered information on her trip to the clinic or talking to Thelma or speaking with Eli or even Rachel.

Page after page, Daisy read until her eyes were tired, her shoulders ached, and she was ready for a dinner with Jonas and a relaxing evening. She was almost ready to give up. Almost. Still scrolling down the page of lawsuits, she spotted something. She read through the information. It seemed serious enough that it could be a passion-filled motive for murder.

She thought about calling Zeke. What if she was wrong? What if there was nothing to her theory? What if she looked like a fool? What if he simply gave her another lecture about the foolhardiness of investigating on her own?

Wouldn't it be better to have ammunition? Wouldn't it be better to ask for forgiveness rather than permission? Her "follow the rules" tendencies nudged her conscience. Still, what if she was right?

After a call to someone involved in a lawsuit that settled the truth in Daisy's mind, she made another call to the person she suspected murdered Hiram.

* * *

The floodlight at the back of the Victorian had switched on at dusk. Daisy passed a motion detector light in the parking area. Standing there with a flashlight, she wondered where Jonas was. He, of course, wouldn't be using a flashlight.

Daisy suspected he had texted Zeke, but she didn't know what the results of that had been. She could only hope. She'd decided to do this without Zeke's initial assistance but with Jonas backing her up.

She didn't think she was in danger as she was merely looking for corroborating information. Her phone in her culottes pocket would be recording the conversation. And Jonas would be a witness.

She knew she stood out in what she'd worn for work today—white cotton culottes and a yellow short-sleeve T-shirt. After all, they both went nicely with the yellow apron with the daisy logo on it. She was thinking about that now because it was a detail to distract herself. Yes, she was nervous. She was tired of being fearful and even feeling panicked. Tired of needing the reassurance that she was safe. Tired of worrying about whether the killer was going to murder her too.

Yes, she could be all wrong about this. Zeke could call her an idiot if Jonas *had* texted him. She didn't care. She knew if the police questioned this person whom she considered a suspect, they might not get anywhere. She felt as if *she* could coax out more information on several different levels.

Daisy's car and her work van were the only two vehicles in the parking lot. The person she was meeting had told her she took a run most evenings and would meet her in the parking lot.

All at once, Daisy heard the pounding of running shoes. When she turned toward the sound with her flashlight, someone blocked her sight line six feet in front of her. That someone was dressed in black running shorts, a black light-weight, short-sleeved hoodie, a baseball cap, and . . . gloves. The gloves should have made Daisy more fearful, but they didn't.

Daisy spoke first. "I'm glad you agreed to meet me, Ramona. I think we should talk."

"Maybe we should," Ramona agreed, taking something from a pouch on her hip, letting her hoodie drop back. "But let's move down the path toward the creek."

That wasn't what Daisy wanted to do at all. But she wanted the truth from this woman who had seemed so caring but might have so much rage inside that it had led her to murder. The long blades of grass were damp around her ankles as they headed down the path toward the creek, Daisy's flashlight showing the way. A pine grove scented the air. Mock oranges and damp willow branches sweetened the rest.

"Let's stop here," Ramona said, moving off the path, closer to the creek's bank.

Daisy's heart raced, knowing she shouldn't be standing this close to the creek's rocky bank. Was that a rustling she heard in the grass? Jonas? Or was it the breeze? She could run from Ramona toward the tea garden if she had to. The truth was, though, that Ramona was the runner.

She could hear the creek rustling over rocks near the shore, the mustiness of the water, moss and algae scenting the air.

"I don't know why you wanted to meet me tonight," Ramona said.

"I thought maybe we should talk, mom to mom." Daisy considered moving toward the grass near the path, but didn't want to become distracted by the questions she had lined up for Ramona.

"Really?" Ramona asked, a bit of curiosity in her tone.

"You wouldn't want Petey to suffer more than necessary for what you've done, would you?" Daisy asked as calmly as she could manage.

"Just what do you think I've done?"

Unable to see Ramona's expression in the dark, she thought about bringing the flashlight up directly into Ramona's face. But that could be interpreted as an aggressive move. Instead of answering Ramona's question, Daisy said, "I spoke with your stepbrother."

"Oh, really. Just what did that imbecile have to say?"

"Among other things, he told me Hiram had a low blood sugar episode during a meeting with you to discuss his father's will. *Fred* is still bitter that you contested it," Daisy said.

"*Fred* is bitter?" The acerbic vitriol in Ramona's tone almost made Daisy take a step back, but she stood her ground.

Ramona flipped her ballcap off and tossed it to the ground as if it bothered her. Anger laced her every word. "I was supposed to inherit antiques from my mother . . . *my* mother. They even had sticky notes on them with my name. My mother had shown me that was what she was going to do." Ramona's voice rose. "They were *labeled*. But do you know what my stepbrother did after his dad died? He trashed them all according to Hiram Hershberger's advice."

The hoot of an owl soared above them. Daisy caught her breath because it startled her. After a moment, though, she tossed a statement at Ramona. "Fred told me that nothing about the antiques was in his dad's will."

"Of course not. My stepfather would have put them in the will if he had thought enough of me. But he never did. Fred was the only one who mattered to him. So I contested the will and that angered Fred. But that had nothing to do with anything else. So why are we here?"

"Come on, Ramona. I'm not naïve. Hiram was the reason you didn't inherit those antiques. Hiram was the reason you lost when you contested the will. Hiram is the reason the Hope Clinic wasn't going to pay for what they let happen."

Ramona was shifting back and forth from one foot to the other, seeming to become more agitated.

Daisy went on, goading her. "I can put two and two together and come up with four. I can understand how upset you were that your dreams were dust. You knew a class action suit wouldn't mean much to the people who were suing, simply the lawyer who brought it against the clinic. Hiram was a good lawyer. He could have defended the clinic well. I could see how you were filled with rage over that. You also knew insulin would kill him."

"Yes, I was mad. Yes, I knew he had episodes of hypoglycemia. You bet, I killed him!" Ramona screamed, her voice ringing in the near silence. "And my admission is going to do you *no* good at all." Suddenly she raised her arm with a stun gun in her hand. It was easy to see she wanted to use it again on Daisy.

As she charged Daisy and Daisy dropped her flashlight, a growl came from the nearby bushes. At the moment Ramona was distracted by it and turned toward the sound, Daisy lunged at Ramona, hitting her wrist and causing the gun to fly into the creek. The problem was, the two of them were near the shore. Ramona grabbed Daisy by her T-shirt and pulled her toward her so she could physically overtake her. But Ramona's ankle turned on the rocky bank and they toppled into the water.

The cold water snatched Daisy's breath. She flailed underwater until she propelled herself up and broke the surface. She heard a splash as Felix jumped into the creek and paddled toward her. His head out of the water, he aimed straight for her. As she doggy-paddled to keep her head above water, she heard, more than saw, Jonas jump in too.

Immediately before Felix reached Daisy, she felt a tug on her foot and then her leg. She was pulled under once more.

She heard Jonas yell, "Let her go!"

The next few minutes were a blur as Felix ducked under the water and she caught him around the neck. She kicked as hard as she could. Suddenly she was free, out of breath, and floating with Felix as Jonas reached her.

There was a splashing and grunts a few feet away. Daisy noticed immediately that the reason she'd been freed wasn't only her kicks. Zeke had gone after Ramona. He dragged her flailing and screaming to the shore.

All at once, patrol officers appeared on the bank and Tommy and Bart cuffed Ramona while Zeke wiped creek water from his face.

In the meantime, Jonas helped Daisy then Felix climb from the creek. The three of them sat on the grass, trying to shake off the fear and panic of what had just happened.

Tommy lifted a plastic evidence bag. Daisy could see something inside of it.

"What is that?" she croaked to Tommy, as Jonas hugged her so close she almost couldn't breathe.

"It looks like a syringe," Tommy answered with no expression at all.

Felix stuck his nose under Daisy's arm while Jonas wrapped his arms around them both.

EPILOGUE

The evening a week later couldn't have been any more pleasant for the barbecue at Daisy's house. When she'd asked Detective Rappaport to join them, he'd insisted on bringing his smoker over the night before. Now it was almost time to check the pork butt, the brisket, and the macaroni and cheese that would be smoked along with the meats.

The detective seemed happy to be there. He was having a conversation with her father while her father stood at the traditional gas grill flipping burgers and rolling over hot dogs. Jonas, Foster, and Felix were playing fetch. Gavin, his daughter Emily and son Ben had joined them too. Gavin held Sammy high in the air, making his grandson giggle. Talking between them, Jazzi and Vi brought out dishes from the kitchen. Daisy's mom, who was already at the picnic table with her Aunt Iris arranging the food, had made deviled eggs and baked home-made rolls. Aunt Iris had brought along chow-chow and a slow cooker filled with baked beans.

Daisy had made the dessert and had gone all out with apple and blueberry fry pies and apple dumplings with maple syrup glaze.

When Rachel, Levi, and their children arrived, Daisy went to greet Rachel. Her friend hugged her close. "You've recovered from your dip in the creek, ya?"

Daisy wondered if she *had* recovered. She wasn't sure about that yet. It wasn't the water from the creek that she'd absorbed into her skin and hair. She was afraid some of Ramona's vitriol and bitterness had rubbed off on her. The police had retrieved the stun gun along with the insulin syringe. It was obvious Ramona had planned another murder.

Closing her eyes for a moment to escape Ramona's image, Daisy opened them and scanned Rachel's pale blue dress, her black apron, and her white prayer *kapp*, along with the pale green and pale lilac dresses of her daughters, the black trousers and the light-blue shirt that her son was wearing. Daisy sometimes longed to fade into Amish life. It seemed simpler and more wholesome.

Giving a smile to her friend, Daisy answered her question. "I'm working on recovering."

A moment later, Zeke emerged from the sliding glass doors, carrying a huge red cooler. Rachel's husband Levi hurried to help him with it, taking one of the handles while Zeke took the other. Two very different men who were sharing in a joint task.

As Rachel's girls ran to play with Felix, Rachel said, "I put the shoofly pies on the counter. From the look of all the desserts, I think you're going to have leftovers."

"I'll send some home with whoever wants them," Daisy assured her.

"How are you really feeling, Daisy?" Rachel asked.

Daisy knew she couldn't duck the question when her friend added, "I just know that look. You seem bothered by something."

What had been uppermost in Daisy's mind came flowing out. "I shouldn't have taken the chance to speak with Ramona," she confessed. "I shouldn't have been so eager to finger the killer. I should have let Zeke handle it."

"And what does Jonas say?" Rachel asked softly.

"Jonas says hindsight is twenty-twenty."

"Listen to him so you can sleep and have peace again. You have a gift for helping, Daisy. I don't think you can run away from that."

The sliding glass doors opened once more, and Tessa and Trevor tumbled out, holding hands and grinning at each other. Tessa called to her, "I'm sorry we're late. Trevor had a blog he had to post."

"Not *my* fault," he said with fake outrage. "You didn't finish the potatoes in time."

Daisy smiled at their banter. She knew Tessa had planned to make sweet and sour hot potato salad.

"I put the casserole in your oven on warm until everything is ready," Tessa assured her.

Glancing around at the friends and family that had gathered for the picnic, Daisy circulated for a while as Gavin and Jonas set up folding tables and chairs. She quickly unfolded white paper tablecloths and stretched them over the tabletops. Next she put out baskets with silverware and napkins decorated with watermelons.

Zeke had taken a soda from the cooler and popped the top as she stacked cups on the table and offered him one.

"Not necessary," he said with a grin and took a swig from the can.

Since she had Zeke right in front of her, she asked, "Has all the paperwork been finished on Ramona's case?"

"She's been charged with murder one for Hiram, two assault charges and an attempted murder on you. She confessed again, no surprise there since there was a witness to her confession with you plus your recording. I can't believe the tech could still get that off your phone even when it was wet. My tech guy is really good."

Then as if Zeke believed she'd like to know, he added, "Her little boy and his dad are moving into the paternal grandparents' house. They're all going to help each other."

Zeke spent a long moment as her eyes misted over. He advised, "Let it go, Daisy. You called Jonas to back you up and he texted me. I wish you hadn't gone after Ramona Lowell yourself, but I understand that you didn't know for sure if she was the killer."

"You're not going to lecture me about it?"

"No. I have to live with my choices and you have to live with yours. In your case, it all worked out well. Be grateful for that."

She and Zeke had always been honest with each other, and he was being honest now.

The sliding glass doors to the kitchen opened once more. Glorie, Brielle, and Nola stepped out.

Brielle ran to Daisy and hugged her enthusiastically.

"What's that for?" Daisy asked, grinning. She couldn't help but be happy that Brielle was happy.

"We settled it. We settled all of it," Brielle said.

"Tell me what you settled," Daisy suggested, amused.

"Grammy is going to rent out her house. My mom and Grammy are going to build another house right there near

Grammy's old one. We'll all live together so we can take care of Grammy. She'll still have all the memories from the house. Won't that be great? By the way, Grammy brought coleslaw and Mom and I brought a whole tray of veggies with a dip."

Daisy kept her arm around Brielle's shoulders. "Let's go talk to your mom and Glorie about this house they're going to build."

A short time later, everyone had taken a seat at a table. After moments of silent thanks, something Levi's family did before every meal, they all dug into the food. It was much later when fireflies danced in the tree branches and near the grass. Jonas and Daisy sat on the glider he'd made for her. Felix rested beside her leg, waiting for any pat she wanted to give him. She looked over at everyone gathered who were interacting as if they'd known each other for a lifetime.

Jonas put his arm around her.

When she turned toward him, she said, "Zeke told me I should be grateful for the way things turned out at the creek."

"What do *you* think about it?" Jonas asked.

"I *am* grateful, and I do have to let it go. I'm even more grateful for my family and friends that are all around us." She gazed into his eyes. "And I'm grateful for *you*."

As Jonas leaned down to kiss her, Daisy thought about the day when she and Jonas and Jazzi would be living in the house together as a family. She would be even more grateful for that.

ORIGINAL RECIPES

Corn Chowder

1 cup chopped red onion
4 tablespoons bacon drippings
1 can chicken broth (14 ounces)
2 cups sliced carrots
1 cup sliced celery
$\frac{1}{4}$ cup chopped fennel (the stalk)
2–3 cups cubed potatoes
1 can whole kernel corn (14 ounces)
1 clove of garlic, grated
$\frac{1}{2}$ teaspoon salt
$\frac{1}{8}$ teaspoon ground white pepper
1 can creamed corn (14 ounces)
2 tablespoons flour
$1\frac{1}{4}$ cups milk

Sauté onion in bacon drippings in a soup pot. Add chicken broth, carrots, celery, fennel, potatoes, can of whole kernel corn, garlic, salt and pepper. Bring to a boil and then simmer until potatoes are tender (about 15 minutes). Stir in creamed corn. Bring to a boil and stir. Return to simmer.

Whisk flour into milk and add to soup and stir well. Simmer 5 to 10 minutes, stirring now and then.

Serves 8.

Crunchy Slaw

Salad ingredients
1 pack coleslaw mix (16 ounces)
½ pack grated red cabbage (4 ounces)
½ cup shaved almonds
½ cup sunflower seeds (kernels, no shells)
1 tablespoon sesame seeds
1 pack ramen noodles broken into small pieces
½ cup chopped red onion
3 chopped scallions

Dressing
¼ cup low sodium soy sauce
Juice of 1 lemon
¼ cup virgin olive oil
2 tablespoons rice vinegar
1 tablespoon toasted sesame oil
2 tablespoons honey
⅛ teaspoon pepper
1 tablespoon grated fresh ginger

   Mix dressing ingredients and pour over tossed salad
ingredients. Stir well and refrigerate for at least an hour.
Stir well before serving.
   This salad will serve about 12 as a side dish.

Chocolate Espresso Cookies

1 cup softened butter
½ cup granulated sugar
¾ cup packed dark brown sugar
2 large eggs
1½ teaspoons vanilla
1 teaspoon baking soda
1 teaspoon salt
1 tablespoon espresso powder
¼ cup Hershey's unsweetened cocoa
¼ cup sour cream
2¼ cups all-purpose flour
6 ounces milk chocolate morsels
6 ounces semi-sweet chocolate morsels

Preheat oven to 375 degrees.

Cream butter and sugar in mixer bowl. Add eggs, vanilla, baking soda, salt, espresso powder, cocoa and sour cream. Mix well. Add flour ½ cup at a time. Stir in chocolate morsels.

Using a heaping dinnerware soup spoon, scoop onto an ungreased baking sheet, two inches apart. Bake at 375 degrees for 10-11 minutes. Cool on the cookie sheet for about 2 minutes before removing to cooling racks.

Makes about 30 cookies depending on scoop size.

Connect with

Us

Visit us online at
KensingtonBooks.com
to read more from your favorite authors, see books
by series, view reading group guides, and more.

Join us on social media

for sneak peeks, chances to win books and prize packs,
and to share your thoughts with other readers.

facebook.com/kensingtonpublishing
twitter.com/kensingtonbooks

Tell us what you think!

To share your thoughts, submit a review,
or sign up for our eNewsletters, please visit:
KensingtonBooks.com/TellUs.

Grab These Cozy Mysteries
from
Kensington Books

Available Wherever Books Are Sold!

All available as e-books, too!

Visit our website at **www.kensingtonbooks.com**